"Who killed the ▮▮▮▮▮▮▮▮▮▮▮▮▮▮▮ he Sky demanded.

Alarm flickered ▮▮▮▮▮▮▮▮▮▮▮ verted his gaze. "*You* wou▮▮▮▮▮▮▮▮▮▮er leave my pony with an Apac▮▮▮▮▮▮ your 'concern' for a dead Chey—"

Swift Canoe was in the middle of the word when Touch the Sky abruptly swept one leg out in a hook, toppling the other man to the ground. Before another two heartbeats elapsed, he had his man pinned. Touch the Sky's obsidian knife, honed to a lethal edge on one side only, Indian fashion, now made a deep indentation across Swift Canoe's neck.

"Who?" Touch the Sky repeated. Quiet, lethal menace marked his tone. "Was it you?"

WARRIOR FURY

"Do you not see it, bucks," Touch the Sky asked his closest warriors, "as clear as blood spoor on virgin snow? They mean to kill Honey Eater and Little Bear, all right. But they mean to kill them in front of me—all for the momentary pleasure of watching my grief before they kill *me*."

The sheer, barbaric heinousness of such thinking struck his comrades dumb. But slowly all three nodded, seeing this thing as it was.

Touch the Sky's lips formed their grim determined slit—the expression that always meant someone was going to die a hard death. "This place hears me," he said solemnly. "And so do the High Holy Ones. I will bring my family home or die with them, and there is no middle way."

"*We* will bring your family home or die with them," Little Horse corrected him, and Tangle Hair and Two Twists approved this with nods.

"Good," Touch the Sky said. He glanced forlornly at his empty tipi, which he had not the heart even to enter. "From this time on we do not follow the path of normal braves. Every step we take from here, we tread only the Warrior Way."

CHEYENNE
VENGEANCE QUEST/ WARRIOR FURY

JUDD COLE

LEISURE BOOKS NEW YORK CITY

JM

JH

A LEISURE BOOK®

June 1999

Published by

Dorchester Publishing Co., Inc.
276 Fifth Avenue
New York, NY 10001

ISBN 0-8439-4531-1

The name "Leisure Books" and the stylized "L" with design are trademarks of Dorchester Publishing Co., Inc.

Printed in the United States of America.

VENGEANCE QUEST

Prologue

Though he sat behind few men in council, the tall Cheyenne brave called Touch the Sky faced a future as uncertain as his past.

His original Cheyenne name was lost forever after a Bluecoat ambush near the North Platte killed his father and mother. The lone Indian survivor of the bloody battle, the squalling infant was taken back to the Wyoming river-bend settlement of Bighorn Falls near Fort Bates.

He was adopted by John Hanchon and his barren young wife, Sarah. Owners of the town's thriving mercantile store, the Hanchons named him Matthew and raised him as their own

5

blood. But their love couldn't protect him from the hostility and fear of white settlers bent on exterminating the Red Peril—especially when, at sixteen, he fell in love with Kristen, daughter of the wealthy and hidebound rancher Hiram Steele.

Steele had Matthew savagely beaten when he caught the Cheyenne youth and Kristen in their secret meeting place. He also warned him: Next time he caught them, the youth would be killed. Frightened for Matthew's life, Kristen lied and told him she never wanted to see him again. Still, Matthew's love for his parents and Kristen kept him in Bighorn Falls.

But Seth Carlson, an arrogant young cavalry lieutenant from Fort Bates, was also in love with Kristen. Either Matthew pulled up stakes for good, he warned, or his parents would lose their lucrative contract with Fort Bates—the lifeblood of their business.

His heart saddened but determined, Matthew Hanchon set out for the upcountry of the Powder River, Cheyenne territory.

He was immediately captured by braves from Chief Yellow Bear's Northern Cheyenne camp. Declared a spy for the whiteskin soldiers, he was tortured and sentenced to die. But just as a young brave named Wolf Who Hunts Smiling was about to gut him, old Arrow Keeper intervened.

The tribe shaman and protector of the sacred Medicine Arrows, Arrow Keeper had recently experienced an epic vision. His vision foretold that the long-lost son of a great Cheyenne chief would return to his people—and that he would lead them in one last great victory against their enemies. This youth would be known by the distinctive mark of the warrior, the same birthmark Arrow Keeper spotted buried past the youth's hairline, a mulberry-colored arrowhead.

Keeping all this to himself to protect the youth from jealous tribal enemies, Arrow Keeper used his influence to spare the prisoner's life. This infuriated two braves especially: the cunning Wolf Who Hunts Smiling and his fierce older cousin, Black Elk.

Black Elk, the tribe's war leader despite his youth, was jealous of the glances cast at the tall young stranger by Honey Eater, daughter of Chief Yellow Bear. And Wolf Who Hunts Smiling, proudly ambitious, turned his heart to stone against all whites without exception. This stranger, to him, was only a make-believe Cheyenne who wore white men's shoes, spoke the paleface tongue, and showed his emotions in his face like the woman-hearted white men. He insisted on calling the new arrival Woman Face and White Man Runs Him.

Arrow Keeper, however, buried his white name forever and named him Touch the Sky. But acceptance did not come with that new name. As he trained to become a warrior, Touch the Sky was humiliated at every turn. Nor did his enemies within the tribe cease their relentless campaign to prove he was a spy for the hair faces.

Through sheer determination to find his place, assisted now and then by the cunning he had learned from white men, Touch the Sky became one of the greatest warriors of the *Shaiyena* nation. His fighting skill and courage won him more and more followers, including the ever-loyal braves Little Horse, Two Twists, and Tangle Hair. And under Arrow Keeper's careful eye, Touch the Sky also made great progress in the shamanic arts.

With each victory, however, his enemies managed to turn appearances against him, to suggest that he still carried the white man's stink which brought the tribe bad luck and scared off the buffalo. And although the entire tribe knew that Touch the Sky and Honey Eater were desperately in love, Honey Eater was forced into a loveless marriage with Black Elk—who chafed in a jealous, murderous wrath, plotting revenge against Touch the Sky.

Arrow Keeper, well into his frosted years, eventually realized he must leave the tribe before Touch the Sky could assume the role of shaman and Arrow Keeper. He left to build a death wickiup, disappearing and thus leaving the question of his life or death a mystery to the others.

Wolf Who Hunts Smiling murdered Black Elk and laid the crime in front of Touch the Sky's tipi. Now the tall brave is menaced at every turn by his enemies. But even more troubling to him is that, since his marriage to Honey Eater, those enemies also mean to kill her and the child she carries inside her. The ambitious Wolf Who Hunts Smiling is on the brink of taking over the entire Cheyenne nation. He then plans to join his secret renegade allies in a war of extermination against the whiteskin settlers.

But one man thwarts his bloody scheme: the tall brave named Touch the Sky.

Chapter One

"Brother," Little Horse said, "I have found sign where other braves saw only bare rock. But I confess I have no power to cut sign into a man's thoughts. Ever since we stopped to rest the ponies at Medicine Bend, you have shed much brain sweat over some secret trouble.

"It is the white man's way to worry in private, the Indian way to counsel among his brothers. Nor have I ever known you to play the fretting woman, even though truly your troubles are legion. So now—put words to this new worry, buck."

Touch the Sky could not resist an ironic grin

at these words—a veritable speech, coming from this normally taciturn friend. He, Little Horse, Tangle Hair and Two Twists had halted well south of Beaver Creek—called Medicine Run by the ancients, for it emptied into the sacred Black Hills to the east. Now their ponies drank from a runoff rill. Sister Sun was well along on her day's journey, and slanted their shadows toward her birthplace.

"My enemies in camp call me White Man Runs Him," Touch the Sky said. "They say I carry the paleface stink that scares off the buffalo, that I learned to mount my pony from the white man's side and to walk in shoes, so that now I can never be a real Indian. Now *you* tell me I even brood like the Mah-ish-ta-shee-da?"

Touch the Sky used the Cheyenne name for whites: Yellow Eyes. The first palefaces their ancestors ever saw were mountain men with severe jaundice.

"I do indeed," Little Horse replied frankly. "I, for one, have learned to admire many of the traits you have wisely retained from your time among the Yellow Eyes. Indeed, my life has been saved by such traits. From them you learned to care for your rifle as you do for your pony, while many careless red men still die in battle after a dirty rifle fails to fire."

"I have ears for this," Two Twists put in. The youngest among them, he was named after his preference for wearing his hair in twin braids. "And I was there in the rifle pits when *this* one"—he nodded at their tall leader—"led us junior warriors in a white men's defense of our hunt camp. He taught us the Bluecoat trick of using enfiladed fire. We stunned the Kiowas and Comanches and sent them fleeing."

"We red men war among ourselves," Tangle Hair said, "while the whiteskins all wisely organize against us. True it is, we have much to learn even from our enemies."

"But comes a time," Little Horse said, looking directly at Touch the Sky, "when you must give over with your paleface ways and remember that now you mount your pony from the Indian side. Tell us. What new trouble cankers at you, buck?"

A long silence followed while Touch the Sky watched his tough little cayuse, having drunk her fill, begin to graze on the grass. The half-wild Indian pony was a palomilla, milk white with a white mane and tail. The Cheyenne and Sioux hunting ranges, occupying the heart of the vast territory the whites called Wyoming, had recently emerged from the short white days of the cold moons. Now the vast stretch between the Black Hills to the east and Shoshone country to the west was ablaze with the promise of renewal. Lush new grass, already well past the ponies' fetlocks, bent in rippling waves under a steady breeze. Bright yellow crocuses and white verbena and blue columbine dotted the vast, rolling plains. A dome of seamless, bottomless blue sky stretched on forever, promising glorious warm moons and good hunts ahead.

But despite nature's hopeful promise, Touch the Sky's lips formed a tight seam, and his eyes, grim and unfocused, saw things far away from the beauty surrounding him.

"Yes," he finally answered. "I have made my stand as an Indian. Perhaps that, after all, has been the main trouble—at least, according to my enemies. If you truly believe in the white man's stink, as they do, then you also believe it stinks forever."

Like his comrades, he had recently abandoned his buffalo-fur leggings and buckskin shirt for a clout and double-soled elkskin moccasins. All four warriors also wore leather bands around their left wrists to protect them from the cutting slap of their sinew bowstrings.

"As to what cankers at me," Touch the Sky repeated, "only the old troubles, but augmented by new omens."

This reference to omens forced all three of his companions to respectful attention. Indians joked incessantly about dying. But their reckless bravado rested on a profound belief in things supernatural. And truly the shaman's sense was strong in Touch the Sky, who had been initiated into the esoteric secrets of the Medicine Way by Arrow Keeper himself—a shaman whose powerful medicine commanded respect throughout the Red Nations.

While he spoke, Touch the Sky turned to look over his left shoulder—toward the northwest, where the sawtooth spires of the Sans Arc Mountains probed into the soft blue belly of the sky.

"If we die young, brothers," he added abruptly, "death will ride out from over there."

One peak alone among the others was obscured by a surrounding blanket of gray-white mist: the peak of taboo Wendigo Mountain, where right now almost two-hundred fierce Comanche and Blackfoot renegades waited in readiness—waited, Touch the Sky knew, to annihilate Chief Gray Thunder's Powder River camp if the Cheyennes did not swear allegiance to them and the ambitious Cheyenne traitor named Wolf Who Hunts Smiling.

Once this power-hungry betrayer of the Cheyenne Way had consolidated all the Plains tribes, he meant to join the Comanche Big Tree and the Blackfoot Sis-ki-dee in leading a war of extermination against all white settlers—those, at any rate, who dared to drift past the invisible line the whites called the hundredth meridian. This was the place where rainfall slackened considerably and the tall grasses gave way to the short-grass prairie, the official beginning of the white man's "West."

"What new augury have you seen?" Little Horse asked quietly. "For truly, Cheyenne, we have just completed a lengthy scout of Wendigo Mountain. You yourself said things appear quiet enough. You said our enemies do not seem to be preparing for any new mission."

"No outward signs from them," Touch the Sky agreed. "But, brothers, back at Medicine Bend I saw another sign. One warning of far more personal dangers. For while I sat stone-still *I saw my shadow get up and move.*"

To a man, his three companions lost some color in their bronzed faces. For all Cheyennes knew that seeing their shadow move while they did not was a portent of grave personal trouble. Indeed, it meant the Wendigo himself had taken a personal interest in making life a terror for the victim.

"So *that* is why you are pushing so hard to return to camp," Little Horse said, nodding as he finally understood which way the wind set.

He did not need to add the thought which immediately flew into each brave's head: Honey Eater was back in camp, several moons along with Touch the Sky's seed germinating inside her—a seed his enemies very much hoped to extinguish before it could sprout life. Now that her impending motherhood was known to all, Touch the Sky had taken steps for her protection—and meant to take more. Still, against enemies as wily and resourceful as Wolf Who Hunts Smiling and the pretend shaman Medicine Flute, no protection could be called adequate.

"My pony has drunk enough," Two Twists said, for he too was thinking of Honey Eater, whom he loved as a sister. This was clear when his dappled gray mare gave the lie to his words—she snorted in protest when he tugged her back from the water by her buffalo-hair hackamore. He grabbed a handful of coarse mane and swung onto her back.

Now, having spoken his worry to his companions, it was as if Touch the Sky's premonition took on even more substance. His vague apprehension began to form a solid ball of cold panic deep in his breast.

Honey Eater. He and his young wife had bested incredible odds—and permanently divided their tribe—when they exchanged the squaw-taking vow. And now they would have to best those odds all over again if their child were ever to breathe life.

This thought put the coppery taste of fear in his mouth. Touch the Sky swung onto his pony and pointed her bridle east toward their summer camp at the confluence of the Powder and

14

Little Powder rivers. He touched her flanks with his heels.

"Hi-ya!" he screamed, unleashing the Cheyenne war cry that always put heat into their mounts. "Hi-ya, hii-*ya!*"

"Do not look across the clearing," Sharp Nosed Woman warned her niece. "As usual *he* is watching you with the fascination of a snake in a trance."

"When you compare Medicine Flute to a snake," Honey Eater replied without looking up from her beadwork, "you do a grave injustice to snakes."

"Speak the truth and shame the Wendigo! But at least Wolf Who Hunts Smiling is not here to goad the coward on."

"I would rather have *that* one here where we can see him. His long absence can only mean trouble."

"Truly, Niece, for our wily wolf is not one to go off and meditate. Child, avoid glancing that way!"

Honey Eater did not require her aunt's warnings—the skinny, lazy, cowardly, yet infinitely dangerous Medicine Flute was *always* watching her. Always watching and always blowing those atonal notes on that infernal "flute" of his—an ugly, discordant instrument made from a human leg bone. As fast as Touch the Sky broke them, Medicine Flute came up with new ones.

Though traces of daylight remained, the first clan fires had already been started for the night. The situation in camp having reached a critical juncture, Touch the Sky now insisted that his wife stay with her widowed aunt while he was away from camp.

Now the two women sat working before the entrance flap of the older woman's hide-covered tipi. A fire blazed in the cooking tripod, warming a pot of wild-onion stew.

"Move back from there, you flea-bitten sack of bones!" Sharp Nosed Woman groused, swiping at a nosy camp dog with the piece of leather she was stitching.

The animal, a shaggy hybrid of wolf and domesticated mastiff, leaped back, growling at Sharp Nosed Woman. Its fur was a dirty yellow, and like most underfed Indian dogs it had ribs protruding like barrel staves. Unlike other Indian dogs, however, this one was aggressive and unfriendly toward most Cheyennes.

However, the moment that Honey Eater spoke soothingly to the dog, it quieted and lay down again, wagging its mangy tail and watching her with clear adulation.

"I swear by the four directions, that ill-tempered beast adores you," Sharp Nosed Woman said, somewhat peevishly. The only way she liked dogs was boiled in rosehips and calf's brains. But Cheyenne camps always kept many around, discouraging surprise attacks. "I see now why Touch the Sky trained it to follow you."

She glanced across the clearing again, though carefully. "I suppose I should be glad for its loyalty. The bone blower over there is a coward, but neither he nor Wolf Who Hunts Smiling would scruple to harm a woman. I only wish that cur did not smell like rancid bear grease."

Despite her preoccupation, Honey Eater

smiled at her aunt's tone. Even the grumpy Sharp Nosed Woman felt an inner tug when she saw that pretty face light up with a smile. The Cheyenne were known as the Beautiful People by other Plains Indians, and Honey Eater was outstanding in a tribe famous for beauties. Those delicately carved high cheekbones, flawless skin the color of wild honey, and big, almond-shaped eyes—all of it was made even more radiant by the approach of motherhood.

"Your belly has barely begun to swell," her aunt remarked. "Yet the entire camp knows by now that you have caught a whelp."

"The entire camp knows," Honey Eater echoed, feeling the weight of Medicine Flute's unbroken stare. "Some women in the Once-a-Month lodge must have guessed I was not bleeding. And at least half in our camp are praying that our child will never breathe life."

"Praying? Well let us hope they go no further, sweet love. For Maiyun will ignore *any* prayer intended to hurt one of his innocents. The High Holy Ones first made the days and gave them to us. They will punish us evil grown ones, but never a child. Only we can hurt our little ones."

"Aunt, you are wise tonight. But I have no ears for this talk of hurting children."

A rare look of contrition crossed the older woman's face. "Forgive me, child. You speak straight. As the twig is bent, so the tree shall grow. An expecting squaw must be careful in her speech and thoughts. For her words and actions shape the child."

A low growl simmered in the dog's throat as footsteps approached them. Both women glanced up apprehensively. But it was only an old grandmother from the Root Eaters Clan.

Sharp Nosed Woman asked, "Where is your husband, little one?"

Honey Eater's preoccupied frown etched deeper.

"Against his will, he and his band have ridden west to scout Wendigo Mountain. Thanks to the lies and treachery of Wolf Who Hunts Smiling, the Council of Forty still refuses to believe a war is brewing there. Many believe that our wily Wolf is only ambitious—they refuse to believe he has raised his battle axe alongside our enemies', that he means to kill our chief and seize this tribe. This incredulity on the part of the headmen leaves Touch the Sky no choice. He and his band must keep a constant eye on our enemy, for no one else will."

Despite her aunt's warning, Honey Eater could not help glancing across the clearing, for the eerie piping had stopped abruptly. She saw that Medicine Flute had taken a rare break from his incessant piping. Now he sat peeling a twig with his teeth, his sleepy, heavy-lidded, mocking gaze leveled on her.

Honey Eater hastily glanced away, unable to voice a thought too horrible for words: She had no doubt of Wolf Who Hunts Smiling's debased treachery. For she believed Touch the Sky's claim that it was this sly Wolf who had killed Black Elk, intending to shoot Touch the Sky. Many still swore that she had given way to raw lust and married her husband's killer.

She tried not to give way before the onslaught of her increasing despair. Oh, how she wished—especially with this new life growing inside her—that old Arrow Keeper had not mysteriously disappeared. Was he even still alive? But at least his wisdom and strong medicine still existed in Touch the Sky.

Yes, but is Touch the Sky still alive? whispered a voice from the edge of awareness. Honey Eater shivered as a cold, invisible finger caressed her spine.

The sun was a dull orange ball on the western horizon by the time the Cheyenne brave named Spotted Tail reached Roaring Horse Creek.

His pony was lathered from hard riding, and Spotted Tail only reluctantly paused to let it drink. He was desperate to reach the Cheyenne summer camp, located north one-half sleep's ride. For clearly a serious trouble storm was brewing.

Spotted Tail had only thirty winters behind him, yet the fearless warrior had covered himself and his Antelope Eaters Clan in glory and now sat behind few men in council. Three times he had the great honor of wearing the Medicine Hat into battle, rallying his brothers to desperate victories against Pawnees, mountain Utes, and the fierce Crow Crazy Dogs—suicide warriors sworn to win a battle or die trying.

His coup feathers trailed on the ground, and his battle prowess had won him election as troop leader of the Bow String soldier society. Only Touch the Sky, Little Horse, Wolf Who Hunts Smiling and Lone Bear, leader of the Bull Whips, bore heavier coup sticks.

A twig snapped in the thickets beside him, scattering his thoughts like chaff in the wind. Spotted Tail's bone-handled knife was instantly in hand. But no more noises followed, and he had no time to investigate. Total darkness neared, and no Cheyenne liked to be outside his camp by night any longer than he must.

Anger once again roiled his guts as Spotted Tail recalled what he had seen earlier. He had ridden south to the Sioux camp at Elbow Bend, for a Cheyenne delegate was always invited to attend major councils held by their close battle allies, the Lakota Sioux. Riding back, he chanced to spot a blue curl of smoke floating out of a cutbank. Slipping up closer to investigate, he found three braves parleying over a loaded calumet: the Comanche trick rider Big Tree, the crazy-by-thunder Blackfoot marauder named Sis-ki-dee, and Wolf Who Hunts Smiling!

Of course they would meet down here, the brave told himself. They knew by now that Touch the Sky watched Wendigo Mountain closely. So they rode in the opposite direction.

Another slight noise from the thicket made Spotted Tail flinch. A rabbit, probably. No time to investigate, for he must get back to camp and bring Touch the Sky this new word. The wily Wolf Who Hunts Smiling would not risk a meeting, down here in the low country, with sworn enemies of the tribe. Not unless a major strike was in the offing—a strike against a vulnerable camp whose braves were too busy warring among themselves to see danger from without.

Spotted Tail had initially, nearly five winters before when Touch the Sky was still called Matthew Hanchon, supported those who wanted this tall captive killed as a spy. But that had changed. Gradually, impressed by the determined outcast's grim strength and growing battle savvy, Spotted Tail had been won over. He now agreed completely with those who argued that Touch the Sky was marked out for a great destiny—and that no other Cheyenne was more loyal to the ancient law-ways and the sanctity of the Holy Medicine Arrows.

Spotted Tail's loyalty had in turn convinced most of the Bow String soldiers to likewise support Touch the Sky. But he knew that his open support of the beleaguered shaman—and his open defiance of Wolf Who Hunts Smiling and Medicine Flute—placed his life in great peril. Already his meat racks had been stripped, his pony string scattered, his hunting kit shredded. Each time he had defied these clear warnings, swearing allegiance to the controversial Touch the Sky.

He tugged on his pony's bridle, preparing to mount. He tensed his legs and immediately felt a white-hot pain slice into the back of the knees—pain so intense a cry was wrenched from this stoic warrior's throat.

One moment he stood rock steady; the next, he felt his legs buckle under him as he crashed to the ground. The pain was a fire raging over his skin, as he felt hot blood rushing down his legs.

He tried to move his legs, but the effort was useless. They no longer answered his will. Spotted Tail, his face a twisted mask of pain, raised his upper body to look at his legs. The sight that met his eyes sent terror and revulsion and grief slamming into him.

A deep and ugly wound marked where the back of both knees had been cut deep. He had been crippled for life, both tendons in the hollow of the knees severed. He was hamstrung, ruined as a man!

Only then did he look up into the eyes of his assailant.

"You!" he gasped.

A rifle butt slammed into his jaw hard, and Spotted Tail felt his head crash into the ground. He was still aware, however, when his attacker spoke the last words Spotted Tail would ever hear.

"Sing your death song if you wish, Spotted Tail; it will do you no good. For it is common knowledge that the soul of an Indian who dies by drowning must remain trapped in the water forever, crying eternally in its loneliness and giving the river its sad song."

By now Spotted Tail had lost much blood. He was helpless to resist when the murderer began dragging him toward the rain-swollen creek.

"He will find you!" he gasped above his fiery pain and numbing fear. "Touch the Sky will see you die a dog's death!"

But cold water shocked his skin, then choked his throat and lungs like vindictive hands. Spotted Tail's world closed down to darkness, and he lost consciousness with his assailant's terrible words mocking him: *Trapped in the water forever!*

Chapter Two

Sister Sun went from dull orange to blood red, and then she quickly sank into her resting place, leaving the sky to a glorious full moon and a generous explosion of stars. Thus blessed with ample light, Touch the Sky's band made good time along the hidden traces known only to red men.

Nonetheless, the tall Cheyenne deliberately slowed down, then halted his mount as they topped the last rise overlooking Roaring Horse Creek.

"Brother!" Little Horse called back impatiently. "Now is no time to play the laggard!

23

Why halt here? A double stone's throw away is water for your pony. See how she fights you to get at it?"

But young Two Twists, who rode nearer his leader, could discern the brave's face better than could Little Horse. Whatever he saw there made him call quietly ahead, "No lagging here, Little Horse. Best to hold for a moment. You also, Tangle Hair."

"You feisty pup!" Little Horse exclaimed, somewhat offended by the junior brave's tone of authority. He whirled his pony and rode back. "If you—"

At that moment Little Horse caught sight of Touch the Sky's face. "What is it, Bear Caller?" he asked softly, using the name that terrified Pawnees had given Touch the Sky after he had summoned a grizzly to rout them. For perhaps the space of ten heartbeats, Touch the Sky stared down toward the old wash that, every spring, swelled with snow runoff and became Roaring Horse Creek. Here and there glittering diamonds flashed where moonlight reflected off the water.

"What is it?" Touch the Sky echoed. "I know only this. The worst sorrow in the world is down there right now, waiting for us."

Not one of them moved, for the awful weight of these words held them. Touch the Sky was not known, as some were, for puffing things up with speech. He came at a thing direct and true. Knowing this, his three comrades felt cold sweat break out at their shaman's words.

Touch the Sky moved reluctantly, gently nudging his palomilla with his knees. But as if she, too, sensed the horror waiting for them below, she tried to crow-hop away from the trail.

The other mounts, too, rebelled. All four braves exchanged troubled looks in the silver-white moonlight. Plains Indians treated their horses as partners, not slaves to their will, and often gave in to them to avoid breaking their wild spirit. They did so now, hobbling them with strips of rawhide well back from the creek. They covered the rest of the distance on foot.

Their elkskin moccasins barely whispered in the new bunchgrass. Touch the Sky's every sense was alert, aware. He felt the gentle breeze caressing his face like exploring fingers; heard the steady chorus of cicadas and frogs, the rustle of cattails down by the water.

Nothing seemed out of the ordinary. He began to hope against hope that, for once, his shaman eye had fooled itself.

Then an anguished groan rose in Tangle Hair's throat.

"Maiyun save us!" he cried, one hand slashing downward across his body, making the cutoff sign for the dead.

Touch the Sky, too, now spotted it, about halfway across the creek: a figure apparently sitting in the creek, water rushing past his chin and the moon glaring in its bloody, empty eye sockets.

However, the figure was not sitting. Touch the Sky spotted the rope which had been thrown over an overhanging limb and tied under the dead man's arms to hold him up.

They still could not, at this distance, recognize the scalped and mutilated man. His reluctant legs as heavy as boulders, Touch the Sky moved down the bank with his friends. They stepped into the cold, quick current and began wading out.

"Look how his face is swollen," Little Horse said. "Blue and bloated. Brothers, this one was drowned before he was mutilated!"

The awful horror of this fate made all of them pause. The white men had their "hell" of fire and brimstone; for the red man, who had no identity except through the group, the only hell was eternal solitude. A drowning victim's soul could never leave the water; indeed, sometimes, late at night, these souls in pain could be heard crying out for help, their cries mistaken for shrieking wind and rushing currents.

Just then Touch the Sky recognized the bone choker painted with the distinctive claybank dye of the Cheyenne Antelope Eaters Clan. And in that moment he knew who the dead man was.

Shock, grief, outrage, and then again grief tore at him all at once. When he managed to swallow the hard stone in his throat, he turned to his friends. His knife was in his hand. Without a word, Touch the Sky suddenly slashed deep into his own arms.

While scarlet ribbons of his blood trailed into the water as he said to the others, "Do you know him now? Brothers, that dead man is Cheyenne. It was he who led the Bow Strings."

By custom Touch the Sky avoided speaking Spotted Tail's name. For it was common knowledge that the dead, hearing their names spoken, might answer.

"You are right," Little Horse replied. His voice was tight with the effort to hold back grief and rage. He, too, slid his knife from his sash and sliced himself, the other two automatically following suit. The warrior way did not permit a blooded warrior to engage in strong shows of emotion. Yet the death of a man as good and brave as Spotted Tail could not simply be accepted, as if his life and dying meant nothing. This blood shed now by his surviving comrades symbolized their grief and love for their dead brother.

All Indians were loath to touch a dead man. But when Touch the Sky said, "Let us carry that warrior one last time to the shore," not one of his friends held back.

"Our comrade was *drowned!*" Two Twists fumed as they lay the body out in the grass. "And look here how he suffered before. He was hamstrung!"

In the glaring moonlight, the deep cuts in the hollows of his knees were clear and stark.

"Drowned," Tangle Hair repeated. "Never can he cross over to the Land of Ghosts. Forever he will wander alone."

This fate was too brutal to comprehend. Inevitably, their sorrow gave way to implacable anger.

"Brothers," Touch the Sky said, "have ears for my words. For now I swear this, and this place hears me: From where we stand now to the Land Beyond the Sun, there will be no place to hide for whoever did this thing."

Arms still trailing blood, he thrust his lance out over their dead comrade. His men followed suit, crossing their streamered lances over his.

" 'Whoever did this thing'?" Little Horse repeated bitterly. The sturdy little brave glanced northwest, toward the now-hidden peak of

Wendigo Mountain. "Is there any doubt who did it?"

"It was the work of the renegades," Touch the Sky agreed. "The one who is no longer with us was openly loyal to me. Now he has been punished for that loyalty. I suspect this killing heralds a major move by our enemies. And no doubt the order was given by Wolf Who Hunts Smiling.

"But who made the actual kill? Was it a Cheyenne, a Blackfoot, or a Comanche?"

His comrades understood this crucial question. No crime known to the Cheyenne lawways was more heinous than the murder of a fellow Cheyenne. In the Cheyenne tongue, the word for *murder* was the same as the word for *putrid,* and the murder of a fellow tribesman caused the internal corruption of the individual and the tribe. Thus the murder stigma was strong. Even if a murderer was not banned (for Cheyennes were truly loath to banish their own) he could never again smoke from a common pipe or eat from a common utensil. He could never participate in the Renewal of the Arrows or the Spring Dance or the annual buffalo hunts.

"Two Twists," Touch the Sky said, finally making up his mind, "you and Tangle Hair will take our fallen comrade back to camp so he can be prepared for his scaffold. Stop and see Honey Eater, make sure all is well with her. Little Horse, remain behind with me. At first light, we will try to cut sign on the killer."

"No 'trying,'" Little Horse put in. "We *will* find his trail."

Touch the Sky stared at all of his companions

in the ghostly moonlight. "I fear this means Wolf Who Hunts Smiling and our enemies on Wendigo Mountain are about to move decisively. If this murder goes unchallenged, their boldness will be insufferable. We *must* punish the killer, and not just to avenge our dead comrade. If we let this thing stand, many more of us will share his silent fate."

"By now," gloated Wolf Who Hunts Smiling, "the deed should be done. He who was the leader of the Bow Strings is wormward bound now! It is the beginning of the end for White Man Runs Him and his toadies."

The new day's sun still held little warmth. Wolf Who Hunts Smiling and the self-proclaimed shaman Medicine Flute sat their ponies in the same cutbank near Elbow Bend where Spotted Tail had seen them one sleep earlier. With them now were Big Tree, Sis-ki-dee, and the blue-blouse captain, Seth Carlson.

" 'The beginning of the end!' " Sis-ki-dee mocked. "Have you joined your tribe's loco peyote soldiers? If the tall Bear Caller had died every time you promised, he would need another lifetime just to fit in all the deaths."

He looked at the other Cheyenne. "As for this sleepy-eyed worm larvae, if he puts that bone in his mouth one more time he will have to swallow it. I have tired of this noise."

Medicine Flute hastily put his flute away after this threat. But Wolf Who Hunts Smiling felt a murderous bile erupt up his throat. This Blackfoot dog sat on *his* hunting ground, yet he spoke with the same masterly, arrogant tone of the whiteskins. Still, the men in Wolf Who Hunts

Smiling's Panther Clan took great pride in not letting any feeling show in their faces.

"The end," he repeated clearly and firmly. "I am weary of this constant cat-and-mouse game. Woman Face and I have tested, tormented, and probed each other's vulnerable places while we wait for the right moment to close for the kill."

Wolf Who Hunts Smiling nursed powerful dreams of glory. When he was still a child playing war with willow-branch shields, he used to watch the chiefs and soldier-troop leaders ride at the head of the Sun Dance parades. Their war bonnets, heavy with coup feathers, trailed out behind them. And they held their faces stern and proud as the people pointed in awe—for were they not warriors who must maintain an aloof dignity around women and children?

But by now he was far beyond mere dreams of glory. There was a gnawing in his belly, a cankering need for power and respect.

However, before the Cheyenne could argue his resolve further, Big Tree interrupted to speak up in favor of Sis-ki-dee's skepticism.

"There is no love lost between my southwestern Comanches and the Contrary Warrior's northern Blackfoot men. But truly, our insane, wild-eyed friend here with the smallpox-ravaged face and ragged hair is no man's fool. How many times have we thought we sent White Man Runs Him to his scaffold for good? You may huff up your chest all you wish, buck! *Talking* our enemy into a grave is easy. You are boasting far in advance of the deed."

"I might say both of you speak straight-arrow," Wolf Who Hunts Smiling shot back, "if I were only speaking of yet another direct attempt on Touch the Sky's life. You are right, we have failed time and again to send him across. But this time, thanks to Medicine Flute's cunning plan, we have turned loose our old and worn-out one-trick pony."

The lupine grin that earned him his name now twisted his lips. The swift-as-minnow eyes stayed constantly and nervously in motion, looking for the ever-expected attack. This parley was being held in a hodgepodge of languages: English—which everyone present understood to varying degrees—and the traditional mixture of Sioux and Cheyenne words used as a trader's lingua franca on the High Plains.

But Big Tree was in a foul mood.

"I have no ears for this talk of one-trick ponies," he complained, frowning. Even in good moods, the huge warrior had little patience with clever speakers. "Only women and squaw-men take the long trail with their tongues. Like white men, you play with language in order to hide your meaning, not reveal it. Get off the long trail and speak words I can place in my sash."

"I am the best speaker in my camp," the Cheyenne boasted.

"So?" Big Tree sneered. "One squaw always has the fattest dugs."

"You call me a squaw-man?" Wolf Who Hunts Smiling said with quiet menace.

"Ahh, for Christ sakes!" Seth Carlson exploded. "It's no damn wonder we can't plant that red son! You bucks're too damn busy locking horns and playing the big Indian with each other. Wolf, what the hell do you mean to say?"

At Carlson's frustrated tone, the four Indians

momentarily buried the hatchet among themselves and exchanged satisfied smirks. This fool in leather boots was only permitted to live because he shared one trait in common with them: a passionate hatred for Touch the Sky, whom he still called Matthew Hanchon from his days among the Mah-ish-ta-shee-da.

"I mean to say only this, blue blouse. Our attempts at murder have all come to naught. But there is a better way to 'kill' him—deprive him of the support he needs in camp, leave him an Indian without a tribe. With the Bow Strings broken up he will have no one left but his little band. And I tell you now, it was the Bow String leader alone who kept the Strings loyal. With him gone, the winds of change will surely blow."

"His supporters will be trapped between the sap and the bark," Medicine Flute put in, speaking in his odd voice that still cracked like an adolescent's. "They will cross over to our side, count upon it. Then, with our supporters among the Bull Whips, the braves on Wendigo Mountain, and a swarm of Bluecoats for added firepower, Chief Gray Thunder's camp will be a bird's nest on the ground."

"Sand hills before a flash flood," Wolf Who Hunts Smiling agreed. "I will give any Bow String who wishes to a chance to swear allegiance to me."

"To us," Sis-ki-dee corrected him, watching him shrewdly. "Surely you meant to say 'allegiance to us'?"

"Of course," Wolf Who Hunts Smiling replied, his eyes sly and lidded now. "They may either join *our* Renegade Nation or die a dog's

32

death as did their leader."

"As to that . . . you say it is done? Who did the killing?" Big Tree asked.

"But, Big Tree. As you say, only women spill unneeded words. Never mind who. Be content that it is done. I gave my word his name would remain unspoken, else he refused to do it."

"Your word!" Sis-ki-dee threw back his head and howled. "Your word is a broken bow. Not one man here cares a gnat's breath for honor, so give over with your haughty Cheyenne rhetoric. Honor is for cowards who lack the manhood to lead."

"Honor has little to do with it, Contrary Warrior. We will need this man after we have combined our camps."

"Who cares a two-penny damn who killed the sonofabitch?" Carlson said. "Just so the plan works."

"It will work," Wolf Who Hunts Smiling said with sanguine assurance.

"Even if it does," Medicine Flute said, "it will not be enough."

The rest stared at him, waiting impatiently. The skinny brave was in the habit of pausing often for dramatic effect. Medicine Flute had no intention of defying the murderous and insane Sis-ki-dee. But from long habit, he held his bone flute as if eager to resume playing his monotonous notes when this annoying talk was over.

"I am talking about Honey Eater," he said. "The proud beauty with the white petals in her hair. If we fear that Touch the Sky may be supernaturally favored, what of his spawn? Or have you forgotten he has sired his whelp in her? Even if we finally kill or drive off the tall one, I fear the issue of this approaching birth—if we are foolish enough to let her bring this child to term."

"Hanchon's squaw has caught herself a baby?" Carlson said sharply. "It's the first I've heard of it."

Wolf Who Hunts Smiling nodded. "Where my cousin failed to sow, White Man Runs Him's seed proved fertile."

Carlson's weather-rawed face slid into a grin. Well, he consoled himself, at least Kristen Hanchon wasn't breeding with the savage. Though it would serve the Injun-loving whore right to be stuck in some stinking tipi with a brood of puling halfbreeds.

"I'll be gone to hell," he finally said. "They say the more things a man loves, the more ways for his enemies to hurt him."

At this, all four braves showed a little more respect for this whiteskin battle leader.

"Then he will surely be hurt," Wolf Who Hunts Smiling said. "No child of his will ever breathe life so long as I walk the earth. And I mean to be sure his wife and babe die before him. Let that licker of white men's boots sup full of sorrow before his own hard death!"

Chapter Three

Even before the critical secret meeting of his enemies began, Touch the Sky and Little Horse had launched their search for Spotted Tail's mystery killer or killers. But before they set out, each took a moment to hack off his long hair with a curved skinning knife—a mark of respect for the memory of Spotted Tail.

Both braves were expert at locating sign, so they split up, each taking a bank of Roaring Horse Creek. The question was not one of locating prints. This ford was popular with white and red men alike. Rather, theirs was the much more difficult task of winnowing chaff from grain, of separating all the signs to find the right ones.

While the air was still grainy with the first light of dawn, Touch the Sky began his meticulous examination of the mud along the south bank.

He paid scant attention to the deeper prints of the heavier, shod horses—made by soldiers and other white men. Clearly, whoever killed Spotted Tail was an Indian. Few white men knew the red man's fear of death by drowning.

Likewise he ignored any unshod prints that were completely dried inside. This killing was recent, and the prints should still be somewhat damp. Up and down the bank he progressed, bent low to the ground, often dropping on hands and knees to peer closely at the ground. Now and then he glanced out across the purling creek. In the gray half-light, he could just make out Little Horse doing the same on the north bank.

Several passes revealed nothing. As the new sun crept higher, he moved from the muddy border near the water back into the grass.

Here the sign was more difficult. Besides their own, he found a few old prints. But the grass within them was barely flattened down—suggesting that none of them was recent enough to be the killer's.

As the sun crept higher, Touch the Sky could not help being aware of his shadow—would he see it move again when he did not? What grave personal sorrow did this omen speak to? Old Arrow Keeper had spoken straight when he said premonitions were sometimes a curse from the Wendigo. Sometimes the warning was too vague to be useful, ensuring even more suffering as one waited in anxious fear.

Stop your womanly worrying, he commanded himself sternly. The best way to avoid a goring is to take the bull by the horns.

Despite this new resolve, his desperation grew as he failed to locate useful sign. If they could not pick up the trail here, chances were they'd never find it.

It was Little Horse who kept their hopes alive. He had stepped into the water and waded downstream perhaps the distance that a good shout would travel. Touch the Sky saw him suddenly stoop to scrutinize the bank. Then he rose and excitedly signaled to his friend.

"Brother!" he shouted when Touch the Sky had sprinted closer. "Our man is wily, but we are walking on his tail now! Come over here!

"See?" Little Horse said after Touch the Sky crossed through the chest-deep water. He pointed to a set of fresh prints made by an unshod horse—fresh, too, judging from the angle of the grass that had sprung back. "The killer stayed well back and then crossed far away from the ford."

"The tracks point north," Touch the Sky said. "You have an eagle's eye, brother. Good work. Now catch up your pony. The longer we stand here discussing the various causes of the wind, the greater our chance of losing our killer."

The trail, once located, was not easy to hold. Clearly the killer had anticipated being followed by experienced trackers. Constantly, the rider had backtracked and sidetracked, causing many time-consuming digressions. Several times he had ridden for long distances along rock spines, forcing his trackers to watch for such subtle clues as slightly displaced stones. He rode through sandy washes, up long draws, deliberately penetrated thick deadfalls and tangled briar patches.

Gamely the two friends persisted, the sun now hot on the backs of their necks. And despite the wildly circuitous route, the trail held steady to the north. Touch the Sky grew more and more convinced he knew exactly where it would end.

However, he held silent until he and his companion finally crested the last ridge overlooking the huge confluence where the Powder River met the Little Powder. Then the two Cheyennes exchanged a long look.

Little Horse nodded down toward their summer camp. From here all appeared peaceful. The tipis were arranged in clan circles, though each was built with its entrance facing east toward the rising sun and the source of all life. The hide-covered council lodge dominated the central clearing, well-worn paths crisscrossing the camp. Enemy scalps dangled from totems that marked the soldier-society lodges. Several adolescent boys played a hoop-and-pole game down near the river.

"There lies our camp," Little Horse remarked quietly. "From here, who would know a black cloud hangs over it?"

"And there," Touch the Sky said, nodding toward the ground in front of them, "lies the trail of our killer. Will you be surprised, brother, if we lose it in a few more heartbeats—lose it among hundreds of other prints leading into the common corral?"

"Disappointed, brother, yes. For it will prove our Sacred Arrows have been sullied again. But surprised? No. Like you, I guessed it long ago."

And so it turned out. There, grazing somewhere among almost 200 half-wild mustangs, was the pony of Spotted Tail's killer.

"Look!"

Little Horse pointed toward a group of braves just then emerging from the Bow String lodge.

"Our comrades must have returned with the body," he said. "For those Bow Strings have cut short their hair."

"Never mind the Strings, brother," Touch the Sky warned his comrade, his straight mouth forming a grim, determined slit. "Take a weapon to hand, and if you must fall, do it on enemy bones."

He nodded toward a group of braves now riding rapidly up the slope to intercept them, led by Wolf Who Hunts Smiling on his pure black pony with its roached mane. Riding with him were Medicine Flute, Lone Bear, and Wolf Who Hunts Smiling's stupid but loyal toady, Swift Canoe.

Touch the Sky eased his Sharp's carbine out of its buckskin boot. For safety when not actually in battle, he always carried it with a ball behind the loading gate and powder in the magazine but no primer cap. He removed one from his shot pouch and placed it on the nib behind the hammer. From long habit he checked his rope rigging to make sure his stone-headed throwing axe was ready to hand.

Little Horse, meantime, checked the multiple

loads in his revolving four-barrel flintlock shotgun. Each barrel was equipped with its own pan and frizzen, making it cumbersome to load. The gun was heavy and limited to short-range fighting. But in a close battle against superior numbers, it packed the authority of several riflemen.

Even as they readied their weapons, Touch the Sky saw Two Twists and Tangle Hair dashing up the slope on foot to cover them. Both carried small-caliber but sturdy British trade rifles at a high port, ready to swing them into firing position in an eyeblink. It was an attack style used by Bluecoat dragoons, and the Cheyennes had used it to good effect before.

"Look here, bucks!" Wolf Who Hunts Smiling called out to his companions as they drew nearer. "Once again Woman Face rides into camp with Little Horse—their long absence a mystery to the Headmen."

"No doubt," Medicine Flute threw in, "they feel deep grief for our dead companion. See, they have shorn their hair and even sliced their arms. All the outward trappings of grief."

"Yes," Wolf Who Hunts Smiling agreed. "All to disguise their guilt at having murdered a fellow Cheyenne."

None of this fazed Touch the Sky—not any longer. His next words instantly proved that.

"Look here, comrades," he called out to his friends. "Here they are, together again—as usual. Loyal as lovers. Tell me, wily Wolf. When are we going to see you hold another woman in your blanket for love talk—another woman besides your squaw Medicine Flute, I mean?"

This apt barb stung Wolf Who Hunts Smiling deep. The muscles around his jaw bunched tight as he fought down an angry response. And look at the stupid Swift Canoe! Grinning like a moon-calf, as if Touch the Sky had said something funny.

"Medicine Flute?" Swift Canoe said, genuinely baffled. "He is not a woman. Are—"

"Sew your lips, soft brain!" Wolf Who Hunts Smiling barked. He turned to Touch the Sky. "Never mind your smoke. Answer my charge. I say you are sending up all this smoke to cover your guilt at murdering a Cheyenne."

"Here is my answer."

He suddenly leveled his rifle dead-center on Wolf Who Hunts Smiling's chest. "Perhaps I did not hear you straight," he said in a dangerously low voice. "For I *believe* you called me Woman Face. Did you, Panther Clan?"

For once the furtive, constantly darting eyes went stone still, staring at the single eye of the rifle muzzle. That eye did not blink, and the situation was as clear as a blood spoor in new snow: Pushed beyond the limits of normal endurance, Touch the Sky would no longer brook even the slightest insult from those he meant to kill eventually. Not now, with the life of his wife and child at stake.

That last thought assured Wolf Who Hunts Smiling that his life was forfeit if he gave the wrong answer.

"I called you Touch the Sky," he said with evident reluctance. But his eyes said: *I will kill you soon, dungheap, so gloat as you will.*

"Is it so? A good thing . . . *Cheyenne.*" Touch the Sky heaped scorn on the last word—making it clear he considered his enemy anything but. "Now, did you also call me a murderer?"

Rage contorted Wolf Who Hunts Smiling's features. But when Touch the Sky's finger eased inside the trigger guard, he finally replied, "Perhaps my tongue flew ahead of the facts, as tongues will do. I meant to say—odd, that our companion was killed while you were gone."

"Odd?" Touch the Sky surveyed the lot of them, his eyes vigilant for the slightest motion, every muscle nerved for action. In that moment he wished one of them *would* start the fight—he ached for the release of violent action. The moment passed, chased away by Arrow Keeper's teachings about the welfare of his tribe. One twitch of the trigger would unleash a massacre here in camp.

"Odd?" he repeated. "What is truly odd is listening to you two-faced cowards calling that good brave *your* companion. You held him in contempt because he refused to lick your feet as Swift Canoe does."

"I have cracked his toes for him," the literal Swift Canoe protested. "But I have never licked—"

"You stone skull!" Wolf who hunts smiling raged. "Open your mouth again and I will cut out your tongue!"

Touch the Sky was tired of this travesty. "Count upon this," he told his enemies. "Somebody else who lives in this camp was also missing when *my* companion was murdered. And when I find out who he is, his guts will string my next bow."

With that stern promise still resonating in the air, Touch the Sky and Little Horse abruptly walked away, Tangle Hair and Two Twists covering their backs from a distance.

"The Headmen are meeting now in emergency council!" Wolf Who Hunts Smiling shouted behind him. "You will not strut away from *their* questions. If you try it, my braves will be ready for you!"

Despite the cool contempt Touch the Sky displayed toward his enemies, a new emotion challenged the outrage caused by the brutal killing of Spotted Tail: fear. For clearly his enemies knew what they were about. They meant to use the current confusion and anxiety to mask some bloody and treasonous move.

And not just against Chief Gray Thunder, he reminded himself as he headed toward the lone hummock where, by tradition, the shaman's tipi stood apart from the rest. Honey Eater had already been alerted to his arrival by the camp crier and had returned from her aunt's lodge, her mangy yellow companion following her with jealous vigilance. Touch the Sky could not resist a smile as he realized it: He understood full well how this lovestruck dog felt, for they loved the same woman.

Honey Eater sat out front in the brilliant sunlight, using a bone awl and sinew thread to stitch him a new pair of strong, double-soled moccasins.

She smiled when she saw him coming and laid her work aside, rising to greet him.

"Maiyun has brought you back to me one more time," she said. "To *us*," she added, modestly casting aside her eyes even as she felt the new life move inside her.

She stepped up into his embrace, eagerly meeting his kisses—a white man's custom he had taught her to savor. But even as he, in turn,

43

savored the woodsmoke and columbine smell of her, tasted the pliant and eager mouth—even then, Touch the Sky saw his loyal men fanning out discreetly all around them, weapons to hand. Realizing the danger, he lifted the bead-inlaid entrance flap aside and led her into their tipi.

"Maiyun will see me back many more times," he assured her. "Several winters ago, when Arrow Keeper sent me to Medicine Lake on my vision quest, one of the voices that spoke to me was your father's."

Both Cheyennes automatically made the cut-off sign at this reference to the dead Chief Yellow Bear.

Honey Eater's eyes widened perceptibly. "What did he tell you?"

"That those who have crossed over to the Land of Ghosts know all that will pass."

Suspended on the feather edge of her next breath, Honey Eater said, "Is it even so? Then . . . what did he tell you?"

"Many things. Some of them easier to understand than others. But one thing he told me was as clear as a marked trail. He told me he has seen me bounce my child upon my knee."

For a long moment, sparks of joy ignited in Honey Eater's eyes. Then, all of an instant, dread invaded those joyous orbs.

"*Your* child? But did he name me for the mother?"

The question caught Touch the Sky by surprise. And indeed, Honey Eater had struck a hard nugget of truth: He had never even considered what she was now thinking.

"My babe will spring from you," he said with

44

finality, "or not at all. And your father has assured me of its arrival. I wish he could have done the same for that good Bow String who was just murdered, for *he* will never know his child."

"Your enemies have remained ominously silent since Tangle Hair and Two Twists returned with the body. But I fear they have treachery firmly by the tail. They mean to try something during the upcoming council meeting."

Touch the Sky nodded. "My wife has a think piece to match her great beauty. They will indeed. Chief Gray Thunder is also in danger."

Honey Eater frowned. "Loyal Bow Strings have been guarding Gray Thunder night and day. But with their leader dead, I fear things may change."

"Things always change. Our enemies are counting on that. That is why they killed the head String. He was to their troop as a needle is to a thread. One is no good without the other."

Honey Eater hesitated before asking, "Do you know who the killer is?"

"Whose hand hamstrung him, whose hand held him underwater until he drowned? No. Not yet. But I know this. His lips have touched the common pipe. Therefore we are all contaminated. Honey Eater, there is blood on the Sacred Arrows."

She could only nod, for the awful force of his words silenced her. Bloodied Medicine Arrows meant a bloodied tribe.

"Wolf Who Hunts Smiling," she said, not making it a question. "If not he, one of his fawning minions."

45

"Straight words, little one. He or one of his lick-spittles. I mean to find out which."

"Yes," she said, another frown invading her pretty face. "And then you mean to kill him."

"I do indeed. And though revenge is part of the mix, there is a greater reason to kill him. For it has come down to this: They are moving to seize the tribe. Leaving this brutal murder unpunished would be a grave mistake. For any sign of weakness now may doom this tribe."

But he saw that the wise Honey Eater had already arrived at these conclusions herself.

"Be careful at this council," she warned him again.

Touch the Sky, however, failed to acknowledge this. For he was busy checking the action of a small two-shot pistol that he had just removed from his possibles bag. Honey Eater's eyes went wide when he handed the white man's "parlor gun" to her.

"I spoke with our friend Caleb Riley. He knows about our child, about the dangers you face in camp. He said you should have this, and I agreed. After I show you how to fire it, we will load it. Then you will carry it—always—in your parfleche. Do you understand?"

At first Honey Eater was surprised. Although her tall brave had grown accustomed to commanding warriors, he seldom used this peremptory tone with her. Clearly, his voice said, he would brook no debate.

But she understood why and approved. She and their child were in serious danger, as was Touch the Sky himself. There was no room for debate. War had come from within this time, and soon Cheyenne would have to kill Cheyenne.

"I understand," she told him, her voice stronger than she felt. "And I will obey."

Chapter Four

"How many times," Wolf Who Hunts Smiling demanded, "must the hunt fail before we admit that the white man's stink dwells among us? How many more good Cheyennes must be found 'mysteriously dead' before the elders pull the cowls from their eyes and admit that a murderer lives among us? When the Day Maker gave us our law-ways, he placed no crime above the murder of a fellow Cheyenne!"

For a moment he fell silent and turned to stare toward the center pole of the council lodge. There, in his usual place in the front rank of blooded warriors, sat Touch the Sky. His face and manner showed a stoic indifference to the proceedings. But Wolf Who Hunts Smiling sensed something else in his archrival's manner: the strong feeling that he was like a cache of gunpowder, about to explode at the first spark.

Truly this Touch the Sky was a dangerous man. Recalling their earlier clash, the wily and ambitious young brave backed away from the direct accusation on his lips.

"Fathers and brothers! Have ears for my words! Here among us now sits a murderer! Our loyal and brave companion was slaughtered like a paleface beef cow! Similarly, my cousin, the greatest war leader this tribe ever knew, was cut down from behind—perhaps by this same killer. How many times, fathers and brothers, must this slayer of our own shed *Shaiyena* blood before we decide that we must follow new leaders?"

An approving shout—led by Medicine Flute and the braves who belonged to the Bull Whip soldier society—greeted these words.

"As for me," Little Horse spoke up from his place in the front rank, "I request that Wolf Who Hunts Smiling stop addressing us as fathers and brothers. I am neither to him, thank Maiyun. Were I his father, I would have killed him at birth and fed him to wild hogs. Were I his brother, I would kill my own mother to prevent her from spawning another monster like him."

Little Horse was not known for speaking out at council. Surprised silence greeted this. Then came a quick burst of laughter from many of the Bow String soldiers.

"Refrain too," Tangle Hair put in, "from re-

49

ferring to 'our' loyal and brave companion. He who is no longer with us was no friend of yours, wolf-barker! Nor are you any friend to truth."

"He has spoken one thing straight," Touch the Sky said, his aggressive eyes trapping those of his adversary. "He said there is a cold-blooded murderer here among us now, and those are true words indeed."

"Yes," Two Twists said, "and a fox smells his own hole first."

"And so," added Little Horse, "does a wolf."

Chief Gray Thunder was seated on a vermillion-dyed buffalo robe in the center of the proceedings. He folded his arms until the belligerent clamor incited by these last remarks finally quieted.

"Some of you, at least," he said calmly, "still seem to recognize who your rightful chief is. Was I not selected by the Headmen? Were all ten bands of the Cheyenne Nation not invited to the Chief-Renewal dance? Have I ever failed to serve all the people to the utmost, or ever put personal gain before my tribe?

"Yet, only look here! More and more of my young men talk like the renegades of the Southern Cheyenne, who follow the Dog Man named Roman Nose."

Even Gray Thunder's enemies listened closely. Though he was well past his fortieth winter, Gray Thunder was still a stout and vigorous warrior. His only "mistake," Touch the Sky thought grimly, was his loyalty to the long-missing Arrow Keeper. For it was Arrow Keeper who advised Gray Thunder and the Headmen to follow the peace road with white men—at least with the decent ones among them, for he claimed many *were* decent. Wolf Who Hunts Smiling, in contrast, argued for an outright war of extermination against all white men, women, and children.

"Roman Nose," Wolf Who Hunts Smiling spoke out boldly, watching Touch the Sky, "is no licker of white men's crotches."

"True it is," Touch the Sky admitted freely, "I have several paleface friends. Unlike you, however, I do not plot with Bluecoat officers to destroy my own tribe. Only tell me this, Panther Clan: Did you yourself actually murder my comrade, or did one of your cowardly lickspittles do the filthy deed for you?"

Rage sparked in Wolf Who Hunts Smiling's dark eyes. Touch the Sky made silent eye contact with the members of his loyal band. One by one, hardly observed by the rest, they fanned out and took up new positions among the councillors.

"Mark this moment, Bull Whips!" Wolf Who Hunts Smiling roared out. "All, mark this! This White Man Runs Him accuses *me* of murder in front of the entire tribe. And does our 'chief' censure him?"

"Why should I?" Gray Thunder shot back, pulling his red Hudson's Bay blanket tighter around his shoulder. "Have you ever once held *your* tongue in check when it comes to accusing Touch the Sky? Neither one of you knows how to respect a council."

Touch the Sky's hunch had been right—Wolf Who Hunts Smiling had meant to make his bold takeover bid during this council. His next words proved that.

"Brothers! Have ears! I have spread our enemies' bones from where I stand now to the Marias River! I have defeated Pawnee, Crow, Ute, and the best fighters the hair faces could send out. And now I say this. A 'chief' who does not enforce the law-ways is no chief at all. What does Gray Thunder mean to do about the killing of our fellow Cheyenne?"

At this Medicine Flute came to his feet. His sleepy, heavy-lidded eyes were now animated from the boldness of what his faction was about to do.

"He means to do nothing!" he said. "And I tell you this. *Nothing* will come from nothing. It is time for a new leader with sap in his veins to lead this tribe against *all* our enemies, white and red! I follow only one leader: Wolf Who Hunts Smiling!"

Clearly, thought Touch the Sky, this "spontaneous" rebellion was all planned. When Medicine Flute finished speaking, Lone Bear and Swift Canoe led shouts of support. A score of Bull Whips produced their weapons.

Triumph gleamed in Wolf Who Hunts Smiling's eyes. With utter impunity, he slid the Colt Navy pistol out of his sash and leveled it on Touch the Sky. In the shocked silence which followed, everyone present heard the metallic click as he thumbed the hammer back.

"No shaman tricks this time, Woman Face," he said softly. "Look into the eyes of the better man who killed you!"

His finger eased inside the trigger guard and curled around the trigger, taking up the slack.

"Before you shoot me, wolf-barker," Touch the Sky said calmly, flicking a bit of dust off his shoulder, "look to Tangle Hair. He has something for you."

Wolf Who Hunts Smiling did look. And he could not miss the single, staring eye of the big muzzle looking back at him—Tangle Hair's cap and-ball dragoon pistol. It fired a huge, conical ball that left exit wounds the size of a man's fist.

"And you, Lone Bear," Touch the Sky said, watching the leader of the Bull Whips. "Look to Little Horse."

Little Horse had borrowed a long cavalry pistol from a loyal Bow String. Now it was aimed center-of-mass at Lone Bear.

"And you, bone blower! Look, mighty 'shaman,' to Two Twists!"

Medicine Flute's face drained white when he saw the old multibarreled pepperbox pistol trained on him.

"Kill me," Touch the Sky said. "Long have you lusted to do it. But know that you three will forfeit your lives for the pleasure. My men have sworn to die with me, so do not think they fear the consequences of their action."

"I have no plans to die in my tipi," Little Horse spoke out, goading Lone Bear. "And the braves in my clan are all a bit crazy. Do what you must, you worm-eating Bull Whip, I am *for* you!"

More silence as the rebels took in their grim situation. Once again Touch the Sky had cleverly anticipated them and moved to block their flank. While he still had everyone's attention, the tall Cheyenne abruptly rose. With a mighty thrust, he rammed his red-streamered lance into the packed-earth floor of the lodge.

"Fathers, brothers, enemies! *All* of you, have

ears. He who may no longer be named was a model of manly courage and decency. Even now his widow is being restrained by her clan from self-slaughter, her grief so terrible she does not wish to live. And therefore, I now say this, and this place hears me!"

He paused, his eyes skewering those of Wolf Who Hunts Smiling. "I will discover just *who* among us killed our comrade. And then I will fight him to the death in a duel of honor. Our Arrows must be washed, and this time only more blood will cleanse them."

A visible shudder passed through all assembled when Touch the Sky suddenly pulled a strip of black flannel from his possibles bag and tied it to the lance. By so doing, he had transformed his weapon into a symbolic "vengeance pole." Black was the color of death and also symbolized joy at the death of an enemy. Doing this before council was a clear vow: Either Touch the Sky would avenge the killing of Spotted Tail, or he was sworn to die as the price of failure.

"You know what to do?" Wolf Who Hunts Smiling asked his lone companion.

The Bull Whip trooper named Skull Cracker nodded his head in the wan light of a three-quarter moon. His only other reply was to slap his thigh with the rawhide-wrapped rock which had earned him his name.

Skull Cracker had a bad habit, as did many Indians, of trusting to medicine to guide his rifle bullets, making him a bad aim. And he was only indifferently skilled with a bow. But his deadly prowess with his crude weapon made him a fearsome warrior. He practiced with it so often that his right shoulder was a knotted lump of muscle—one blow from horseback could drop a buffalo bull or smash a human skull like an egg shell.

"White Man Runs Him is still chortling from his bragging session during council," Wolf Who Hunts Smiling said. "But I *gave* him that little battle. Let him have a sweet taste of the hump steak before we make him eat the horns! Finding his little Honey Eater with her brains oozing from her ears will drive the cool and goading smile from his lips. In his rage, he will move to kill me here in camp. With my supporters warned, he will be marked for certain death."

"Just so it is you he goes for," Skull Cracker said. "I fear few men, but this Touch the Sky is one of them. No man is a coward to admit it, only wise."

"As you say. But he is mortal, buck, and I will smear the blood of him on my body."

The two Bull Whips had met near a salt lick in an elbow bend of the Powder River. The river whispered steadily behind them, water bugs skimming the placid surface. Slightly east of their position, where the cottonwoods thinned out, the clan fires of camp showed lurid, flickering images in the night. Now and then loud cheers erupted—the younger braves betting on pony races and wrestling matches, shouting encouragement to their favorites.

"No man is a coward to fear *him*," Wolf Who Hunts Smiling admitted after a long moment of brooding. "Only a soft-brain would not. I once mocked him for a squaw-man. And truly, he *is* womanly in his weakness for showing his feelings in his face for all to see. Have you seen him gaze on his woman? This is a weakness in a man, this needing of women."

"A man must rut," Skull Cracker objected.

"If he *needs* it, buck, it is a weakness that can be used against him. But it hardly matters with Woman Face, for once he raises his battle axe, there is no soft place in him. Still, for once the Bluecoat soldier chief Seth Carlson spoke straight. The best way to hurt a man is to hurt the thing he loves most."

Wolf Who Hunts Smiling glanced farther back past camp. Downstream, the river formed a little backpool, out of sight from here. A thick screen of willows afforded good privacy, and the pool was set aside as a bathing area for the women. The Cheyenne were the most modest of the Plains tribes. By strict custom, Cheyenne males always steered wide of the area.

Wolf Who Hunts Smiling did not bother mentioning a more practical reason for sending Honey Eater under—the new life beating inside her. Medicine Flute was a coward, certainly. But he was no fool. Any son spawned by Touch the Sky would be as deadly to Touch the Sky's enemies as a smallpox blanket. So would a daughter, a potential breeder of his line.

"He has her watched constantly now," the ambitious Cheyenne went on. "But no guard will stray too close to the women's bathing pool. Honey Eater likes to go there after dark, when it is private."

He nodded toward a log lying near the water's edge. "Roll that into the current and you can float up to the pool unobserved. Take a care, however, moving through the reeds which separate the pool from the river. Show her no mercy, buck! Even after the killing blow drops her, deliver a few more. Turn her pretty face into bloody pulp, and let her tall brave practice his 'kissing' on that!"

Skull Cracker hesitated. He was as brutal as his name implied, and for this reason Wolf Who Hunts Smiling sought him out for this killing. But the taboo against killing a fellow Cheyenne was strong. Even stronger was Skull Cracker's fear of Touch the Sky.

"As to killing a woman," he boasted, "I agree with our Sioux cousins. Are *they* called cowards like the Ponca? No, yet they prize a woman or a child's scalp even higher than the rest, for the hair is of better quality.

"But a thing troubles me. I would rather give her a tap to silence her, then drown her. This thrashing of her face, it ensures the murder stigma."

"Yes," Wolf Who Hunts Smiling agreed. "It does. And it thus ensures that none may call it an accident. Let the tall pretend Cheyenne know that we have snuffed out his wife *and* his child in one lethal stroke. His hurt will be topped only by his rage. Caught between those emotions, anger clouding his vision, he will make his fatal mistake.

"Now go, Bull Whip, and may your thoughts be bloody or nothing!"

Honey Eater unbraided her hair as she stepped past the thick willow brake and breathed a grateful sigh.

The bathing pool, deserted now as the air began to cool, lay silent and inviting. New moonlight reflected off it like glowing foxfire. Touch the Sky thought she was still visiting with Sharp Nosed Woman. He had asked her to start bathing earlier, when other women from her clan were present.

She had meant to do as he asked. But though he thought only of her safety, he had neglected her Cheyenne modesty. Honey Eater was proud of the new swelling of her body. But it was still difficult to abide the smiling, slanted glances of the other women when they saw her naked. And surely *this* place, at least, was safe. Must she give up all her little pleasures?

But that thought triggered another stab of guilt—her new pistol! She had it with her now in her parfleche, as she had promised Touch the Sky. However, surely she could leave it here with her clothing? Certainly the water would ruin it.

Frogs lulled her in a raw-throated serenade. Honey Eater took one last, sweeping glance around in the grainy darkness. Then she lifted each foot to slip out of her moccasins before shrugging out of her fawnskin dress. A womanly rounding of her stomach—noticeable only now when she was naked—made her smile self-consciously even in this solitude.

Both hands placed lightly over the swelling, as if protecting the chrysalis of life within her, she waded into the pool. The water had cooled, and at the first shock of it she halted for a moment. A sharp intake of breath hissed across her lips.

A log drifted lazily past farther out on the river. Honey Eater's first hesitation passed and she waded out up to her knees. The bottom here was smooth sand and small pebbles, pleasant under her feet. The gentle fragrance of wild roses teased her nostrils. Honey Eater tried to empty her troubled mind of all worry, savoring this peaceful and pleasant moment.

A stick snapped, somewhere in the reeds beside her, and Honey Eater whirled around. Instead of thinking of her new firearm, long habit took over. Her hand flew automatically to the rawhide thong around her neck. It held a short, wide-bladed knife. The threat of surprise attack was constant, and no Plains tribe valued chastity more than the Cheyenne. By long custom established by the Cheyenne women themselves, these knives would be used to commit suicide when threatened with rape and a fight was useless.

But it wasn't fear of rape that sent Honey Eater's blood throbbing into her palms. Like a she-grizzly with a new cub, there was no fear in her—only the instinctive determination to protect this life which depended on hers.

But there was no further sound from either the willows or the tall reeds that separated the river from the pool. Besides, the frogs still chorused. Touch the Sky had once warned her: When the frogs fall silent, danger is near.

Another twig snapped. She heard the noises of someone breathing, and Honey Eater's heart leaped into her throat.

The reeds beside her abruptly parted, and she nearly screamed—until she recognized the intruder.

"You!"

Honey Eater laughed outright, her relief was so great. For there, tongue dangling from one side of his snout, was the loyal camp cur that had lately become her shadow.

He lowered his head between his front paws, sensing that this area was taboo even to him.

"Well, I am glad to see you," Honey Eater admitted. "Though you are a male, you may stay."

She waded out until the cool water reached her hips. She stooped under and soaked herself clean to her hair. She let the water brace her skin. Then she rose, saw the moon swim into focus, heard the chorus of frogs.

Again she dipped, rose, and noticed something different: The frogs had fallen silent.

Her breath snagged in her throat. Before she could move, a figure lunged through the reeds and grasped her hard above her left elbow.

A snarl of canine rage, sudden splashing as the cur charged closer, a brindled streak of fur in the moonlight. It leaped hard on the attacker, driving him back. Crying out as she broke free, the lithe Honey Eater spun around in the water and raced toward the safety of camp.

Chapter Five

"I have heard a thing," Touch the Sky said, riding up beside the young herd guard named Hump Medicine.

The youth was instantly wary and a bit nervous. He knew this tall one's black reputation, knew of the many charges against him, and this made Hump Medicine cautious. But he was also aware that Touch the Sky's coup feathers trailed the ground behind him when the shaman donned his crow-feather war bonnet.

So he held his face expressionless, in the warrior way, and said only, "I have ears for this thing." His tone was respectful but not friendly.

"I have heard," Touch the Sky said, swinging down off his palomilla and dropping her hair bridle, "that one may use gunpowder in place of salt. But count upon it, little cousin: Salt will not fire a rifle."

Touch the Sky said this in a conversational tone, meantime running his eye over the fine blue dome of seamless sky and the sawtooth pattern of the distant mountains on the horizon. All around them grazed the half-wild mustangs the tribe had driven down out of the mountains at the end of the cold moons. Some of them still had not shed their winter coats. And because they still had a tendency to stampede, herd guards like Hump Medicine constantly patrolled each flank.

Clearly, Touch the Sky's odd words puzzled the young warrior. The braves of Hump Medicine's clan, the Crooked Lances, remained independent of the two soldier societies, the Bull Whips and the Bow Strings. But they were sharply divided over the current power struggle.

Some favored Wolf Who Hunts Smiling and Medicine Flute, others swore allegiance to Chief Gray Thunder and their controversial shaman, Touch the Sky. In his secret heart of hearts, Hump Medicine felt Touch the Sky was the better man. But truly, appearances always seemed to indict him past any reasonable explanation.

So now he only frowned and said, "Gunpowder? Salt? You have spoken like a true shaman, for I cannot place such talk in my parfleche."

"Perhaps not. Perhaps in saying them I only mean to remind you to be careful with appearances. But you can pick my words up and examine them later. The truest words seldom fly direct to their meaning."

Touch the Sky, still in no hurry, knelt to pluck a tall-grass wildflower. He nibbled on the pleasantly bitter stem as he surveyed the herd around them. But his thoughts ran far from the view.

He again saw Spotted Tail's dead and bloated face, eyes ghastly with the horror of dying unclean. And he again saw Honey Eater's face last night in the orange glow of the firepit—drained of color, still fear-distorted, as she told him of the aborted attack at the bathing pool.

So now he took his time with Hump Medicine. This tribe was on the verge of bloody revolt. The young braves whose loyalties were still undeclared—those like Hump Medicine—were therefore critical. Not only would it be the young warriors who would decide the looming battle—the path they chose now would shape the tribe's future, a future which held special importance for Touch the Sky now that *his* child was to have a place in it.

"Now you tell me a thing," Touch the Sky said.

"If I can."

"You can, buck, if you are a man. Name the braves who have cut their ponies from the herd and ridden out in the past few sleeps. Ridden out by themselves and stayed gone for at least one sleep. Never mind the scouts and runners."

Hump Medicine frowned in spite of his resolve to show no feelings. This thing was awkward. He knew full well about the vengeance pole that Touch the Sky had recently set up. So he also knew why he asked this question.

Hump Medicine had admired Spotted Tail greatly. Truly he wanted to see his murderer punished. But what if it *had* been Touch the Sky, as Wolf Who Hunts Smiling claimed? What if Touch the Sky's show of emotion was merely smoke to hide his guilt? In that case, Hump Medicine feared he might be helping a killer set the trap for an innocent man.

"By what authority," Hump Medicine said, his eyes slanting evasively off toward the horizon, "can I be compelled to answer this? I have passed my initiation and am now a warrior, not a child. You are our shaman and Arrow Keeper. Thus, I owe you respect. But only soldier chiefs or a war leader may compel an answer from an initiated warrior. Even Gray Thunder does not have this power."

Touch the Sky felt no anger at this reply. Indeed, he respected it. A warrior was expected to resist undue authority, and Hump Medicine spoke true words.

"Several winters ago," Touch the Sky said, "I was severely beaten by the Bull Whips during my first hunt."

Hump Medicine nodded solemnly. "Everyone knows the story. Wolf Who Hunts Smiling was a hunt policeman. He said you violated hunt law by hunting alone. Others say you were only trying to drive a small herd back to the main group when they went over a blind cliff."

"Yes, as you say. And although they could not stop it, not one Bow String laid his whip against me. Do you know why?"

Again Hump Medicine nodded. "Their leader, the one who may not be named—he cried out,

'Bow Strings, if you honor justice, turn your ponies!' "

"You have the story well, buck, and you have it true. *That* was a brave who honored justice above all else. *That* was a brave who saved my life. Now look at me, *Shaiyena!*"

Startled, Hump Medicine did as commanded. Indeed, Touch the Sky's tone brooked no defiance. The shaman's dark, powerful orbs seemed to glow with a preternatural power. Hump Medicine felt a shiver move up his back as he realized that there *was* a touch of the supernatural to this one.

"I esteemed him as a brother. Can you look in these eyes and tell me I killed him?"

For perhaps ten heartbeats Hump Medicine did look. And by the tenth heartbeat, he was ashamed for his suspicion.

"Yes, you killed him," Hump Medicine replied in a tone of self-mockery. "It happened on the same day the Powder flowed backwards. Now forgive a buck with green fur on his antlers, shaman, and ask me what you will. I will tell you what I can, for I too want to see this killer do the hurt dance!"

"We must bring this killer to justice!" Wolf Who Hunts Smiling fumed. "Every great tribe falls, and falls hard, once there is no manly will left to punish tribal law breakers. It is not just the putrid stink of murder that is on us. Did you see Woman Face openly defy our law-ways at the council? Did you? Gray Thunder warns us about the Southern Cheyenne Dog Soldiers. But is this tall renegade of ours any less danger than Roman Nose?"

65

He and Medicine Flute had stopped by to visit the war lodge of the Antelope Eaters Clan. Like the Crooked Lances, most of the Antelope Eaters remained aloof from the two main soldier troops. And also like the Lances, their members were torn in their loyalties. The two visitors knew that.

"Indeed, he is more dangerous than Roman Nose," Medicine Flute put in, his voice cracking like an adolescent's. "And more cowardly. Roman Nose at least declares his rebel's status openly like a man. He first snapped the common pipe. Then he took his followers and left the main camp. Our 'Dog Soldier' pays lip service to our law-ways, still lets his lying lips touch the pipe, while secretly defying our ways. This is the excellent treachery he has learned from living among whiteskins. Their chief skill is at talking from both sides of their mouth. They use language to disguise their true meaning."

Medicine Flute's words carried weight. While still young, the intelligent and perceptive youth had realized that visionaries were highly respected by red men, that *they* did not have to hunt and fight and work as other braves did. So he pretended to have visions and eventually convinced most of his clan that he possessed medicine. With Wolf Who Hunts Smiling goading him on, he had once awed the entire tribe by performing a miracle: setting a star on fire and sending it blazing across the heavens.

But in fact, Wolf Who Hunts Smiling had talked to a reservation Indian educated in a whiteskin school. This so-called miracle was really a comet, and the whiteskin shamans had predicted its passage. Nonetheless, Medicine

Flute claimed credit for the spectacular celestial demonstration, which had struck many in the tribe dumb with awe.

Despite Medicine Flute's influence, however, a middle-aged brave named Shapes the Bow had begun frowning. He was a respected warrior and was looked up to by the younger men of his clan. But like many competent warriors, he was not able to speak up confidently as leaders such as Wolf Who Hunts Smiling could do.

Seeing him frown, Wolf Who Hunts Smiling sent a high sign to Medicine Flute. Then he said, "What is it, Uncle? Our words do not fly straight enough for you?"

He was careful to keep his tone friendly. Wolf Who Hunts Smiling had no complaints against the Antelope Eaters. True, some of their braves were squaw-men who let their women nag them in public. But when the war cry sounded, none was ever found hiding in his tipi. He would rather win them over by persuasion than by coercion. But if it came to that, coercion would do.

The older brave scowled at Medicine Flute. "*Your* words fly straight enough, Wolf Who Hunts Smiling. But that one there with the legbone flute in his skinny fingers. All right then, he moved a star across the sky. *Ipewa.* Good. But did I alone just now hear him call Touch the Sky a coward? Say what you will about the tall one who arrived among us wearing shoes, except to call him a coward. Call a grizzly a flea and speak more sense."

"He would not call him a coward," volunteered a younger brave, "if Touch the Sky were within hearing of those words."

Medicine Flute was about to object, demanding more respect as the shaman-by-right. But Wolf Who Hunts Smiling silenced him with a warning glance.

"Medicine Flute spoke carelessly, bucks, as we all do from time to time. He knows better. We both admit that Touch the Sky shows a manly grain clear through. Indeed, he may well be the best warrior on the Plains. But bravery does not preclude treachery. The Pawnees who stole our Medicine Arrows were brave enough. And a good warrior may still be a pretend Cheyenne."

Wolf Who Hunts Smiling was a beguiling speaker. The rest were forced willy-nilly to nod at this wisdom.

"He heaves a good axe, scars ridge his strong body. But when you look on that 'noble' form, see this also. See an 'Indian' who drank whiskey with whites inside the trading post. This, while a bounty was on our hair and his red brothers risked death outside, waiting for him. I was there, I saw it!

"See this too. See an 'Indian' who deserted his tribe at a vulnerable time, just so he could go fight battles for his paleface parents. See an 'Indian' who counts among his blood brothers a Bluecoat soldier chief!"

"An 'Indian,' " Medicine Flute chimed in, not to be outdone, "who has taken a white woman into his blanket for love talk and then ruts on a Cheyenne woman."

None of this could be denied. Hearing all of it like this, bald and unadorned, made Shapes the Bow's frown etch even deeper. At a quick sign from Wolf Who Hunts Smiling, he and Medicine Flute left.

"Leave things as they are for now," Wolf Who Hunts Smiling said as they crossed the common clearing. A wide smile tugged at his lips. "I am content."

Wolf Who Hunts Smiling had recently traded a bar of pig lead and a bullet mold to a Sioux for a powerful slingshot. Made by the Apaches down south—masters of the silent kill—it featured a strong osage-wood handle and a powerful sling made from buffalo sinew, treated with lime for increased tensility. It lacked the effective range of a bow or rifle. But loaded with a palm-sized stone, it could drop a full-grown elk, at closer range, dead in its tracks.

Wolf Who Hunts Smiling had taken to practicing often lately. Now, before he resumed the conversation, he removed a small stone from the pouch over his left hip. To their right, a red-winged blackbird darted from one tree to another. The wily Cheyenne drew a careful bead and let fly the stone.

Medicine Flute pulled his instrument from his lips, duly impressed, when the bird promptly fell to the ground. A few feathers trailed it lazily down.

"Yes," Wolf Who Hunts Smiling said, resuming his former theme, "we have sown the seeds of doubt in the Bow Strings. Soon we shall reap the harvest in new followers. Carlson's men are in position by now. When the renegades ride down from their stronghold, we will show them the secret escape trails. Our village will be surrounded by soldiers with new carbines and big-thundering wagon guns. All escape will be cut

off. When that time comes, you will see Gray
Thunder and Woman Face's supporters slink
away to join us."

"That is all I can tell you," Hump Medicine
finally told Touch the Sky. "Those are the only
ones I saw riding out. You must talk to the other
guards."

"I have already, little brother," Touch the Sky
assured him. "I have learned what I need to
know. Ha-ho, ha-ho. I thank you."

Indeed, Touch the Sky had spent the better
part of the day engaged in meticulous question-
ing. He had established exactly who had ridden
out recently enough to have killed Spotted Tail.
And then he had narrowed that list down to
those he considered capable of the heinous
crime of killing Spotted Tail.

Now, as he headed back toward camp to
check on Honey Eater, he ran the names
through his mind once again. There were only
four likely suspects. Lone Bear, Medicine Flute,
Swift Canoe, and last but never, ever least—
Wolf Who Hunts Smiling.

Chapter Six

However, fate had no plans for granting Touch the Sky an easy vengeance quest. He and Honey Eater still lay in their robes, naked limbs entwined in close slumber, when a familiar voice shook them awake like a strong hand.

"Brother! Be up with the birds, for I would speak with you. I shall wait for you in the common corral—you will be needing your pony!"

Little Horse. Touch the Sky shook off the last cobwebs of sleep and then sat up, instantly alert. Most Indians were late sleepers when in their peace camp, he reminded himself. Light barely showed in the smokehole at the top of the tipi. His band would not be astir this early unless some serious new threat loomed close.

Honey Eater, too, had woken in a heartbeat. She said nothing as he tied on his clout and battle sash. He pulled his rifle out from under the old buffalo robe that protected it from dew at night. He checked to verify that there was a bullet behind the loading gate and dry powder in the magazine. Then he worked the action, the precision sound of the well-oiled mechanism solid and decisive in the early stillness.

Honey Eater said nothing with words. But her eyes, as she watched him, clearly asked the question.

"I know as little as you," he said, trying to keep the bitterness out of his voice. But the hard little nubbin of resentment and anger burned tight and hot inside him, like a slug festering in pus. The unspoken thought plagued him: Did it matter anymore what the latest danger was? Every day, for him and those foolish enough to love him, was like a brutal initiation rite. Other men could lie in peace with their women, perhaps. But for him "peace" was an illusion created by the Wendigo to drive men mad—as elusive as the fabled white buffalo whose birth would mark the coming epoch of the Red Nations.

Though he gave voice to none of this, she read the discontent in his eyes clearly enough.

"When we were both prisoners in the whiskey-sellers' camp," she told him gently, "I fully expected both of us to die. I was *ready* to die, for that night you swore your love for me out loud, you sang it to the stars and the trees.

"Now only look. We did not die. Our paths

since then, they have been so very hard. Where we had no right or chance of ever being together, our *hope* was the waking dream that kept the possibility alive. Despite the bent words of our accusers, we never disgraced our Arrows by dishonoring my marriage.

"Now—our child grows in me! Here is the spot where you just lay, still warm with you. *Let* our enemies plague us like locusts. Every moment with my tall brave is a gift from Maiyun. I would not trade this danger I share with him for peace with any other man. And the promise of lying in his arms again—and of presenting him with a healthy child—is all I need of a reason for living."

These words filled him with love, and not a little shame for his momentary discouragement. Honey Eater's eloquent words reminded him again. He did not fight for himself, or for glory and coups as some warriors did. He fought for Honey Eater and every Cheyenne child, woman, and elder in this camp. The warrior's first sworn duty, higher than the quest for glory and honor, was to protect the people. The braves, they could make their choice and then fight it out if need be. But the noncombatants depended on the warriors, and they must be protected.

He held her close for a few moments, feeling the vitality pulse inside her. Then, after her solemn promise to go stay with Sharp Nosed Woman, he left to join his companion.

Little Horse had already cut out his palomilla for him. Touch the Sky caught her up and slid the bitless bridle on, then seized a handful of pure white mane and swung onto her. Only now did Little Horse speak. By custom, he avoided opening on the serious topic directly.

"Buck," he said, "you are a warrior to be reckoned with. But you never truly lost your clumsy white-man's fingers—you plait bridles like a spindly-legged Ponca! I will make you a new one before that one falls apart. If the Day Maker gave you sense, perhaps you will watch me and learn something."

They bantered thus, speaking of a few more inconsequential matters while Little Horse pointed them toward the broad tableland to the south and they cleared the camp area. But soon the hard pace, after they crossed the gravel ford and pushed their well-grazed mounts to a run over the dew-damp grass, discouraged further conversation.

Approaching a redrock headland, the trail narrowed and entered a series of ascending cutbanks. Only now, as they slowed to a walk for the climb, did Little Horse speak again.

"Trouble is overleaping itself this time, Cheyenne! Especially for you. First our comrade, the best Bow String warrior, is brutally murdered. Now these attempts on Honey Eater's life. Rebellion threatens to turn our camp into a killing ground, and you are sworn to either slay our comrade's killer or sacrifice your own life. All this in your parfleche already, and now only look!"

They rode up out of the last cutbank, and Little Horse pointed ahead into the gathering light of morning. "Tangle Hair has been training his new pony for night riding. He spotted them earlier."

That first sight was indeed discouraging. Far

below, spread out in pyramidal ranks, were the fat-in-the-middle Army shelters known as Bell tents. At least fifty big cavalry horses filled a temporary rope corral behind the tents.

Then Touch the Sky recognized the swallow-tail unit guidon snapping under the Stars and Stripes, and cold fear kissed his nape: the pennant of the First Mountain Company, Seth Carlson's elite Indian-fighting unit.

"Carlson," Little Horse said, spitting the English word out like putrid meat. "A paleface girl with sunlight trapped in her hair preferred you over him. Now his blind pride has turned him into an implacable Indian killer."

"Exactly why he is here," Touch the Sky agreed, nodding. "That truce flag on their flagpole means they are supposed to be staging war games. But no 'game' brought Carlson here so soon after our comrade's death."

"No," Little Horse agreed. "It was a wolf in Cheyenne's clothing. A Wolf Who Hunts Smiling."

Touch the Sky kept his pony back behind a spine of rocks, for he had spotted sentries below at lone picket outposts ringing the camp. There was still no sight of Carlson. But while he watched, the unit bugler walked to the middle of camp and blew reveille. Gradually, soldiers began to emerge from their tents and form into their messes, building fires for breakfast.

"Our enemies mean to leave us on our scaffolds this time," Touch the Sky said. "We must keep an even closer watch over Gray Thunder. And we must watch these carrion birds"—he nodded down toward the soldier camp, now swarming with activity—"constantly."

75

Little Horse agreed. But his usual tone of insouciant recklessness was noticeably muted now when he spoke.

"Brother, we scaled the cliffs of Wendigo Mountain together. I shirk back from no challenge. But a thing troubles me greatly. It is one thing to grease my face against a Pawnee or a Ute. I am keen for such sport, and neither tribe is one to fool with. But have you seen how the Bow Strings are beginning to quarrel among themselves since their leader was killed? It sickens me to think of using Cheyenne skills to kill my fellows."

"The Star Chamber is meeting even now to select the Strings' new leader," Touch the Sky said. "But you speak straight, and I fear even a strong leader will not be able to staunch the avalanche. I despise Wolf Who Hunts Smiling and Medicine Flute as I loathe the yellow vomit. However, no man can fault their think pieces."

He nodded toward the Bluecoat camp below. By now the men had separated the metal halves of their bull's-eye canteens and were using them to fry bacon. Even as both Indians watched, Seth Carlson stepped past the fly of his tent, still strapping on his saber.

"Nor are these capable insurgents alone. Now you behold a soldier who believes Indians are nits—and of course, nits make lice. Once he was content to kill *me*. Now only the annihilation of our tribe will ease his troubled sleep— or at least, annihilation of that part loyal to me. And still there is more, for this time our enemy means to do what the Yellow Eyes call the coup de main. The full attack in force."

He slewed around on his pony's back, staring

toward Wendigo Mountain. "The insane Contrary Warrior and the Comanche Butcher will join their renegades to the slaughter. For this reason, I must name and then fight the murderer of our comrade. The Strings will follow the man who avenges him. But either I do it soon, or we lose our only allies."

"Either you do it soon," Little Horse said grimly, "or we lose *you*. This swearing on a vengeance pole—you went too far, buck! When Siski-dee stole our Arrows and demanded your head for their return, the choice was not yours. This time you have shot a hole in your own canoe! Is your life so short of dangers that you, too, must add to the list?"

"And *I* will paddle that canoe, shot or no," Touch the Sky assured him. "But never mind the future dangers and look sharp now. The hair-faces are about to drop a bead on us."

They watched below as Carlson slid a pair of brass cavalry fieldglasses from his campaign bag and began to scan the surroundings. The two Cheyennes backed up toward their ponies and disappeared again into the cutbank.

Concerning the brutal murder of Spotted Tail, Touch the Sky had already carefully mulled his list of prime candidates.

Of the four, one was a coward—Medicine Flute. But truly, Touch the Sky reminded himself, many murderers were also cowards. So he considered that all four—Lone Bear, Swift Canoe, Medicine Flute, and Wolf Who Hunts Smiling—were capable of murdering a fellow Cheyenne. Indeed, he was convinced that Wolf Who Hunts Smiling had killed his own cousin, among others, in his relentless quest to control the common pipe and destroy Touch the Sky.

But Wolf Who Hunts Smiling was also one to play the big Indian whenever possible. It would be his way to order the killing done by a subordinate. And chief among his fawning lickspittles was the not-so Swift Canoe. Stupid, but competent with weapons and loyal to his master, he was a reasonable choice for an assassin.

So with Swift Canoe, Touch the Sky began the critical process of elimination. In his private, inner circle of unvoiced thoughts, Touch the Sky had already picked the killer. But from a leader, Arrow Keeper had always instructed him, justice must be swift, sure, and above all, impartial. In this, the Cheyenne Way converged with the white man's ideal of innocent until proven guilty—a standard most whites suspended when dealing with Indians.

Nonetheless, time was critical. And unfortunately, justice could be time-consuming.

He already knew that the braves of Swift Canoe's clan were currently on guard duty for the group of tribal women who roamed far afield gathering nuts and the cherries that gave good flavor to pemmican. Soon after Touch the Sky returned from his scout of the blue-bloused soldiers, he found Honey Eater and asked where the women would be working.

If she was curious, it was not her way to press into a warrior's business. He would tell her what she needed to know, and he always had. She told him they had left early, heading toward the fertile bottom land surrounding the place where the Powder ox-bowed west of camp. Touch the Sky turned his palomilla loose in the common corral and covered the distance on foot.

He soon spotted the bored-looking Swift Canoe. He had propped his cap-and-ball trade rifle, the cracked stock reinforced with a strip of buckskin, against a tree. He himself perched on a fat log, indifferent to the women fanned out all around him. After all, his manner said, was he not a warrior? Warriors took no interest in the affairs of women and children.

"Swift Canoe!" Touch the Sky called out from behind him. "I would speak with you!"

The simple brave, caught in some private reverie, flinched with a violent start. He struggled off the log, almost tripping himself, and snatched up his rifle. Touch the Sky seldom approached him, so he assumed this visit meant trouble. He held his muzzle leveled at the brave's chest.

"Here is your chance," Touch the Sky told him affably. He made no move to draw any of his own weapons. "One twitch of your finger, and Woman Face is sent under! A pinch of black powder, and White Man Runs Him crosses the Great Divide. You will be the new hero to your wolf-barking master who always chides you for a dolt."

Indeed, there was a hard nugget of truth in all this, and Swift Canoe was clearly tempted to take up his trigger slack. But the moment passed.

"I could, but I will not," he replied coldly. "It would indeed be an honor to kill such as you. Because of your glory seeking, my brother is dead!

"However, I am the first to concede that your

79

band are all warriors to be reckoned with. My guts would be fed to the dogs before your blood was done soaking into the ground."

"I said it before, slow boat. It was the treachery of your renegade master that killed your twin. As for the skill and loyalty of my brothers, you are wise to respect them. However, they are not the reason why you must forbear from killing me now."

Touch the Sky nodded at the British trade rifle. "The sun is behind you. With your hammer cocked, sunlight is streaming through the chamber and out your muzzle. Bold killer, you have a primer on your nub but no bullet in your chamber! Blast away."

Swift Canoe's deep copper skin flushed even darker. He scowled, glancing down to verify this.

"This is some of your shamanism," he muttered sheepishly. "I had a bullet when I left camp."

"Is it even so? Perhaps it leaped out to 'graze'?"

Swift Canoe missed the pun. His scowl cut deeper as Touch the Sky tossed his head back and laughed. But instantly, his face was grim and menacing.

"Who killed the leader of the Bow Strings?" he demanded.

Alarm flickered in Swift Canoe's turgid eyes. He averted his gaze. "*You* would ask me this? I would sooner leave my pony with an Apache than believe your 'concern' for a dead Chey— *Anhh!*"

Swift Canoe was in the middle of the word when Touch the Sky abruptly swept one leg out in a hook, toppling the other man to the ground hard. Before another two heartbeats elapsed, he had his man pinned. Touch the Sky's obsidian knife, honed to a lethal edge on one side only, Indian fashion, now made a deep indentation across Swift Canoe's neck.

"Who?" Touch the Sky repeated. Quiet, lethal menace marked his tone. "Was it you?"

"No. I swear it!"

"You swear it by Maiyun, the Good Supernatural?"

Swift Canoe had trouble swallowing the hard lump of fear in his throat. "Yes, I swear by Maiyun and the Medicine Hat!"

"Do you know who did it?"

When Swift Canoe hesitated, Touch the Sky flexed his right arm—just enough to draw a neat line of blood across Swift Canoe's throat.

"No! I swear by Maiyun I do not!"

Touch the Sky had learned to study a man's eyes close for lying—most Indians were not as adept at lying as was Wolf Who Hunts Smiling, for lying was far less accepted among red men. Swift Canoe's eyes did not run from his or reveal that telltale inner twinge of conscience.

Touch the Sky believed him. In fact, he had never considered Swift Canoe a very likely candidate in Spotted Tail's killing. He had hoped, however, to coerce some useful clues from him. Clearly the stupid dolt knew nothing.

Touch the Sky stood up and sheathed his knife. "Have ears, soft brain! The choice is yours, and it is a clear as white man's glass. Our right peace chief is Gray Thunder, our war leader River of Winds.

"So far you have made the choice to follow a

traitor. And like that traitor, you are going to die. But spread the word among your dishonorable peers: Any Cheyenne is welcome to join those who follow the ancient law-ways. Those who choose to sully the Arrows will die.

"And say this too: I will kill the maggot who sent my comrade over. Just as I will kill the next man who even insults my wife!"

Chapter Seven

Despite his bold words to Swift Canoe, however, Touch the Sky knew that the jaws of a powerful and dangerous trap were closing on Gray Thunder's summer camp.

One jaw was Seth Carlson and his pony soldiers, now bivouacked within easy striking distance of camp. The soldiers' presence had been discussed at council. But the current treaty allowed right of passage as well as "training missions" to temporarily occupy outlying Cheyenne ranges. So the council had decided to limit their reaction to constant monitoring of the hair-face unit.

But a mere sentry could not save the tribe in time, Touch the Sky knew. Because it wouldn't really matter if they had brief advance warning when the "war games" turned deadly serious. A warning would hardly matter because the trap had a second deadly jaw: the renegades massed on Wendigo Mountain.

"They are coming," young Two Twists announced grimly shortly after Touch the Sky's confrontation with Swift Canoe. "I have followed your orders and constantly scouted the northern slope of Wendigo Mountain. They are slipping down in pairs and small groups. They are remaining separated and scattered apart to avoid causing much notice. But each group is heading to a staging area in the pine bluffs north of our camp."

Two Twists and Touch the Sky had joined Little Horse and Tangle Hair for a badly needed parley in the relative safety of the common corral. Two Twists's dappled gray and Touch the Sky's all-white palomilla rolled in the lush grass, drunk on the brimming sunshine. Their innocent joy almost saddened Touch the Sky—it was such a jolting contrast to the tension and fear which now gripped his tribe.

"A trap is no good," he told his companion, "unless both jaws spring shut together. Our wily wolf is eager to seize this village. But he is like a man who is willing to wound, yet reluctant to strike."

"Of course," Little Horse said. "For when he does strike, he must not fail. The price of his failed treason will be death. So he will only strike when the victory is assured."

Touch the Sky said, "Your thoughts fly on the

same wind as mine, buck. So our mission, while daunting, marks itself out clear: We are not enough to disable both jaws of the trap. Yet we can try at one."

"And if one is blocked, the trap will not spring," Tangle Hair said.

Touch the Sky nodded. "Even if we can ruin this trap, much still depends on my effort to expose our comrade's killer. We are rapidly losing more Bow Strings to the traitor's side. But if they see the killer of their leader brought to a hard justice soon, it may add to their courage. If not—I fear they will cross to those who promise to avenge it. And when enough go over, the Wolf Who Hunts Smiling will howl."

"It may be," Little Horse pointed out, "that those who promise to avenge our comrade's death will not need to even pretend. For they have blamed you for the killing, privately if not publicly. And if you fail, you will fall on your own knife, and they will have their man—at least, according to the lies they live by."

"Then we have only one solution," the ever-sanguine Two Twists said. "Our shaman will indeed cut his stag out from the herd and slaughter him."

"Do you have solid news there?" Little Horse asked his leader.

Touch the Sky shook his head. "Nothing you may heft. But as to that, I have another visit to make soon. The best news this day, brothers, was the selection of River of Winds to head the Bow Strings. The Star Chamber showed wisdom in this. He is already our war leader. Such double authority sits well on a buck as fair and loyal as he."

"Truly," Little Horse agreed. "Fair and loyal—as was our departed brother."

All three braves caught the ominous implication of this remark.

"All of this," Tangle Hair said, shaking his head in bitter frustration, "it cannot stand! Look there. Even now loyal Bow Strings ring Gray Thunder's tipi, protecting him from assassins. Touch the Sky's wife—where is she? Hiding under guard and leaving our tall shaman one more thing to worry on. Now River of Winds will need protecting. This cannot stand."

"Nor will it," Touch the Sky assured him. "The hair-mouths have a saying: 'When the worst is reached, things must mend.' Remember, bucks. The time is long behind us when killing Wolf Who Hunts Smiling could end our troubles. I wish now I had followed my desire! But he now has too many allies, like surplus beasts in harness, to pull their scheme along even if he drops dead in the traces. There is no easy path up from this muddy swale. We must slog up one step at a time."

Little Horse nodded. "Straight-arrow, shaman. We must wage holding fights for now. Feints, ambushes, violent disruptions of any kind we can manage. Whatever will run them off a blind cliff each time they mean to stampede."

Now that he had a better grasp of their battle plan, Little Horse began to show his famous swagger.

"I have been worrying like an old grandmother," he scoffed. "We are merely up to our usual sport here. Either we cover ourselves in glory or we die in battle. What man could want more?"

It was mostly bravado. But Touch the Sky knew that, for warriors, sometimes bravado and a little craziness were enough.

"You are all an embarrassment to your mothers," Touch the Sky told them proudly. "And as ugly as runt pups in the rain. But you are stout men to die beside. *Ipewa.* Good."

A moment later, however, the mirth left his eyes and Touch the Sky was all business. "Little Horse!"

"I have ears!"

"And a bold heart, too, buck. Ride south and make a picture in your mind of the pony soldiers and their locations. Tangle Hair! Relieve Two Twists at spying on the renegades."

"What?" Two Twists objected. "Do I stay in camp and stack up dog turds?"

"Trouble enough for all, double braid, pipe down. I have a job for you too. You are the best dissembler among us. Figure out some lure to get Medicine Flute away from camp—alone. He knows I mean to brace him, so now he surrounds himself with a pack of Bull Whips. When you have him cut out alone, hold him prisoner and sound your war whistle to summon me."

All three of his companions grinned, liking the sound of this.

"Do you mean to kill the skinny bone-blower?" Little Horse demanded, his voice making it clear that *he* would not weep at the funeral scaffold.

"In good time, yes, he will feed the worms. For now the dishonorable dog will live. Now turn to, stout warriors, and like Cousin Owl keep your eyes to all sides! Death is trying to cut sign on all of us. Circle your robes at night with dried pods, keep your back to a tree, and sleep on your weapons.

"Go, and may the High Holy Ones ride with you!"

Not long after this parley, Touch the Sky heard a long, shrill blast not unlike the cry of a loon—Two Twists sounding his reed war whistle. It came from a secluded willow thicket downriver from camp.

Touch the Sky, his Sharps tucked under one arm, battle axe swinging from his sash, took one of the well-concealed escape paths that ran through the cottonwoods and cattails near the water. Nonetheless, he felt hostile eyes monitoring him from camp until he was finally out of sight.

"Quick work, little cousin," he praised Two Twists. His loyal minion still held a knife to Medicine Flute's throat. He sheathed it as his leader came up. "How did you snare our weasel so fast?"

Two Twists sneered. "As you might catch a bear with honey. Do you know the maiden called Raven's Wing?"

Touch the Sky nodded. "Only a blind man could not." If any woman in camp rivaled Honey Eater for beauty, it was this comely lass.

"Our Bow String companion murdered at Roaring Horse Creek was her favorite uncle. When I told her we were trying to snare the killer, she was eager to help."

Two Twists' eyes beamed contempt at the

scowling Medicine Flute. "So I bade her remark to her sister, in front of this pathetic stag-in-rut, that she was going down to this place to bathe in the deeper water. Naturally, dungheap here deserted his guards to sneak down to spy on a naked beauty."

"At least," Medicine Flute retorted, "I am a man with sap in my veins. I like to look at naked women. So? The whole world knows you prefer watching the bucks."

"So you are a man, are you?" Touch the Sky repeated. "With sap in his veins? Let us tap this sap."

Medicine Flute's vehement protest died on his lips when Touch the Sky abruptly grabbed the bone flute from his hand and snapped it across his thigh, throwing both halves into the brawling river. Moments later, Medicine Flute squawked like a crushed bird when Touch the Sky swept his legs out from under him.

"Here, Two Twists, help me. Hold his braid back like this."

The skinny shaman-pretender was trapped and helpless. Touch the Sky, nearly twice his size, had laid aside his rifle and straddled Medicine Flute's scrawny chest; Two Twists, grinning like a happy baby, pinned his head back motionless by gripping the long braid as if it were a leadline.

"What . . . what outrage is this?" Medicine Flute demanded, his voice cracking like winter ice. "My medicine has set a star on fire! I deserve respect."

Both dark eyes protruded in fear when Touch the Sky slipped a rifle cartridge from his parfleche and chewed the cardboard end open.

"What . . . what are you doing? What is that for?"

"The coward *would* have to ask what a cartridge is," Two Twists sneered. "He has never had need of one."

"I am merely going to blow open a rotten gourd," Touch the Sky informed his prisoner. "And you, pig's afterbirth, will be right there close to see it."

"So close," Two Twists promised, winking as he had seen white men do, "that you will swear it is all taking place inside your head."

Without further parley or ceremony, Touch the Sky suddenly tipped the open cartridge and tamped the grains of black powder into his victim's left nostril. Before a totally surprised Medicine Flute could dislodge it by expelling a breath, Touch the Sky pinched the nostril shut.

Two Twists had already twigged the game, seeing his leader work it once before. Despite his warrior training, his stoic face divided itself in an ear-to-ear smile.

"Best have ears now, white liver!" he said. "For soon you will not have ears. Nor brains, nor eyes. You killed our comrade, reptile, and now we will blow you across the Final River."

"K-k-killed your comrade? I? But, Two Twists! Woman Fa—uhh, Touch the Sky! I swear by the sun and the earth I live on, I killed no one!"

"Nothing but the green diarrhea spurts from your mouth," Touch the Sky said. "Two Twists, let me have one of your lucifer matches. *This* one has told his final lie. Now we shall employ a trick learned from the white buffalo hiders and scatter his skull like a clay pot!"

"Bucks! G-g-give over with this madness!" In his abject fear, Medicine Flute's voice rose so high it squeaked. "Take counsel of this rash behavior. I have k-killed no one!"

"Puh-puh-perhaps," Touch the Sky said, mocking his fear stammer, "you did not do the black act itself. You are squeamish and would vomit if blood spattered you. But you know who did it. You are one of the worms who planned it."

"No! I swear by all things holy! No!"

Medicine Flute did seem sincere enough. Touch the Sky believed him. Wolf Who Hunts Smiling had learned long ago that men of few words seldom took any back. Nonetheless, Touch the Sky decided to make sure. He nodded at Two Twists.

"Strike the match, brother. This one has threatened my wife to her face, has spoken of his pathetic and base lust when no man was there to kill him for it. Now he crosses over."

"No! Please, dear Maiyun, *no!*"

By now the lower part of Medicine Flute's body flopped around like a nerve-twitching snake. Touch the Sky struck the lucifer on the rough sole of his moccasin. A spear-tip of flame leaped up, and Medicine Flute went as white as moonstone.

Two Twists snorted. "Careful, brother. He might wet on you in his fear."

"Say the killer's name," Touch the Sky told Medicine Flute, "and your head stays on your shoulders."

"If I knew I would say! I swear this thing!"

The words sounded comical thanks to his plugged nostrils.

" 'I tware dis ting!' " Two Twists mocked him. "Your word is not worth a spavined pony!"

Even so, Touch the Sky could read beyond a man's words. And he was convinced that Medicine Flute did indeed speak the truth at this moment. He had never favored this fungus-spine for such a brutal, hands-on attack as the one that maimed and killed Spotted Tail. And if he did know the killer's name, he would have spoken it by now.

Still . . . this was a rare chance for sport at the expense of a "man" he loathed to the very core of his being.

Touch the Sky gave the nod to Two Twists, abruptly letting go of the nostril. Two Twists dropped the match, brief sparks snapped, and Two Twists roared, *"Boom!"*

Medicine Flute screamed—a long, shrill, womanish scream that must have alerted the entire camp. Despite this, both Touch the Sky and Two Twists dropped to the lush river grass, convulsed with laughter. For most of the "black powder" had in fact been sand, with a few grains of real gunpowder mixed in to cast sparks.

"We terrified her!" Two Twists managed between gales of mirth. "Look at her lip quivering still!"

"Enjoy your child's game," Medicine Flute raged. He scrambled to his feet and began backing quickly away. His face twisted under the weight of his anger—so much anger that he could not bite his tongue before going too far by adding, "I wonder how you will laugh, Woman Face, when your whelp is untimely ripped from the dead Honey Eater's womb!"

Murderous rage instantly chased the mirth from Touch the Sky's face. Medicine Flute already had a good start on him. Now his willow-stem legs flew with impressive speed toward camp.

"Brother, watch out!" Two Twists shouted behind him as Touch the Sky tore blindly—blood filling his eyes—after the traitorous pretend shaman. Two Twists was astounded, for his leader was not one to succumb to goading. But this time he had, and he was not looking toward that hidden figure in the reeds!

Too late, Touch the Sky glimpsed motion in the reeds and cattails off to his right. There was a sharp fwipping sound, a bit deeper than the twang of a bow string. Then Touch the Sky's world exploded in a bright orange starburst when a blow like an iron fist slammed into his skull.

Chapter Eight

With the watchful eyes of Little Horse never leaving them, the unholy trio met just outside the newly erected breastworks of the Army field camp: Captain Seth Carlson, the Blackfoot Contrary Warrior named Sis-ki-dee, and the feared Red Raider of the Southwest Plains, Big Tree of the Quohada Comanche.

"Both of you listen to me and listen good," Carlson told the Indians. His years spent working with aboriginal scouts had made him proficient in sign language. Now his hands stayed in motion, filling in when he couldn't find the words he needed.

"I went to West Point. The best training in the world for war leaders. Heap big war makers! And I tell you this: a wise battle leader always strikes at the earliest opportunity. He who hesitates in battle is lost, for he surrenders the element of surprise and gives his enemy time to prepare.

"This Wolf Who Hunts Smiling. Granted, he is no coward. But a burned baby fears the fire. Hanchon has whipped him so many times he's got that Cheyenne spooked. We don't *need* to wait for his order. With my men and yours, we can raze Gray Thunder's camp."

" 'Heap big war makers.' " The brass rings in his nostrils flashed in the sun when Sis-ki-dee tossed back his head to laugh. "I have heard talk of this 'war school.' The young bucks spend four winters at this place. And yet they neither fight one battle nor kill one enemy in all this time. Four winters! They are called 'warriors' once they learn to cipher on paper and speak through their noses in French. *My* bucks are all tempered in the heat of battle. None rides with Sis-ki-dee until he has drunk the blood of his first kill."

"Do those kills include the babies you brain against trees?" Carlson said, his broad, bluff face divided by a sneer of contempt.

"Only the white ones," Sis-ki-dee shot back.

Big Tree had heard enough of this. "Are you both girls in their sewing lodge?" he demanded. "Only women and farting old men jabber on like this and say nothing of weight. Carlson, you say right about surprise. We Quohadas always try to attack out of the sun. But do not lose faith in our wily Cheyenne wolf."

95

Big Tree shifted his huge bulk around in his stolen Texas stock saddle with its bare saddle tree. He nodded toward the ridges behind them.

"The brave called Little Horse is up there. My scouts tell me Tangle Hair is similarly watching the pine bluffs where our men are massed. At the first sign of attack, they will use mirror signals to warn the main camp. Are you truly eager to enter a forewarned Cheyenne camp? They are not called the Fighting Cheyenne for nothing. Every man, every woman, even the smallest child will pick up weapons from the dead and attack. When you fight them in their camp, there is no surrender. The battle is never over until the last Cheyenne is dead."

Even Sis-ki-dee, quick to call a hesitating man a coward, nodded at these words.

"We could win," he said. "No doubt we would win, eventually. But the cost would be a hard sort of 'winning.' Wolf Who Hunts Smiling and Medicine Flute are both working at Woman Face's loyalists from within. Better to trap a badger in his hole. Once the battle of words is won, the tribe will side with Wolf Who Hunts Smiling."

Carlson mulled all this and had to admit that these two renegades knew shit from apple butter. Behind him, in camp, his men sat crimping cartridges and cleaning their new Spencer carbines. It would indeed be awkward to explain—before a board of inquiry—how a "defensive" battle took place in an Indian village!

"I'll hold off a bit longer," he conceded. "But even if every buck, bitch, and papoose in that village throws in with Wolf Who Hunts Smiling, don't forget—there's at least four we'll have to kill. Hanchon and his band will fight like a regiment."

"Four we need to kill?" Big Tree said. "Not four—six. The wily Wolf recently told me another attempt will soon be made to kill Honey Eater."

"She only makes five," Carlson said.

Big Tree bared his huge white teeth in a grin. "As you say, Long Knife. She does. But her swollen womb makes it six."

Honey Eater was shelling peas in front of her aunt's tipi when she saw Two Twists run up from the river, his face frantic, and charge across to the Bow String lodge. Her face drained of color as the wooden bowl of peas in her lap spilled its contents onto the ground.

"Niece!" Sharp Nosed Woman scolded. "Look what you have do—Niece? Honey Eater? What—?"

The look of sudden fear on the pretty girl's face shocked her aunt into momentary silence. Honey Eater stood up, the bowl clattering to the ground unnoticed, as Two Twists and three other braves raced back toward the river.

"Honey Eater! Remember the child inside you! Come to your senses at once!"

Even as the four of them disappeared in the distant willows, Honey Eater watched another figure abruptly debouch from the thickets further upriver. He hurried across camp toward Medicine Flute's tent. There was no mistaking the lupine gait of Wolf Who Hunts Smiling.

"Oh, Maiyun help me!" Honey Eater cried out, buckling to her knees as her legs failed her.

"Wolf Who Hunts Smiling has killed my husband!"

As if to confirm these terrible words, the four braves came into sight lugging an apparently lifeless Touch the Sky.

"Maiyun give me strength," Honey Eater said. "Aunt, help me. Help me to my tipi. For my legs refuse to heed my will, yet I must go to my husband."

Curious onlookers began to straggle closer as the braves, Two Twists directing, bore toward the lone hummock where stood Touch the Sky and Honey Eater's lodge. Immediately, Catch the Hawk and some other loyal Bow Strings came forward and formed a guard outside the tipi.

Two Twists greeted Honey Eater at the entrance flap, his face a mask of relief.

"Once again, sister, he has eluded the Black Warrior. He has an ugly bruise over his right temple. He may have been struck by a bullet fired from a distant gun—or a weak one, for luckily it did not penetrate. It only stunned. He is awake and clearing up in his mind, though in pain."

Her first reaction was a warm flood of relief. Then, close on its heels, came frustrated anger.

"Pain?" she said bitterly before going inside to her brave. "His life has known little else. And of all the enemies eager to mete it out, none is more zealous than his own people!"

"I did not expect to kill him," Wolf Who Hunts Smiling said. "Be glad I even got a shot off. Had I missed, Woman Face would be making new ropes from your hair."

This was undeniable, and Medicine Flute nodded in the flickering light from his firepit. A double ring of armed Bull Whips now circled his tipi.

"But know this, shaman. You went too far, saying what you did to his face. Even *I* forbear from publicly insulting or threatening his she-bitch whore wife. Would you charge a grizzly cub in front of its mother?"

These words sobered Medicine Flute even further. "I was a fool," he admitted. His eyes cut toward the entrance flap when it stirred in a breeze, and he flinched violently.

Wolf Who Hunts Smiling threw his head back and roared with derisive laughter. "You white-liver! Do you squat to piss? Woman Face no longer has blood in his eyes to strangle you. He gave vent to emotions in the heat of rage. But colder blood will guide him now in this divided and dangerous camp."

Wolf Who Hunts Smiling patted his sling-shot. "This is the very thing to confound them close to camp. It is silent, yet powerful. With the right weight of stone and enough time to aim, I am sure it will kill a human."

Medicine Flute seized at the drift of his thoughts. "Honey Eater?"

"Among others. Who knows what use it may serve. Only you and Lone Bear have seen me practice with the sling. No one else knows I have it."

The skinny shaman frowned when from long habit he reached for his leg-bone flute. "That sanctimonious, woman-faced intruder has ruined another flute! Now I must make a new one."

"Fitting if his squaw should provide the bone for it."

Medicine Flute grinned, liking the sound of this. Then his heavy-lidded eyes went gloomy again. "Fitting, perhaps. But hardly likely, buck. He is in camp much lately to protect her. When he is not, she sticks to her aunt like black to a crow."

"He is in camp much," Wolf Who Hunts Smiling agreed. "But that must change now. Little Horse rode in today with news of the meeting of his enemies. He knows that the hair-face Seth Carlson is waiting only a mirror flash away. The Contrary Warrior and Big Tree are also pressing in. Woman Face will not long abide this. He hates Carlson as he hates the red-speckled cough. And so much as he hates, so does he fear. Count upon it, he will ride out."

Wolf Who Hunts Smiling rolled his head over his right shoulder, indicating Touch the Sky's tipi on its lone hill. "And when he does . . . do not forget that Skull Cracker is out there in the night, watching for his chance, waiting."

Although Touch the Sky had regained awareness and clarity of thought, his right temple had swollen into an angry red lump the size of a fat walnut. His pain was immense. Honey Eater prepared a soothing, soporific brew from yarrow and sassafras and red-willow bark. She made Touch the Sky drink a generous amount. Now, as Uncle Moon passed his zenith and the camp began to quiet, her brave slept fitfully.

Lying beside him, Honey Eater held Touch the Sky tightly, fighting back tears as she listened to the things he muttered in his drug-induced sleep. All the fears that strong Cheyenne men were taught to hold down inside—out they came now: his fears for his people, for his white parents, and most of all, for her and their unborn child.

It comforted her now to press her swollen belly into him, the three of them snuggled in tight together. But what, she worried yet again, was going to happen? The tribe was now like a beast caught in a trap, trying to gnaw its own leg off. If—

Her heart leaped into her throat when a stick snapped just outside. And did she hear breathing?

"Touch the Sky," she whispered. But for once, thanks to the soporific drink, he failed to respond.

Another stick snapped, and now she definitely heard breathing. Fighting down a cold panic, Honey Eater fished under the robes. Her fingers made reassuring contact with the two-shot parlor gun.

She untangled her limbs from her husband's. She rose silently and found the elkskin entrance flap. The sound of breathing was unmistakable now.

Fear pulsed in her temples and palms. She stepped closer to the flap, the small gun thrust out before her.

The flap bulged inward, and her breath snagged in her throat. But she moved her finger inside the trigger guard and began taking up the slack.

Oddly, despite her welling fear, a voice spoke at the edge of awareness: *If you must kill, let it be Wolf Who Hunts Smiling.*

The flap bulged more, quivered, then moved aside. But instead of a wolf, it was a wolf-dog: her shaggy, yellow, adoring camp mutt, looking guiltily up at his Adored One with his head thrust between his paws.

How could she have forgotten? Honey Eater was so relieved that she could not resist scratching his ears a moment before she ordered him outside. Delighted by the unexpected affection, he took up his spot right outside the entrance.

But it was a long time until morning, Honey Eater thought. And the darkness around them was deep.

Chapter Nine

"Tangle Hair's latest mirror flashes give support to my own observations," Little Horse said. "The Kiowa-Comanche force in the pine bluffs to the north is battle ready. They are sleeping on their weapons, ready to attack when Carlson does."

Touch the Sky, alert though still propped up in his robes, nodded. The huge knot over his temple had receded. A grape-colored bruise had replaced it. Touch the Sky had decided the missile which struck him was probably a stone flung from a slingshot. He knew of no one in camp who possessed one, but the weapons were not unknown to Plains tribes.

As to who fired it—that was a pointless question in a camp where his enemies outnumbered his friends.

"As usual," he said, "Carlson is the main boulder. Only when *he* rolls does the rockslide begin."

"As you say," Little Horse agreed. He watched his friend, knowing more was coming. It came.

"Therefore," Touch the Sky said, "we must keep the main boulder from rolling."

Little Horse grinned. "I am always ripe for trouble. But no fight is more pleasurable than with a whiteskin pony soldier. Does your wound give you pain, brother?"

"I saw you with your knee shattered on Wes Munro's keelboat," Touch the Sky replied. "I was there when his men smashed it so hard that even today you limp. Not once did you cry out or cooperate with your enemy. This wound of mine hurts, certainly. But I am ashamed to say so to you, stout buck."

The comment pleased and embarrassed Little Horse. As was the warrior way when directly praised, he accepted the compliment in silence. After all, he had earned it. He quickly changed the subject.

"How fares your attempt to name our comrade's killer?"

"Based on their movements in and out of camp, I have ruled out the two least likely to have done it, Swift Canoe and Medicine Flute. Sadly, the two who are left are Wolf Who Hunts Smiling and Lone Bear."

"Either man," Little Horse said bitterly, "has both cause and capability."

"As you say. Nor would they scruple to add my wife—and child—to their list of victims."

"You have set up a vengeance pole. Either the killer dies or you do. At first I thought your brain was soft for doing this. But now I see this thing better. Not only does the killer among us have the guilt-worm cankering at him—add the fear-worm to the list."

Touch the Sky nodded. "A man who is afraid begins eventually to show that fear."

Little Horse said, "But will it show in time? Our tribe is coming apart like shoddy in the rain."

"Time enough, buck, if we can delay Carlson, and thus, the renegades. As to that, I have seen the hair-face camp and have a plan in my parfleche."

"*Ipewa.* Good." Little Horse grinned again. "I have no desire to count my teeth falling out in old age. Let us leave a few more white widows east of the Great Waters!"

Once again Touch the Sky's band was forced to ride out of camp under cover of darkness. Each brave had rigged his pony with a full battle kit. For this night mission, Touch the Sky had selected the darkest pony on his string—a well-trained blood bay with no markings. The warriors smeared each other all over with thick claybank mud to cut reflection.

Touch the Sky's plan—if all went well— would not include a skirmish with the soldiers. Carlson's men were expert marksmen, unlike most soldiers on the frontier, and carried highly accurate carbines. Instead, the Cheyennes would rely on their skill in stealth to silently throat-slash the cavalry horses. With luck, they would thus make it impossible for Carlson's men to attack their camp any time soon.

Uncle Moon tracked higher across the sky as they drove their ponies hard toward the Blue-coat camp south of them.

"It all comes down to this night," Touch the Sky told his warriors when they stopped briefly to water their ponies at a rill. "This may be the most important strike we have ever mounted. For if we fail, our tribe is ruined."

Seth Carlson seldom had trouble sleeping. But it was only midnight when he rolled out of his blankets, suffering a rare case of the nervous fidgets.

He had spent much of his military career, after West Point, fighting the Indian Wars. Unlike the war with Mexico, described by his hero General Winfield Scott as "a perfect little West Point war," this out here was a dirty, makeshift, seat-of-the-pants kind of struggle. In America's sagebrush heartland, the "front" was all around and the "rear" was nowhere.

He stepped past the fly of his tent, fully dressed and armed. He slept that way in the field, for in the heat of an attack a man could die while groping for his trousers or pistol. Carlson glanced warily all around him.

Trouble was coming. He sensed it. He knew Matthew Hanchon well by now. And by now, that red son should have launched some kind of strike. Carlson's unit had been bivouacked here for days with no sign of Indians. The officer couldn't help thinking of some good advice heeded by the best Indian fighters: *Be careful when you see redskins. Be even more careful when you don't.*

It reassured him somewhat to reflect on how battle-ready the camp was. A series of defensive obstacles—trenches, pointed stakes, wire entanglements—ringed the rows of tents. Two-wheeled caissons laden with ammunition had been strategically placed to be handy in a battle. A pyramidal stack of thirty-pound artillery shells stood ready between two muzzle-loading artillery rifles mounted on wagons.

While he stared toward the dark mass of the folded ridges to the north, the words of an insult surfaced from memory. An insult Hanchon had once hurled at him: *Kristen Steele would rather mate with a Cheyenne dog than kiss your filthy lips.*

Hot rage boiled up inside him, making his temples throb violently. Although he planned to kill the savage for that remark, it flew close to the truth. That high-hatting, uppity she-bitch *had* rejected him in favor of a full-blooded Cheyenne! Him, a scion of the first families of Virginia and a graduate of the U.S. Military Academy!

Carlson crossed toward a nearby tent, crouched under the fly, and called inside, "Sergeant Padgett!"

In a few moments, the sleepy voice of his orderly responded. "Yo!"

"Did you personally select and post the pickets like I ordered?"

"That's an affirmative, sir. Cunningham's squad. Not a shirker in the lot, and them boys keep a tight asshole when there's trouble."

"They know the order?"

107

"No campfires, no matches, stay covered down out of the moonlight."

"Good. But I want you to roust out enough men to double the guard."

"Now, sir?"

"Now!"

"Yessir. Expectin' trouble?"

"Let's just say it's too damn quiet out there. Hanchon has four-flushed us before. Don't give him or that bunch of his the slightest opportunity to infiltrate this camp. And, Sergeant?"

"Sir?"

"Post more sentries around the corral. I expect the attack on Gray Thunder's village to commence tomorrow. In the meantime, nothing must happen to those horses."

"It is useless," reported the frustrated Little Horse. "Not only have Bluecoat sentries ringed the corral, they are linked by fine wires. One tug and they will all be alerted."

He had just returned to a little copse on a ridge above the Bluecoat camp, their hastily selected staging area.

"The camp, too, is a bastion," Touch the Sky said dejectedly. He had just finished scouting it. "Had we not wrapped our eyes, preparing them for night vision, I would have missed their pickets."

"What can we do?" Tangle Hair said. "See? Uncle Moon is climbing down from his zenith, and the Always Star grows dimmer in the north. If Sister Sun catches us near here, we are in for some sharp work."

"What can we do?" Touch the Sky repeated. "The thing we came to do. Kill those horses."

"But, brother," Two Twists objected. "You heard Little Horse just now. He said it is impossible to enter that corral. If a squaw-man like Medicine Flute called it impossible, I would scoff. But when Little Horse shies back from a deed, it is best left to Maiyun."

But Touch the Sky's lips were pressed into a tight, straight line—a sure sign his mind was made up, that now it was root hog or die.

"Maiyun will help us," he averred, "if we first help ourselves. Little Horse says we cannot now enter the corral. But with great caution, one of us might penetrate the camp itself. Then a diversion can be used to draw off the corral sentries. The rest must move quickly to enter that corral and throat-slash as many mounts as possible. But it must be done quickly, before they recover in the camp."

"What manner of diversion?" Little Horse demanded. "And who will penetrate the camp?"

"A military camp offers diversions enough, buck, as we have proved in the past. Buffalo hiders make camp like soldiers, too, yet look how we once slipped up on some. As to who . . ." Here Touch the Sky switched to English. "Can even one of you plug-ugly red Arabs savvy what I'm saying right now?"

The rest understood his point, if not his words. They reluctantly agreed it was only logical, for the success of their mission, to send the one man who could quickly comprehend the soldiers' language.

"Here," Touch the Sky said, holding his Sharps out to Little Horse. "It will only be in my way."

Touch the Sky tasted the familiar, coppery

taste of fear. But Arrow Keeper had taught him how to turn his fear into a ball and toss it outside of himself. He slid his knife from its beaded sheath and held it low against his thigh, knowing from experience that a knife fighter must slash upward to rip vitals.

Then he started down the ridge, and each step brought him closer to his enemy's camp.

It seemed to Touch the Sky that he had crawled for hours. He inched toward the fortified camp on elbows and knees, ignoring countless cuts from sharp chips of broken flint and shale. Only by constantly keeping his ears strained could he pick up the subtle sounds— breathing, whispered words, a man clearing his throat, the rumble of digestive gears—that warned him to steer wide of picket outposts.

A laborious climb through a defensive trench was followed by several lines of pointed stakes. Most difficult of all, however, were the coiled tangles of wire designed to trip attacking men and horses. He could not always avoid them; then Touch the Sky was forced to roll onto his back and press low under the wire, sometimes widening the passage by digging into the ground with his knife.

His various labors and cramped positions left him weary and aching by the time he cleared the final siege barriers. But nonetheless his heart surged in triumph. For there ahead of him, smoking a cigarette in the silver-white moonlight, was one of the white men he despised most on Maiyun's green earth: Seth Carlson.

Touch the Sky had already made a good

mind-map of the camp during daylight observation. Staying well clear of the shadowy humps that marked the squad tents, he also avoided drifting too close to the well-protected corral.

A bright moon lit the way. From time to time, after staring straight ahead, he would observe the same area from the side of his eye. Such peripheral glances sometimes revealed shapes or movements that straight-on vision could not.

That same bright moon that lit his way also came close to killing him.

"Halt!" came a sentry's uncertain voice out of the darkness near the huge cook tent. "Who goes there?"

Touch the Sky ducked back into the shadows. He forced down the tight lump of fear that rose like a bubble into his throat.

"Goddamn Army," he groused. "Man can't even drain his snake in peace."

He heard the sentry chuckle. "Sounds like grumpy old Hoby Winslowe. That you, Hoby?"

"Naw. I'm a Cheyenne renegade about to blow this camp up Salt River."

The sentry chuckled again but remembered the order for silence and said no more. Loosing a long, nasal sigh of relief, Touch the Sky continued heading toward the pair of muzzle-loading artillery rifles and the pyramidal stack of shells he had spotted earlier.

As he had hoped, the limber wagon which supported the guns included a keg of charging powder. It was only a few minutes' work to saturate the shells with black powder. Touch the Sky saved just enough to pour out a thin line along the ground as a fuse.

At one point a vedette, a mounted sentry, surprised him. Touch the Sky barely managed to roll under one of the wagon-mounted guns in time. But the man passed on. Quickly, Touch the Sky pulled his flint-and-steel from his possibles bag.

He did not realize he had cursed in English when the first few sprays of sparks failed to ignite the line of powder. Was the powder damp? If so, there went their great diversion—and Gray Thunder's camp.

He struck downward with his steel, a spark leaped, and a moment later more sparks exploded as the fuse ignited. Caught off-guard by the suddenness of it, Touch the Sky was late leaping to his feet.

The ear-shattering, skull-jarring, crack-booming explosion knocked him down with the force of a hot tornadic wind. For a few heartbeats, the camp lit up like a desert at high noon. He could read the markings on the tents, see the fear and awe starched into the faces of the corral sentries. Then it was raining dirt and debris, and he could hear troopers shouting confused orders in the chaos.

But Touch the Sky had little luxury to admire the effects of his destructive handiwork. As tents went up in flames, corral sentries poured into camp to help their comrades.

Do it, brothers, he silently urged his own loyal comrades who were waiting to turn that corral into a charnel yard. *Do it for your tribe and for my child!*

Chapter Ten

Even before Sister Sun woke for the day, the Bull Whip trooper named Trains the Hawk raced his pony across camp toward the Panther Clan circle. He leaped to the ground in front of Wolf Who Hunts Smiling's tipi and threw back the entrance flap.

A heartbeat later, a lethally honed blade was pressed against his neck.

"You fool! Never enter my tipi unless told to do so!"

Wolf Who Hunts Smiling sheathed his knife, instantly forgetting his anger. Trains the Hawk was one of his most reliable runners, and the look on his face said the news was bad.

"How goes it at the soldier camp, Trains the Hawk? Are they ready to attack?"

His subordinate shook his head, clearly dreading to be the bearer of bad tidings. "No attack soon. The camp is a shambles. Almost all their horses have been throat-slashed. A vast explosion has silenced the big-talking wagon guns and ruined much equipment. Few men were killed, but many were burned, and fires were still raging when I left to bring you this word."

Wolf Who Hunts Smiling had indeed heard an explosion during the night. But he had hoped it was a cannonade directed against Woman Face and his followers. Wolf Who Hunts Smiling was not one to panic at every setback—after all, few worthwhile victories came along an easy path. But this devastating report made his jaw drop open in astonishment.

"White Man Runs Him?" he asked in a voice so low it made Trains the Hawk step back a pace in nervous fear.

"I did not see him or his band. But neither do you see an Apache once he decides to kill you. Truly, Panther Clan, who else but White Man Runs Him?"

Medicine Flute, Swift Canoe, Skull Cracker, and Lone Bear, all on alert in these final hours before the takeover, hurried across camp, warned by the sound of Trains the Hawk's arrival. They were just in time to see their leader livid with rage.

"You bird-hearted fools!" he seethed. "I charged all of you with one task: keep Woman Face away from those soldiers! See how well you obeyed me. He has left the pony soldiers without ponies. Once again our attack in force must be delayed. Look around you."

They did, and saw many braves with guns moving about.

"See them?" Wolf Who Hunts Smiling demanded. "Loyal Bow Strings. Armed and ready to sing the death song. True, since a certain brave was murdered, their numbers are steadily dwindling. But those who still fly Touch the Sky's streamer have staked their sashes to the battleground. We can beat them, yes. But we would cut down the tree to harvest the nuts! The victory would leave us little to celebrate."

"It is one thing," Lone Bear spoke out boldly, "to *tell* a man he must stop Touch the Sky from doing such and such. It is another thing to *do* it. How does one stop the wind from blowing? How does one describe the taste of water?"

By now the calculating Wolf Who Hunts Smiling had calmed himself somewhat. Strong leaders, he reminded himself, did not show feelings of frustration in front of their followers. Did the cunning Sis-ki-dee ever throw a tantrum like a child? No, nor Big Tree, either.

So the wily young Cheyenne assumed his usual sneer of cold command. "Straight words, Lone Bear! My braves are good men, all of you. We have been slowed, but not stopped. I refuse to order the final movement until all three factions are ready: the Whips here in camp, the renegades to the north, Carlson to the south."

Whatever else he meant to say was forgotten. Wolf Who Hunts Smiling had just noticed a dog crossing near his tipi.

"Brother," he said to Skull Cracker. "Is that

the skulking cur that lives to follow Honey Eater?"

Skull Cracker frowned and rubbed the bite marks on the back of his thigh. "The very beast. The unmannerly wretch! It even snaps at Touch the Sky when he throws meat to it. It has already sunk fangs into me."

"A noble animal," Wolf Who Hunts Smiling said with contempt.

Swift Canoe looked puzzled. "Do you truly think so, brother? Why, the stink blowing off it would raise blisters on leather. Just a few sleeps ago, you called it—"

"Swift Canoe," Wolf Who Hunts Smiling cut him off, forcing down his rage. "You rabbit-brained dolt! I spoke in jest. Get out of my sight before I feed your liver to that dog."

As his lick-spittle slunk away, pouting at the rebuke, Wolf Who Hunts Smiling turned to Lone Bear.

"Brother, you say that cur bit you? It sounds like distemper to me. We need our dogs, but not a distempered cur."

He stepped back into the entrance of his tipi, tucking the flap between lodge poles to hold it back. This way, the Bow Strings scattered about could not see the slingshot he pulled from his parfleche. He had done some more experimenting with it. Now he did not load it with a stone, but with a deadly, half-ounce, .53 caliber buffalo ball from his shot pouch.

The sling fwipped, there was a sound like rawhide splitting, and the yellow wolf-dog leaped straight up as if snapping at a hovering fly. It dropped heavily, nerve-twitched for a few moments, then died where it fell.

"Impressive work!" Lone Bear approved. "A clean head shot. You have gotten deadly with that weapon. And I once called it a toy."

"Hold your praise, I did not shoot it for target practice, buck."

Wolf Who Hunts Smiling turned to Skull Cracker.

"Woman Face and his band have yet to return from the night's mischief. That means Honey Eater is hiding with her homely aunt. That dog was the favorite of Woman Face and his squaw. First make sure you throat-slash it, so the tall one understands. Then dump it in their tipi—on the same robes where they conceived their child."

It was the Indian way to boast after a victory. At the first water hole, their lathered ponies pushed their heads underwater up to their eyes. Their owners, meantime, agreed among themselves that four fiercer braves never donned clouts.

"Brothers!" Little Horse boasted. "If Carlson was half a man, Touch the Sky would have killed him by now. For now, we will leave him at his mother's tit. Some day, perhaps, he will grow to a soldier."

"Did you see the blue-blouses scatter like chickens?" Two Twists demanded. "Not one thought for their horses. They were in a hurry to return to their tents. They feared for the safety of their devil water!"

"You three bucks!" Touch the Sky said, admiration clear in his tone. "Hair-face buffalo hiders could not have worked more quickly. It was hard to believe you were pony-loving Cheyennes, watching you soak that corral in hot blood."

"Docile nags, lazy and fat from graining," Little Horse scoffed. "*Our* lean ponies would give intruders a merry chase. These spirit-broken nags stood shivering while they waited their turn to die. Thus it is when you beat and water-starve a horse, when you shove iron into its mouth to hurt it every time it tries to be wild in answer to its very nature."

And so it went. Their boasting affirmed the foolishness of whiteskin culture. But as they arrived at camp in the gathering light of dawn, all four braves were reminded that winning one battle falls far short of winning the war.

"All seems quiet," Little Horse remarked as they topped the last rise above the river valley. The camp lay spread out below them, wrapped in long white feathers of morning mist.

"Too quiet," Touch the Sky said. His eyes flicked to Sharp Nosed Woman's tipi, but he said nothing else.

They turned their ponies loose in the common corral. Despite their own exhaustion, they first rubbed their tired mounts down good with clumps of sweet sage.

Touch the Sky decided to return to his empty tipi and sleep—Honey Eater would be safer with her aunt, anyway. Little Horse, whose lodge lay in the same direction, fell in beside him.

"Do you resume your quest today, brother?" Little Horse asked. "The quest to name our comrade's killer?"

Touch the Sky nodded. The dew-damp grass

was silent under their moccasins as they neared his tipi.

"It is narrowed down to two, Lone Bear or Wolf Who Hunts Smiling. Both men hated him who is no longer with us."

"Which do you favor for the crime?"

Before Touch the Sky could answer, the wind shifted. A familiar odor was wafted to his nostrils from inside his tipi: the unmistakable, sheared-metal odor of deathblood!

"Honey Eater," he said out loud, unaware that he was speaking. "She defied my order and stayed at our lodge!"

Little Horse, too, had sniffed the familiar odor of death. At his companion's words, his face went as pale as scrubbed marble.

Touch the Sky would gladly have repeated his crawl through wire entanglements and pointed stakes, rather than cross these last few paces to his tipi. A black foreboding descended over him and turned his eyes to dead wood. So this was the sorrow promised by his omen? But somehow, his stout comrade at his side, he reached forward and gripped the entrance flap.

"Courage, Bear Caller," Little Horse said when he faltered. And then Touch the Sky, his face set in a grim mask, threw back the flap.

Honey Eater was gone. When he recognized the dead dog, its throat gaping in a bloody death rictus, his first reaction was a flood of warm relief. It was not Honey Eater, and in that moment no other fact mattered.

Then came the rage, and it was Little Horse who caught first spark.

"Brother! This desecration cannot stand. They have violated your home, your very marriage bed. Let us rout the cowards from their robes now and name the culprit!"

Touch the Sky shook his head. "No. It will stand, for now, assuming my wife is safe, which I am about to make certain. I cannot retaliate. As things stand now, it would only ignite a slaughter of the innocents."

"Then what? What can we do?"

"We keep an eye to the main chance, buck! Have you forgotten we already have a man to hunt? I have a killer to name. And once he is named, I must fight him to the death. For only his death might shock some sense into those Bow Strings who are wavering."

Chapter Eleven

"The thing of it, sir, they're cavalry," Sergeant Padgett said. "And I swear, a pony soldier is just like a cowboy in one respect. He'd rather die of the drizzling shits than be caught walking. The men ain't too keen on the idea of riding shank's mare back to the fort."

The orderly for the First Mountain Division fell silent, knowing his C.O. was in a foul mood.

"Shank's mare? They can put that thought away from their minds."

Carlson said this while sifting through the ashes of his command tent. It had caught ablaze in the explosion the night before. "The Queen of England will sing 'Loo-loo Girl' in public before I *march* my men back to Fort Bates in disgrace."

Carlson lost the thought when his fingers brushed something metallic. He pulled his favorite pair of gold-gilt spurs—now ruined past recognition—out of the ashes.

"God *damn* that aboriginal heathen!" he roared. He threw the ruined spurs down in disgust. "Winfield Scott himself wore those spurs when he rode into Mexico City victorious. That red sonofabitch is walking on his own grave, Sergeant Padgett!"

"Yessir," the unit orderly replied, not sounding too convinced. It was a familiar litany by now.

Across the way, the unit's cook was likewise cursing. The mess tent had gone up in blazes, and now the fragrant smell of crisp bacon—several entire sides of it—hung thick over the camp.

"I mean it," Carlson vowed. "No one returns to Fort Bates until that red son is sent under."

"Right, sir," Padgett said, waiting for his commander to get over his latest tantrum.

"He's pushed me as far as he's going to, Sergeant Padgett, you mark my words this time! Hanchon *and* his flea-bitten bunch are worm fodder. The whole damn bunch are long overdue for a comeuppance. We'll by God put paid to the lot of them. And if we can't get *them*, we'll at least turn that Cheyenne camp into a happy hunting ground."

"Sir?" Padgett said when his ranting commander finally paused to take a breath.

"What?"

"How we gunna do it, sir? We got no grub nor horses."

"I have a remarkable grasp of the obvious, Sergeant. This area is rich in elk and antelope; we'll send hunters out. As for horses . . . soon we *will* have some. I sent Cunningham to get Trader Buck."

"That half-breed swindler? He's crooked as cat shit."

"He's a horse trader, isn't he?"

Padgett frowned. "So he claims. You can put a feather on a rock and call it a bed, too. But I wouldn't sleep on the sonofabitch."

"We haven't got a hell of a lot of options. When you're standing in the bread line, you don't ask for toast."

"But how do we pay him, sir? He calls himself a trader, but I know for a pure-dee fact that he only accepts cash."

"Never mind that, it's not your problem."

Two years earlier, while stationed further north in the Bear Paw Mountains, Carlson had worked in cahoots with a group of hard-case highwaymen. Privy to inside information about gold shipments, the officer came up with a perfect scam: the white thieves disguised themselves as renegade Cheyennes for the robberies.

Carlson's generous share of the swag now lined his heavy money belt: thousands of dollars worth of high-grade gold dust. He had meant to use it to buy into the new, booming railroad industry once he left the Army. But those plans could wait—his men needed horses in order to deal misery to the savages. And by God, they were going to have them.

"Cap'n," Padgett said uncertainly, "Trader

Buck don't hardly break them green horses to leather. You *might* get some to take a saddle. Hell, they're mustangs, same stock as the Indian ponies."

"Well? They say the best way to fight fire is with fire. Savages may be too ignorant to harness the wheel, but they do know how to break ponies for battle. Genghis Khan did not have a better cavalry than Plains Indians. We'll let the men work the horses for a day or two to get the feel of them."

Padgett just sucked his teeth, saying nothing. But he definitely did not like the sound of any of this. His commander was taking this situation with Matthew Hanchon far too personally.

"The thirty-pounders was both ruint," he reminded his C.O. "So was the limber wagons with the support equipment for the guns."

"Won't need the big guns, you know that. There'll be enfiladed fire from us on the south flank, the renegades on the north flank, and skirmishers within the camp itself. True, the big guns would scare and disorient them. But so will a massed attack."

"All due respect, sir," Padgett persisted. "It's got a bad look to it."

Carlson knew better than to pull rank. He was breaking treaty laws nineteen to the dozen, and Padgett knew it. So instead, Carlson reached one hand into the pocket of his blue kersey trousers and removed five newly minted double-eagle gold pieces: a hundred dollars, over three months' pay for a sergeant.

Padgett's eyes lit up, catching fire from the sun-burnished gold as he stared at them in his leader's palm.

"How do things look now?" Carlson asked him.

Padgett broke into an ear-to-ear smile. He quickly pocketed the gold.

"Who wouldn't be a soldier?" he said, winking.

Newly animated with a sense of duty, Padgett whirled around. "You men!" he shouted to a group of slackers pitching horseshoes in front of their charred tents. "Uncle Sam ain't a-payin' you to cool your coffee! Get a new rope corral up, we got fine horses coming!"

"There goes yet another Bow String," Little Horse told his companions. He nodded out across the central camp clearing. A brave named Goes Beyond walked between Wolf Who Hunts Smiling and Medicine Flute. These two both had their arms around him.

"See? He holds new black streamers to tie to his pony's tail. He has joined the Whips. Lone Bear has made the announcement: Any Bow Strings who wish to change loyalties may join the Whips without an initiation."

"Goes Beyond has joined them," Touch the Sky conceded, gloom clear in his tone. "And if Goes Beyond has left the Strings, his brothers and cousins will soon follow him. He has always been a leader in his clan."

Touch the Sky, Little Horse, and Two Twists sat in the grass before Touch the Sky's tipi, filing arrow points while discussing the death of Spotted Tail. They already had a good stack. But, clearly, more would soon be needed.

Or perhaps not, Touch the Sky thought—and

it was not a comforting notion.

"Brothers," he said, giving voice to this new worry. "You have heard Arrow Keeper say that enough butterflies can kill a man? Only think. We have all of us been preparing for a bloody takeover. But see here how a large pool is forming from steady drops. More and more Bow Strings are being lured to join the Whips."

"Lured and intimidated," Little Horse said. "The Whips are making ugly remarks about what might happen to certain squaws and young children if their husbands and fathers stay with the Strings."

"Lured, intimidated . . . if it cuts wood, you may call it an axe. One way or another, we are losing our supporters. We may end up like braves in a burning canoe. Either we douse the flames in time or the water engulfs us. Even now I am not sure that enough Strings remain to even consider a fight against the rest."

"You truly believe all the Strings would capitulate?" Two Twists asked. "They would let our chief be slaughtered, they would desert the ancient law-ways to join this renegade nation? These Kiowas and Comanches, our fathers fought them at Wolf Creek!"

"All the Strings?" Touch the Sky said. "No. A few would never cross to the traitors. As for the rest who are crossing over—count upon it, Wolf Who Hunts Smiling is doing his best work now. He and Medicine Flute have put a honeyed layer of lies over their true motives and plans. Right now he tells our tribe nothing about the murdering pigs Sis-ki-dee and Big Tree. Not at first. He will beguile the Strings into their first downward step. Once on the icy slope, the fall will be rapid."

"And what of us?" Little Horse said.

Touch the Sky smiled grimly, chipping his flint so hard that sparks flew. "What of us? They will either kill us or drive us from the tribe."

"One fate mirrors the other," Two Twists said. And truly, an Indian without a tribe was a dead Indian.

"It comes down to this," Touch the Sky said. "I have delayed too long in challenging the killer of our comrade. I confess I have reached a chokepoint in the stream, for I am convinced the killer was Wolf Who Hunts Smiling or Lone Bear. Either one would relish the deed. One may trifle with Medicine Flute or Swift Canoe. But these two are neither simple nor scared. I favor Lone Bear for the killer, but have no easy means to prove it."

"Of course not," Little Horse said. "Both of them are hard, tough, vigilant men. You have narrowed it down, like a hunter isolating a buffalo from the herd. How can you close for the kill until you are sure of the bull?"

It was a good question. Touch the Sky's precarious position in the tribe—and the strict Cheyenne sense of justice—made it essential that he name the right man. Yet neither brave was likely to make a mistake now and reveal his guilt. What, Touch the Sky wondered, could he hope to prove in time?

"At any rate," Little Horse said, trying to cheer his companion, "we have put the blue-blouses out of the game. Even now, Tangle Hair is watching the renegades. At their first movement, he will alert us."

"Yes," Two Twists said, "And recall your own words, brother. 'A man who is afraid begins eventually to show his fear.'"

"Eventually," Touch the Sky repeated. He watched Goes Beyond enter the Bull Whip lodge with his new companions. A loud cheer of welcome erupted. "But eventually may be too late. For time is a bird, and the bird is on the wing."

Chapter Twelve

"Brother," Lone Bear said nervously, "this thing must be considered! When you and Medicine Flute spoke of this plan with the killing, I counseled for holding off. But you and the skinny flute-player here insisted it be done. 'Do not shed brain sweat worrying,' you both assured me. 'Woman Face will either be killed, or the tribe under new leadership, before he can name the killer.' "

Lone Bear paused, irritated by the droopy-lidded, bored gaze of Medicine Flute. He sat peeling the bark from a twig with his teeth. The big troop leader suddenly reached over and pulled the twig from his mouth.

"But only see what is happening," he continued. "Woman Face still walks above the ground, sassy as ever. This tribe still calls Gray Thunder chief. As I speak, Carlson's men are as useless as teats on a boar. Bucks, would any of *you* willingly face that one in a fight to the death? Yet that shall soon be my fate if the rest of you do not stir your stumps."

They sat in a parley circle in a little glade halfway between Gray Thunder's camp and the rolling pine bluffs to the north: Lone Bear, Wolf Who Hunts Smiling, Medicine Flute, and the renegade leaders Big Tree and Sis-ki-dee.

Sis-ki-dee's copper brassards glinted in the slanting sunlight, matching the insane glint in his eyes as he took the measure of Lone Bear. Evidently he approved of what he saw, judging by his next words.

"This Lone Bear is a stout Cheyenne covered with battle scars. No coward here! And he speaks true. We had best stir our stumps, or the tall shaman will pick us off one by one."

Big Tree, too, was a believer today. "I would not piss in Carlson's ear if his brains were ablaze. But he is a capable enough soldier, hardened by years on the Plains. Yet, have you seen that camp? The Bear Caller left it a smoldering ruin without firing one bullet! We have met our match in this Northern Cheyenne warrior, bucks!"

At this, Wolf Who Hunts Smiling bridled. " 'This Northern Cheyenne.' Contrary Warrior, have you forgotten *my* blood? I am far more Cheyenne than he."

"You are talking to *three* Northern Cheyennes

right now," Medicine Flute said.

At this Big Tree roared with laughter. "Such noble red men, so proud of their tribe! Well, skinny sissy, you have counted in error. Lone Bear and Wolf Who Hunts Smiling make two Northern Cheyennes. As for you, count one droopy-lidded Papago squaw-man who gnaws on bones."

This was a good shot, and despite tribal loyalty Lone Bear and Wolf Who Hunts Smiling could not help momentary grins. Medicine Flute blushed crimson with rage. But he took in Sis-ki-dee's insane, smallpox-scarred visage and Big Tree's massive chest. Wisely, he abstained from the insult on his lips.

"Never mind our cowering shaman," Lone Bear said. "He is worthless as a man, but he puts on a good show for the superstitious. But that is not the issue here. Tell me what we are doing to head off this fight. I killed our man as you requested, and I feel no regret. I will regret it deeply, however, if Touch the Sky names me for the killer."

"He will not because he *can*not," Wolf Who Hunts Smiling insisted. "How would he prove it? More important, Carlson will be ready before that happens. He has sent for Trader Buck, and now his men have mounts again. As soon as the soldiers have worked them a bit, the attack goes forward."

"We cannot count on all the new Bull Whip converts to actually fight against their old comrades," Medicine Flute said.

"No," agreed Wolf Who Hunts Smiling. "But they will at least refrain from stopping *us*. That camp will be ours. I will kill Gray Thunder, of course, and don his headdress. The takeover, with our camp surrounded, may otherwise be bloodless."

"What is wrong with blood?" Sis-ki-dee demanded. "Are you squeamish because they are your people?"

"Of course not. But my goal is to exterminate the white man, not the red."

"I still do not like the smell of this," Lone Bear insisted. "You are telling me that my fate relies on Carlson's acting in time. Granted, he is capable. Ask all the dead Mandans to the north. But he is up against a true demon, as are we. I need more assurance than this vague talk of pony soldiers saving me."

"You have more than vague talk in your camp, Bull Whip," Wolf Who Hunts Smiling assured the troop leader. "If it does come down to a fight, you will not be alone."

Lone Bear frowned. "Speak words I can heft. You know the way it is once a vengeance pole goes up. Remember when Scalp Cane's brother was killed by a drunk Lakota? It will be one on one: Touch the Sky against the man he names, and woe betide that man. The fight will be from horseback with lances and battle axes only."

"Lances, battle axes, and *this*," Wolf Who Hunts Smiling said as he pulled the osage-wood slingshot from his parfleche.

"I have gotten good with this. It is silent, accurate, and when loaded with a buffalo ball, even deadly. If you must fight, I cannot promise to get close enough to hit Touch the Sky. After all, I must stay hidden. But I can surely drop his horse. Then Woman Face will be a fish in a keel."

Sis-ki-dee and Big Tree shared a disdainful grin.

"If you cannot gut your Indian then, Lone Bear," Sis-ki-dee scoffed, "you are far less of a man than you appear."

Touch the Sky had consulted every mortal means to prove who killed Spotted Tail. Arrow Keeper had often taught him that no shaman worthy of the title was quick to bother the Good Supernatural—not until all earthly wisdom and resources were exhausted.

He had reached that point. He was on his back, arms pinned behind him as a mountain lion went for his throat. Now he could only hope for enlightenment from Maiyun.

But first he made a quick survey of the camp to assess the danger. Gray Thunder, seeking to head off a flashpoint, had virtually confined himself to his tipi. Loyal Bow Strings (a dwindling breed, Touch the Sky thought dejectedly) watched his tipi.

Two Twists had relieved Tangle Hair again on sentry duty at the pine bluffs. Loyal Little Horse sat within sight of Sharp Nosed Woman and Honey Eater. These two were stretching thin sheets of elk meat on a drying rack behind Sharp Nosed Woman's tipi.

He found River of Winds, the new leader of the Bow Strings, locked in urgent discussion with a group of braves before the Bow String lodge. At a sign from Touch the Sky, the two ducked into the empty lodge.

"How goes it?" Touch the Sky said.

River of Winds shook his head. "They are polite. They respect me. But to a man they loved

133

their former leader, and who would not? They are enraged that his killer has not been punished."

"Yes, they feel betrayed."

River of Winds nodded. "As you say. They tell me, 'This Gray Thunder, what manner of chief is he that kin-murderers are permitted to live among us?' They will recognize no authority that lacks the will and strength to punish killers. In contrast, Wolf Who Hunts Smiling is all talk about quick action to punish the wrongdoers."

"Did you go to Gray Thunder?"

"I did, shaman. As you requested, I emphasized the urgency of monitoring this soldier camp. But Gray Thunder is understandably preoccupied. He only shook his head. 'The talking papers permit this sort of thing,' he kept repeating."

"And when you told him about the meeting between our wily Wolf Who Hunts Smiling and Seth Carlson? He said nothing to *this*?"

River of Winds looked uncomfortable. He glanced away. "He did. He said, 'Tell me proof besides the word of Touch the Sky and his band.' And truly, you are the only ones who claim that Wolf Who Hunts Smiling is collaborating with the whiteskin army. You must understand. Wolf Who Hunts Smiling watched Bluecoats turn his father into stew meat with a double shot of canister fragments. No Cheyenne hates soldiers more than he."

"Perhaps," Touch the Sky said. "But he hates me even worse. He would cross his lance with that of anyone who wants to kill me. And Carlson wants to kill me at least as bad as he does."

River of Winds, who strove always to be fair

and impartial, only said quietly, "I know little of this."

"River of Winds, tell me a thing. Never mind our chief. Do *you* believe my claims, preposterous as they may seem?"

It was a long time before this careful man answered.

"Touch the Sky, not so long ago I was one of those who lay dying of mountain fever. You risked every manner of danger to return to this camp with the whiteskin vaccine. And then, when the hair-face doctor said you were too late and all hope was lost, you refused to accept this. You hung from a pole for hours to convince Maiyun otherwise. Why would you do this if you were the white man's dog your enemies claim? To answer you, then, buck: Yes. I believe you, and I have decided that Wolf Who Hunts Smiling is a murdering traitor and that he killed his own cousin. However, what I believe as a man, and how I must behave as a troop leader, are not the same. I believe it of him, yet I lack any proof that will stand."

These were important words coming from an important brave. But River of Winds followed them immediately with a more sobering truth.

"However, I fear that all is lost. Our old system of authority has fallen. I cannot even verify your report about renegades in the pine bluffs because Lone Bear is sending out all the scouts. Without formal verification, the Headmen will not act. I have little power over the Strings unless . . ."

He trailed off. But Touch the Sky knew what he meant to say: *Unless Spotted Tail's killer is brought to justice quickly.*

And so, having exhausted all mortal means to do this, the tall shaman walked down to the sweat lodge to quiet his mind.

It sat beside the river, a simple frame of bent saplings over which buffalo hides had been stretched. Touch the Sky built a fire inside within a circle of rocks. When they were glowing, he used a rawhide pail to scoop water from the Powder. He stripped, stepped inside, and poured the water onto the glowing rocks.

At first the steam that enveloped him was too hot for comfort. But then, as the sweat oozed from his pores, his thoughts slowed until the trance glaze owned his eyes. He did not "think" in any conscious sense. He only kept his mind quiet, his senses alert, and asked Maiyun with quiet dignity to send him an immediate sign.

Touch the Sky was not sure how much time passed. He only became aware, with a start, that he was chilled—that all the steam was dissipated.

He stepped outside, wiped himself down with clumps of sage, rinsed quickly in the river. He had dressed again and started climbing the long slope to camp when the Day Maker answered his request.

Lone Bear had just joined a group of his Bull Whip brothers around a fire where they were roasting a dog on a spit. Suddenly, while Touch the Sky watched, a flock of crows detached themselves from a nearby cottonwood tree and flew in a straight line toward Lone Bear.

The birds swooped down on him, then circled his head while the startled brave swatted at them. His companions stepped back, shocked —wrens might act this way, or starlings during their nesting time. But not lazy and stupid crows!

Their only function, as any Cheyenne knew, was to mark out the guilty. For crows themselves had the eternally furtive, guilty manner of all criminals and scavengers.

So Touch the Sky knew full well what this sign meant. And without hesitation he crossed directly toward the group of Bull Whips. One look into Lone Bear's pallid face confirmed it: This was the traitorous coward who killed Spotted Tail.

"You are lower than the whiteskin pigs who place a bounty on Indian hair," he announced. And with that he stepped boldly between Lone Bear and the campfire: the ancient Cheyenne way of announcing that he meant to kill him.

Chapter Thirteen

Chief Gray Thunder—pressed hard in his own camp, virtually confined to his lodge—did not and could not give the nearby Bluecoat camp the priority he secretly felt it merited.

Such matters normally fell to the war leader and his assistants, the soldier-troop leaders whose men were, in effect, the tribal police. River of Winds was presently both war chief and the leader of the Bow Strings. Despite the obvious emergencies in the camp itself, he did order a spy to watch the soldiers. But he could do little else.

As for Lone Bear, Gray Thunder had noticed

a thing. This troop leader seldom felt any urgency lately when it came to the Long Knives. Why? Especially when his (unofficial) master, Wolf Who Hunts Smiling, made great show of his implacable wrath toward the beef-eaters.

Gray Thunder sat alone in his commodious tipi, where once a wife and babes had livened the silence. His woman fell, fighting hard to save the children, in the same Pawnee attack that had killed Honey Eater's mother, the wife of Chief Yellow Bear. The children had indeed been saved—until a white trader brought cholera to their camp, and he lost all three of them in one cruel stroke of fate's blade.

All that sadness, however, did not drive him into the sullen, cynical, drunken ways that some braves fell into after such a trauma. Gray Thunder saw *all* the people in the village as his family. He had lost some of his little ones, yes, and it was the saddest pain in the world. But others remained, depending on him. And now their lives were in peril.

He shuddered to think of the full extent of the treachery going on right under his nose. Clearly the ambitious Wolf Who Hunts Smiling was about to move and move decisively. But how far would the traitor go? Did he now parley with white soldiers and Indian enemies of the tribe?

Touch the Sky said so, and Gray Thunder had no proof that Touch the Sky was a liar. Yet, often he *appeared* to be a liar. So neither could the chief exactly prove that Touch the Sky was honest. But Gray Thunder trusted no man more than he had trusted Old Arrow Keeper. And that erstwhile shaman had been convinced that Touch the Sky was Fate's warrior—sent by the

Holy Ones to fulfill a great destiny.

However, it was difficult now to believe that Touch the Sky was headed anywhere except to the Land of Ghosts. Gray Thunder threw the entrance flap back and peered out at his troubled camp. His thick hair—cut short now for Spotted Tail—showed streaks of silver, and deep lines creased the corners of his eyes.

A huge ring of Bull Whips crowded Medicine Flute's tipi. Something new was afoot. Gray Thunder called out to one of the Bow Strings guarding his tipi: "Cousin, what is all the commotion?"

"Serious business, Father! Touch the Sky has stepped between Lone Bear and the fire. A bloody fight is coming."

Gray Thunder considered this in silence. Then he said, "Why did Touch the Sky pronounce his death sentence?"

The String looked at his peace chief, clearly having trouble believing it himself. "Remember his vengeance pole? He claims it was Lone Bear who killed my troop leader."

However, once again mercurial destiny intervened and forced a delay in Touch the Sky's vengeance quest.

Even as the young Bow String and Chief Gray Thunder spoke, the sentry watching the soldiers returned to camp with urgent word.

"Brother!" Little Horse said, running up to Touch the Sky in the clearing. "Carlson has hunkered in the dirt with Trader Buck. His soldiers have ponies and are making signs of mounting the attack!"

This new word stopped the tall Cheyenne in

his tracks. Little Horse heaped on more bad news.

"The renegades, too, are keen for some bloody work. They are drunk on strong water and clearly mean to terrorize our camp. They wait only for the soldiers to charge. We are about to be overrun!"

Little Horse was not one to panic. But his dire words and manner showed how hopeless their situation had become. Nonetheless, many had noticed a thing about Touch the Sky: He thrived on trouble. The bleaker the prospects, the more calm and cunning he became, as if egging his enemies on to their best mischief.

Little Horse stared when all this grim news evoked a smile from his companion. "Brother, did you hear me straight? Or have you just enjoyed a visit with the Peyote Soldiers?"

"I heard you straight and true, Little Horse. I heard you mention Trader Buck. That means our white enemy now rides Indian mustangs."

Little Horse frowned. "All the more reason to worry. These are not grain-fed, lazy, timid animals beaten and spurred into submission. They are ponies whose spirits will rise with the tide of battle."

Touch the Sky glanced out toward the common corral and their tribe's own spirited ponies. "As you say, for they have wild mountain blood singing in them."

He suddenly made up his mind. "Go get Two Twists," he told Little Horse. "Then select five Bow Strings you would trust with your mother's life—if indeed there are five such men left to us. Bring them here at once, ready to ride."

Little Horse found his fighting fettle now that

he knew his mission. But he was clearly puzzled. "Why, brother? What is on the spit?"

"Why?" Touch the Sky grinned. "Are you keen for sport, buck?"

The familiar tone rallied his companion. "Only if I have a good chance at dying."

"Excellent odds! Now go get our men, and the crazier the better—this is no job for sane men."

"As good as done, Bear Caller. But tell me something of this plan, or how will I entice these crazy braves?"

Touch the Sky nodded toward the two hundred ponies now taking off the lush grass. "That herd of ours—we are going to steal half of them and set them free."

In the pine bluffs, Sis-ki-dee sat his big clay-bank and stared south toward the rock spine known as Stone Ridge. Wolf Who Hunts Smiling was strategically located there. From that spot the Cheyenne could see the first dust puffs further south that would mark the onset of the cavalry attack. Spotting them, he was to release a smoking arrow—the signal for the renegades to complete the pincers. From Stone Ridge, Wolf Who Hunts Smiling could easily return to his camp in time to direct the takeover from within.

Big Tree nudged his blood bay up beside his comrade. Behind the two battle leaders, Comanche and Blackfoot braves mingled in circles, sharing strong water and boasting of their plans for the slaughter to come. They were particularly aware, as the devil water flowed, of the extraordinary beauty of Cheyenne women.

Big Tree said, "The prelude was long, Contrary Warrior. But finally the fast and dance are over, the battle is at hand. As things stand now, we command Wendigo Mountain. But what of that? The wily Wolf is right! Only our combined might will rule over so many whiteskin guns."

"Never mind the whiteskin guns, Quohada. One world at a time."

Sis-ki-dee raised his sheathed North & Savage rifle toward the Powder River camp, out of sight in the river valley.

"We call him White Man Runs Him," he said. "But to you, stout bucks, I will say it plain. No man runs that one. Not one of us is safe so long as he—or his bloodline—walks the earth."

Big Tree's oval, homely face showed nothing. He wore two foxskin quivers, both bristling with arrows. "You know your quarry, hunter! Perhaps he will elude death this day, perhaps not. I have learned not to announce his death in advance.

"But as for his bloodline . . . we will soon be making things lively in that camp. And, buck, I know his woman, I held her prisoner in Blanco Canyon. I will search her out first thing and cut the roe out of her."

A collective cheer abruptly erupted from their men. Both battle leaders glanced toward Stone Ridge and saw why at the same time: a black parabola of smoke arced across the bottomless blue of the sky.

Touch the Sky's plan was bold and reckless, and so ambitious it could well fail utterly, leaving the Cheyennes to die hard. But after he quickly explained it, the crazy-brave nature of the effort infected his fellow Cheyennes. They

143

pitched into the game with zeal, not one of them stopping to calculate the risks.

They worked so quickly that few in the main camp even knew what was afoot until it was too late. The braves, all experts at herding mustangs, first bunched and pointed the animals. Then, firing their weapons and yipping the war cry, they quickly cut the herd in two and stampeded half the ponies in the direction of the Bluecoat camp.

"Hi-ya! Hii-*ya!*"

A rolling thunder preceded them, yellow-brown dust roiled up to black out the sun, and the very earth shook from the pounding hooves.

"Jee-zus Christ with a wooden dick!" Sergeant Padgett exclaimed. "Are them buffalos stampeding?"

It had taken several commands to do it, and it was not a smooth execution. But Seth Carlson finally managed to halt his charging unit. He, too, stared at the approaching wall of dust. Then he broke out his brass fieldglasses.

"That's not buff! Those are horses. Indian stock. There's a handful of braves driving them."

A few seconds later, Carlson swore roundly. "That goddamn Hanchon is one of them. Five, maybe six more with him. No battle rigs, no war paint."

"Horses?" Padgett stared at his commander. "Cheyennes always paint for a skirmish. That red nigger must be dumber than you credit him, sir, if he thinks he can stop cavalry with a pony herd. They'll spook before they hit us. Even if they don't, they can't hurt us. 'Member that buff stampede we got caught in near Laramie? They was a hunnert times more of them than these critters. Meaner, too. All we lost from it was one horse gored."

Carlson nodded vaguely during all this, wanting to be reassured, needing it. But even as Padgett belittled Hanchon's strategy, Carlson's ginger mustang began nervously sampling the air with quivering nostrils.

Behind them, the men had increasing trouble gentling their new mounts. They had been difficult to control from the very outset. But now they crow-hopped, sidestepped, tried to buck their riders.

"Never mind holding sets of four!" Carlson shouted. "Close up and form a wedge! Asshole to belly button, close it up there. Second squad dress on the fourth, then guide center! We'll make this herd break around us, then we make our final movement to the camp."

Come on then, Hanchon, Carlson thought. He slid his carbine out of its boot and tried to prop the butt-plate on his thigh. But by now his little mustang was giving him grief six ways to Sunday. She was nearly impossible to control.

The stampeding mustangs drove ever onward, the Cheyennes whipping them to a frenzy. Behind Carlson, a trooper cursed when his mount suddenly bucked him and bolted off toward the approaching herd.

Only then, when it was too late, did Carlson fully understand: Hanchon wasn't attacking, he was driving those mustangs around them and back toward the mountains they came from! Every step closer put the smell of freedom into their nostrils. And these mustangs his men rode—they, too, were answering the call of the wild.

But now his carbine went flying as Carlson barely managed to stay in the saddle. The ginger bucked hard, again, again, jarring Carlson's teeth and tailbone. Cursing men were forced to simply leap from horseback and give it up as a bad job, for their mustangs followed their companions back toward the mountains.

In his rage, Carlson forgot how dangerous it was for a cavalryman when his horse was shot out from under him. Blind with fury, he unsnapped his stiff leather holster and drew his .44. He dropped the mustang in her tracks with one shot behind the ear. But he'd neglected to remove his legs from the stirrups first.

Carlson heard a sound like green wood breaking as the dead pony fell hard on his awkwardly twisted left leg, snapping the bone in several places. But his humiliation wasn't quite complete. As he lay trapped under his dead mount, forced to cry out like a child at the fierce pain in his ruined leg, the dust cleared out ahead.

Long enough for Matthew Hanchon to meet his eye from astride his all-white pony.

The Cheyenne laughed with savage contentment. "Kristen Steele sure as hell lost a good man when she refused you, Soldier Blue!" he called out, giving the blade an extra twist before he escaped with his companions to safety.

Chapter Fourteen

"The Headmen refuse to act against Touch the Sky for stealing our ponies," Wolf Who Hunts Smiling fumed. "All because they herded them back again, their numbers grandly swollen by the stolen cavalry herd."

"Indeed," a worried-looking Lone Bear chimed in, "the talk all around camp is about the brilliance of the maneuver. This is some more of Woman Face's excellent treachery. And so much for your faith in whiteskin soldiers."

"At least the renegades withdrew in the nick of time when the attack failed," Medicine Flute said. "The tribe remains ignorant of that threat."

"Lone Bear is right to chastise me," Wolf Who Hunts Smiling said. All noticed this, for admitting mistakes was rare in this one. "It became too important in my mind to plan the attack around Carlson's unit. Like an old woman holding a rifle, I was far too cautious."

Lone Bear fidgeted, clearly nervous. He, Wolf Who Hunts Smiling, Medicine Flute, Swift Canoe, and Skull Cracker sat molding bullets in the Bull Whip lodge.

"Brother," Lone Bear said, "I have no ears for all this chest-pounding and agonized cries of apology. Is your manhood growing as faint as Swift Canoe's intelligence? Do you understand that the tall one has stepped between me and the fire? I have no choice but to fight him."

Swift Canoe frowned. He realized he had just been insulted, but he wasn't sure precisely how. As for Wolf Who Hunts Smiling, normally he brooked such a tone and manner from no man. But his rage was focused elsewhere: on that white-stinking, pretend Cheyenne who had once again ruined his bid for power.

He looked at Medicine Flute. "Your thoughts share a canoe with mine, shaman. You are right—the tribe suspects nothing so far as the Kiowa-Comanche force is concerned. And Lone Bear here is so far gone with fear he is missing the main point. This fight with Touch the Sky is not bad fortune. It is our best chance yet to both kill him and move against the tribe."

Lone Bear stared at his fellow Whip. He was used to his companion's wily speaking skills, and they held little sway over him.

"Are you still harping on that familiar 'best chance yet' theme? Buck, how many times have you assured a man that Touch the Sky's time was at hand? And of those men you duped, how many can you still name among the living?"

"All right, then," Wolf Who Hunts Smiling said. "Play the big Indian. Never mind my plan. But recall your own words, troop leader: 'I have no choice but to fight him.' Face him on your own."

Now it was Lone Bear's turn to swell with rage. And Lone Bear enraged was a fearsome sight—even Wolf Who Hunts Smiling felt a cool lick of fear and placed one hand loosely on his knife. Lone Bear *was* a "big Indian." He carried twice Wolf Who Hunts Smiling's weight, and little of it was fat.

"Face him on my own? You treachrous wolf-barker! You swore on your father's scaffold that the killing of the Bow String leader could not be laid at my tipi!"

Swift Canoe suddenly giggled. "His father *had* no scaffold, for he was kill—"

A murderous glance from his master silenced the lackey.

"Now," Lone Bear raged on, "the crime has been laid at my tipi, and you leave me to die a hard death? Perhaps I will tip my lance sooner—and in your direction!"

"Come down off your hind legs and hear me out. I say again this fight between you and White Man Runs Him is our great chance. And you will be as safe as a Cherokee in church, I swear it."

Lone Bear looked skeptical. But, indeed, at this point what other choice did he have but to listen? Time was nipping at his heels, and so was a forlorn death.

Wolf Who Hunts Smiling slid the slingshot from his parfleche.

"You all know the custom in such matters. The duel will go forward at the place the women call Flower Meadow. Almost the entire tribe will turn out to witness it. I will not be able to get so close that I can ensure a fatal hit to Touch the Sky. But if not, I know I can drop his horse."

Medicine Flute pitched into the persuasion game. "Lone Bear, you are no yearling colt. Of course this Touch the Sky is a formidable warrior. But he is not a god! And are you such a faint combatant? Your coup feathers trail the ground, and every Whip in camp respects your battle prowess."

"He will be on the ground," Wolf Who Hunts Smiling said. "And you mounted. Is this so daunting? Only think what respect awaits the brave who kills that stinking dog."

"Once you two manage to kill Touch the Sky," Medicine Flute said, "his band will be demoralized. The Whips can move instantly to kill Chief Gray Thunder. The renegades will swoop down from the bluffs to help us take control of the camp."

"Of course it *should* work," Lone Bear said. "Every plan to kill him seems foolproof in the telling of it. Yet, they all seem to fail in the *doing* of it."

"Spoken straight," Wolf Who Hunts Smiling conceded. "But know this. Never before have we two teamed up against him. Of the failures so far, which two of them could equal our scalps and trophies, our cunning?"

This outrageous wheedling was calculated to appeal to Lone Bear's remarkable vanity, and it worked. After a few heartbeats of brooding silence, he finally nodded.

"As you say, Panther Clan. Timid men die young in rags, yet I plan to dress well in old age. This plan you mention, it is not without its merits."

"Stout buck! It only needs men of strong will. We must have done with this incessant game of getting nowhere. Skull Cracker!"

This worthy brave, his rawhide-wrapped rock dangling from his sash, shook himself awake. "I have ears."

"And a strong arm, warrior. Know this. Honey Eater will avoid the duel. She cannot stand to see her tall stag fight. You, Skull Cracker, will pay her a visit under cover of all the distraction. Woman Face will leave a guard, but what of that? Your deadly rock makes no noise.

"Bucks, no more eking it out like dust-scatters over their crops! We are going to get it done in one fell swoop: Woman Face, Gray Thunder, and Honey Eater."

"How many times," Honey Eater implored her brave, "have I ever asked such a thing? Always I have refrained from intruding in the affairs of warriors."

"You have," Touch the Sky replied fondly. "Refrain now, too, and your record remains unsullied."

His words infuriated her. But the handsome warrior's insouciant grin made it impossible for her to sustain her anger.

151

She lost the battle to look stern, and they both broke out laughing. She and Touch the Sky sat cross-legged on the grass between their tipi and the meat racks. He used a whetstone to hone the blade of his battle axe. Now and then he held it up in the light, squinting to judge his work.

"You make light of my premonition," she said, "because I am a woman."

"I make light of nothing, wife. It was Arrow Keeper who first told me that you, too, have a touch of the shaman's sense. He was right. You come to me and ask me to call off this fight. You tell me you fear some disaster will befall me."

Touch the Sky shifted his gaze from the blade to her. "So? At least I am warned. As you well know, disaster is the creek I—now *we*—camp near. But the fight must go forward. If it does not, you will see a bigger disaster. You will see an end to the Cheyenne heritage. At least to the honorable and decent part of it. And how will our child fare then, in a world of hatred and killing ruled by Wolf Who Hunts Smiling?"

His words, and even more, his determined tone saddened her. And yet, sad or no, they were true words, words even a soft brain could pick up and examine.

"My father told me your path would be hard and lonely. But he said you were a man whose life was meant to *matter*. 'He will never run quickly into trifling danger, daughter,' my father assured me, 'and when he is finally forced to kill, the dying will be important.' I understand his words better now."

She suddenly took the axe from his hand and laid it aside, gripping his hand.

"I see it now. Arrow Keeper knew all along. Maiyun has marked you out, and you more than any other man live by a flame within—the flame of justice and honor and courage. If such as you finally fall, this will be no world for our babe. I am happy to have your child inside me. It will be the high honor and joy of my life to see that child go forth into the better world you have made for it."

These profound words were spoken in Honey Eater's simple and direct manner. They made pride and gratitude and loving adoration brighten his eyes.

"If I have any proof at all that Maiyun has favored me," he replied, "it is only you. But, sweet love, only think. They have put the murder blood on our very robes! You worry about me. Well and good. But my enemies no longer draw a line between me and mine—to kill you is to kill me, and they know it. Do you, too, know it?"

She nodded. "Of course. Because likewise, to kill you is to kill me. They can cleft two hearts with one chop."

"It is good that you see this thing clear. Because we are not merely going to cower in our tipi, wife of a warrior! We are both going to fight. On the morrow, while I am at the Flower Meadow, young Hump Medicine will guard our tipi. But that is not good enough. Do you have the weapon I gave you?"

She nodded and patted her parfleche.

"*Ipewa.* You had *better* have it, pretty, or I will tell Sharp Nosed Woman you are not eating the nourishing mother's soup she sends over."

Honey Eater enjoyed a rare moment of teasing laughter with him.

"You have no heart to swat me," she said. "But Sharp Nosed Woman will box my ears for me."

"As you say. Now break out this short iron, and let us see one more time how you handle it."

Chapter Fifteen

Soon after the old grandmothers sang the Song to the New Sun Rising, the people began filing out of camp. They bore toward the huge, open expanse called the Flower Meadow just past the river confluence.

It was here, on solid, flat ground devoid of prairie-dog holes, where the braves often worked their green ponies. The field was also used for the huge Sun Dance parade—and on the rare occasions when two warriors fought a duel to the death.

Most walked, leading ponies attached to travois to transport the very young or very old. As the law-ways required, Gray Thunder was on hand, a ring of loyalists surrounding him. The Whips and their supporters crowded one side of the meadow—Lone Bear was lost in the crowd.

The Bow String side was noticeably less busy.

"Brother," said a worried Two Twists, "I know Lone Bear's riding style. He is a big man and will sit high, for he uses a saddle and his roan is high across the withers."

"He is heavy, and thus a bit slower," Little Horse coached. "Dodge, twist, maneuver, use your greater speed to advantage."

"He is not *that* slow," Tangle Hair warned. "Once Lone Bear gets the kill gleam to his eye, the lethal instinct animates him. And never mind his speed—he is *strong*. A glancing blow from my lance would be a bone-crusher from his."

Touch the Sky grinned ironically. "I thank all of you for such encouragement. Ha-ho, ha-ho! Best embrace me now, for evidently you all expect me to die."

"Today is a poor day to die—for *you*," Little Horse scoffed. "Lone Bear, however, had best lay out new moccasins for his funeral. He is formidable, granted. But I have seen our shaman here dispatch better men."

Little Horse made a great show of yawning, as if he were already bored. "Take care of it quickly, brother," he added, "then I will teach you how to plait a proper bridle."

Touch the Sky was indeed worried about this fight with Lone Bear. He took few opponents for granted, this Bull Whip leader least of all. But despite the nervous belly flies stirring within him, his attention kept wandering. Once again he glanced back in the direction of camp—and Honey Eater.

Little Horse caught that glance and easily read its meaning.

"This Hump Medicine," he said casually. "You left a good man to watch Honey Eater. He is young, but what a lion in battle! Sharp, too. You know I am famous for my good hearing? Well, once I said to him, 'Hear that faint squeaking noise? It is a whiteskin wagon caravan passing ten miles north of here.'"

"And *that* feisty pup replied: 'Yes, I know, for the third wagon in line needs grease on its hubs!'"

This levity caused all four Cheyennes to laugh. But the mood suddenly changed when Touch the Sky said, "Where is Wolf Who Hunts Smiling? He was here when the crowd began assembling. Now I can spot him nowhere."

"Trouble," Little Horse said instantly, losing his grin. "It can only be trouble. He would not miss this for a wagonload of tobacco. This explains why Lone Bear is strutting about so confidently, boasting how he will dress Touch the Sky out like a deer. Somehow, someway, they mean to make it two against one."

If true, this news was serious enough. But Touch the Sky was not so sure *he* was the target of this latest treachery—not directly, anyway. Again, his troubled gaze swept back toward camp.

He took some comfort in two facts: Hump Medicine was stalwart and vigilant, and Honey Eater was armed. Nor was she the timid, mincing type—already she had the mother's powerful urge to protect her young, and there was no stronger protection in Maiyun's creation.

But he was a warrior, and the warrior survived from fight to bloody fight by focusing down to one thing only: the fight at hand. His wife must fend for her capable self right now, for he must close for the kill. It was his *duty* to win, and that meant hardening all the soft places inside him. Thus, he denied his enemy a spot to wound him.

River of Winds served as reluctant referee. Now, as the new sun ignited sparkling diamonds out on the Powder, he walked out toward the center of the meadow.

"Where is Wolf Who Hunts Smiling?" Two Twists repeated desperately.

But it was too late to wonder. After a long pause, River of Winds raised both arms straight overhead, and a massive cheer erupted from the Bull Whip end.

"Remove the hobbles from your pony, brother," Little Horse said quietly, the bravado worried out of him now. "And unsheath your lance. Once again it is time to fight. May the High Holy Ones ride with you!"

Skull Cracker frowned when he peeked around the corner of the deserted council lodge. No one stirred in camp, and it would be easy enough to cross it unseen. Except, there sat Hump Medicine in front of the very tipi where Skull Cracker's quarry hid.

Hump Medicine was young, but no brave to fool with. So Skull Cracker recalled the many lectures in cunning and deceit preached by Wolf Who Hunts Smiling and Medicine Flute.

Always mystify and surprise your victim. Never lose the element of surprise, and kill him when he least expects it.

Thinking this last thought, Skull Cracker grinned when an inspiration hit him. Without further delay, he simply began walking toward the tipi as if nothing unusual were going on.

Hump Medicine spotted him while still about thirty paces away. But the sight was hardly alarming: Skull Cracker seemed to approach as if he bore a message. His only weapon was his rawhide-wrapped rock, and it was tied to his sash. He would have to get close to kill with it.

So to be safe Medicine Hump halted him at ten paces out by lifting the muzzle of his rifle. This brave has no business here, not now or ever, and Hump Medicine knew it.

"Bad time for a visit, uncle," he told the older brave. "Come back when Touch the Sky is here."

"My business is not with Woman Face. Nor should you be so confident he will return this day. At any rate, I have something for his squaw. Will you give it to her?"

Skull Cracker dipped his left hand into his parfleche as if to retrieve something. But this was only a feint to distract the younger brave, for the right hand reached up and quickly untied the rock from his sash.

Hump Medicine's brow wrinkled in a frown. "You have something for Honey Eater? What?"

"This, dungheap!"

Skull Cracker spent time every day hurling his deadly rock at targets. Now his right arm—the one propelled by that massive lump of shoulder muscle—shot out like a powerful

159

spring uncoiling. The fist-sized rock chunked with savage force into Hump Medicine's skull, caving in his forehead and killing him instantly.

Skull Cracker's breath whistled in his nostrils from his exertions. Quietly he stepped over the prostrate figure and reclaimed his rock. He wrapped the rawhide several times around his wrist to secure it for a killing blow at close range.

Then, his lips twitching into an anticipatory grin, he reached out to lift the entrance flap.

From his hidden position behind a briar deadfall, Wolf Who Hunts Smiling commanded a good view of the Flower Meadow. He could see the people lined up on both of the long sides, the two combatants at either end being coached by their supporters. Then River of Winds lifted both arms, and the fight was on.

Touch the Sky's pure white palomilla looked magnificent, her mane riffling as she picked up speed in the charge, her muscles defined like taut ropes. Divots of grass and soil flew from beneath her scrambling hoofs. Lone Bear's powerful roan was less graceful, more brutal, lowering its head like a charging bull. Both men held their stone-tipped lances braced under one arm.

Wolf Who Hunts Smiling already had his slingshot to hand. Now he dipped a few fingers into his shot pouch and removed a heavy buffalo ball. He dropped it into the sling's load pouch.

Let them make one pass, he told himself. Lance fighters seldom ended it at the first pass, for that was the coup-count. Then, on the second pass, the killing pass, he would finally free Woman Face from his "noble" red soul.

Touch the Sky slid forward and hugged his pony's neck tightly with both knees. Lone Bear hurtled toward him like a downhill locomotive, his face grim and determined, a juggernaut of death. Touch the Sky felt the palomilla's muscles heaving beneath him, felt his band watching on the edge of their next breath. Closer the two enemies hurtled, and Touch the Sky shifted his lance for the first strike.

The "shaman ear" could suddenly hear the dry-leaves voice of old Arrow Keeper: *Not for honor and not for personal glory. For your tribe, your wife, and your child, take this coup!*

It almost appeared as if the two stubborn ponies would collide head-on. At the last moment, however, Touch the Sky's palomilla twisted to the right. Neither man could get a solid thrust off. They both settled for hard sideways swipes, and both connected.

Touch the Sky made first contact. His lance whacked Lone Bear across the shoulders, giving Touch the Sky the coup. His band and many Bow Strings erupted in cheers. The blow, however, lacked force because it was in the same direction as Lone Bear's motion. Lone Bear's lance, in contrast, caught Touch the Sky across the chest with a force opposite his motion.

For one horrible instant, Touch the Sky felt himself lifting from his pony as the blow threatened to unseat him. Desperate, he lowered his upper body and jammed both feet into his pony's rope rigging to brace himself. The blow knocked him flat, and a mighty shout of triumph went up from the Bull Whips when he rolled off his pony's back. But the rigging held, and though one shoulder scraped ground painfully, he was able to struggle back into position.

However, the near miss had cost him his lance. Now, as he turned his pony for the second pass—the killing pass—he pulled his battle axe from its rigging.

Disgusted with his performance so far, despite winning the coup, Touch the Sky set his lips in the straight, determined line that always meant death to his enemies.

"Hi-ya!" he urged his mount and himself. "Hii-*ya!*"

He braced himself for the killing blow as his enemy raced ever closer. His arm drew back to strike, and then there was a flat, solid, sickening sound of hard impact. His palomilla gave one massive shudder. An eye-blink later, Touch the Sky hurtled from his downed mount and bounced off the grass.

The fall rattled, but did not hurt, him. But his last weapon had flown off somewhere. He barely had time to stand again before Lone Bear, eyes sheening with savage triumph, bore down on the horseless, unarmed brave.

Honey Eater had tensed when she heard Hump Medicine speaking outside her tipi. But his voice, while wary, did not sound unusually angry or alarmed. Some tardy spectator leaving for the great spectacle, perhaps. When he fell silent again, she relaxed somewhat and resumed her labors with a piece of beadwork.

This busywork was merely desperate activity. More than anything, she wanted this horrible morning to be over and her tall brave at her side again. If only—

Light flooded the tipi when the entrance flap was thrown further back. Startled, she looked up, expecting Hump Medicine. But it was Skull Cracker who stepped inside. His deadly raw-hide-wrapped rock dangled from his right hand—and it dripped blood and fresh gobbets of brain matter.

"No dogs to sic on me," he told the frightened woman. "And no tall shaman to protect you. He is already sleeping with the worms, and now I will send you to him. First, take off your dress. I would look on your naked flesh."

Honey Eater fought down the panic as he took his first step into the tipi. The pistol Touch the Sky gave her was in her parfleche, all right—but there the parfleche lay, on the other side of the center pole among their sleeping robes! Why had she neglected to tie it on when she dressed?

Skull Cracker's huge knot of shoulder muscle flexed in anticipation of the crushing blow. He slapped the rock repeatedly into his left palm as he advanced.

"Sing your death song while you can," he advised her.

Fearing he would grow lust-impatient, kill her quickly, and strip her himself, Honey Eater hastily shrugged out of her fawnskin dress. The sight brought him up short. The delay gave her a desperate inspiration.

"Do not do this thing," she said suddenly, "and I will give you all the yellow dust my husband has earned as a spy for the whiteskins. We have been hoarding it. There is enough to buy many fine ponies and weapons."

Skull Cracker hesitated. This was the first he had heard about whiteskin gold. But truly it made sense. Why else would Touch the Sky have been leaving messages in trees for soldiers?

At that moment, as he stared at her taut, heavy breasts and copper-burnished skin, most of the blood in his brain had rushed elsewhere. Why not at least see this gold? he reasoned. So what if it was a hoax to buy time? Either way she was dead.

"Get it," he said. "But I am watching you. Don't make me kill you before you sing your death song—kill you brutally as I killed your favorite cur."

He was indeed watching her. But all the wrong parts held his attention. And the parfleche she picked up was too small to hide any weapon but a knife. He dismissed it, staring at her nipples the color of lush plums.

"Do you know what my husband once told me?" she said conversationally as she slid one hand inside the parfleche to get the gold.

"Why not tell me what he said, honey flesh?"

"He told me that when you stab a man, you should go between the fourth and fifth rib, for that way it is straight to the heart. And he told me that when you shoot a man, you must never 'aim' a pistol. One only points it as if it were an extension of one's finger, he said. And finally, Skull Cracker, he told me you were a pig's afterbirth!"

Skull Cracker never heard the shot that ended his snarling charge and made Honey Eater's ears ring. And even as she leaped out of the way of his dead body, she marveled at the ironic justice of it: Skull Cracker was falling dead on the very same spot where he had thrown the murdered dog.

The warrior's reflex brought Touch the Sky instantly to his feet after his pony was downed. But he had fallen hard, and the instinct to keep fighting could not clear his head immediately. Nor was there time for any plan—in a mere heartbeat, the determined roan was on him.

A hard pivot to his left barely eluded the stone point of the lance. In the same motion, Touch the Sky flung himself down. But he was not trying to duck—he was instead employing a desperate trick perfected by Cheyennes in the days before they moved farther west and became renowned horsemen. In those days they had sometimes been forced to fight mounted warriors from the ground.

He wrapped himself, clinging with all his might, to the roan's right foreleg. For one heart-stopping moment his grip almost gave out. Then, with a thudding slam that audibly snapped the pony's neck, the roan crashed down at full gallop. Touch the Sky felt a few moments of exhilarated victory before a blow like a mule's kick ended his side of the fight.

With one dead man inside her tipi and another outside the entrance, Honey Eater had no choice but to join her people at the Flower Meadow. Reluctantly, she mounted her little pony and set out.

Dread made her hearts heavy as she cleared the willow thickets and spotted the dueling ground. It was over, and both men were down!

But hope surged in her soul when she realized that it was Little Horse leading all that cheering! Only look—there lay Lone Bear, horribly twisted and broken, killed by the weight of his own dying horse—and Touch the Sky, though clearly bruised and shaken, rose and began walking unassisted off the field.

And now Honey Eater understood why so many of the Bow Strings, those who had gone over to the Whips, were united again behind River of Winds, Gray Thunder, and Little Horse: a huge flock of crows, the traditional sign of guilt, were circling Lone Bear's body. Thus Maiyun affirmed Touch the Sky's claim that Lone Bear was indeed Spotted Tail's killer. Now, as her husband had prayed, the Bow Strings were again strong and united.

More wild cheers erupted when she halted her pony, dismounted, and walked slowly out to meet her victorious brave in front of all the people. But the Bull Whips were not cheering. And even as she felt her little one stir inside her, Honey Eater resolved to remember her warrior husband's words: *For a Cheyenne, the end of one battle only marks the beginning of the next.*

WARRIOR FURY

Prologue

Though he sat behind few men in council, the tall Cheyenne brave called Touch the Sky faced a future as uncertain as his past.

The ill-fated brave's tragedy began in the year the white man's winter-count called 1840. A U.S. Cavalry ambush killed the great Cheyenne peace chief Running Antelope and his wife, Lotus Petal. Only one Cheyenne survived that Platte River massacre: Running Antelope's newborn son.

Pawnee scouts were about to brain the infant against a tree when the lieutenant in charge stopped them. The baby was taken back to the river-bend settlement of Bighorn Falls near Fort Bates in the Wyoming Territory. There he grew up the adopted son of John and Sarah Hanchon, owners of the town's mercantile store.

The Hanchons named him Matthew and loved

him as their own blood. The first sixteen years of his life were happy ones. Early on he went to work for his parents, stocking shelves and delivering goods to the outlying settlers. Though some local whites hated this full-blooded Indian in their midst, many others eventually accepted and even befriended him.

Then his life's path took a fatal turn when he fell in love with Hiram Steele's daughter, Kristen.

The richest and most powerful rancher in the area, Steele caught the young lovers in their secret meeting place. He ordered one of his wranglers to savagely beat the youth and promised to kill him if he caught the couple together again. Fearful for Matthew's life, Kristen forced herself to a difficult lie. She told him she could no longer love an Indian.

Humiliated and heartbroken, Matthew soon faced even greater troubles. A proud and arrogant lieutenant from Fort Bates, Seth Carlson, had staked a claim to Kristen's hand. He visited Matthew with a merciless ultimatum: Either Matthew pulled up stakes for good or the Hanchons would lose their contract to supply Fort Bates—the very lifeblood of their mercantile business.

Thus trapped between the sap and the bark, a miserable but determined Matthew said good-bye to the only life he knew and lit out for the upcountry of the Powder—Cheyenne Indian country. But his white man's clothing and language and customs doomed him. Captured by braves from Chief Yellow Bear's tribe, he was immediately accused of being a Bluecoat spy and sentenced to torture and death.

Two young braves especially hated him: Black Elk, the tribe's war leader, and his cousin Wolf Who Hunts Smiling. Black Elk's loathing of this intruder deepened when Chief Yellow Bear's daughter, Honey Eater, took too keen an interest in the accused spy's fate.

Wolf Who Hunts Smiling was about to plunge a knife deep into Matthew's vitals when an authoritative voice stopped him. The speaker was old Arrow Keeper, the tribe's shaman and protector of the four sacred Medicine Arrows.

Arrow Keeper had just returned from experiencing a crucial vision at holy Medicine Lake. In that vision, a mysterious youth—the son of a long-lost Cheyenne chief—eventually led the entire Cheyenne nation in its greatest battle victory. This mystery warrior would be recognized by a distinctive mark, and Arrow Keeper spotted it buried in the hair over the prisoner's right temple: a mulberry-colored birthmark in the shape of an arrowhead, the mark of the warrior.

Over the strenuous objections of many, Arrow Keeper and Chief Yellow Bear spared the prisoner's life. His old name was buried in a hole forever and he was renamed Touch the Sky. Even more shocking, Arrow Keeper insisted that this pathetic intruder must live with the tribe—and even train as a warrior.

Despite a constant campaign to destroy and humiliate him, Touch the Sky became the most formidable warrior in the tribe. But after Chief Yellow Bear died, Honey Eater was forced into a loveless marriage with Black Elk. Her star-crossed love for Touch the Sky—which he returned—drove Black Elk to a murderous jealousy that his cousin Wolf Who Hunts Smiling constantly encouraged.

With the mysterious disappearance of Arrow Keeper, Touch the Sky was narrowly voted as the tribe's new shaman and Keeper of the Arrows. But Wolf Who Hunts Smiling joined forces secretly with Comanche and Blackfoot allies. He also selected another clever and scheming brave, Medicine Flute, and called him the tribe's only true shaman.

Aiming for Touch the Sky in dense fog, Wolf Who Hunts Smiling mistakenly killed Black Elk. Although he cleverly convinced many that Touch the Sky was the killer, Touch the Sky and Honey Eater defied their tribal enemies and exchanged the squaw-taking vows. Now the tribe is deeply divided and the battle lines clearly drawn. Wolf Who Hunts Smiling and his allies—who now include Hiram Steele and Captain Seth Carlson—are determined to destroy this tall warrior and his loved ones.

Chapter 1

"Over here, brother," Little Horse called out to his comrade, Tangle Hair. "Anthills. Let us clean our blankets."

The two young Cheyenne warriors sat their ponies in the lee of a long ridge. Below them, the Powder and Little Powder rivers formed their huge confluence west of the sacred *Paha Sapa*, known to the whiteskins as the Black Hills. Tucked into the wedge of flat tableland between the two rivers was the sprawling summer camp of Chief Gray Thunder's band of the Northern Cheyenne.

Little Horse rode a sturdy paint mare with a roached mane. He swung down and hobbled her, foreleg to rear, with rawhide. Then he undid his rope rigging and pulled off the red Hudson's Bay blanket. He joined Tangle Hair beside a huge

9

mound crawling with red ants.

Both braves threw their blankets onto the mound. Within a few heartbeats the blankets were alive with furious, ravenous ants. In mere moments the ants had devoured all the lice infesting the blankets. The two friends pulled the blankets off, snapped the ants away, and returned to their ponies.

"If only," Little Horse remarked, staring down toward their camp, "the human lice that infest a village could be so easily eliminated."

"Straight words, brother. But a louse is one thing, a wolf another," Tangle Hair said. "Especially a Wolf Who Hunts Smiling."

Little Horse secured his rigging and said nothing. Nor did his stoic face reveal the new worry storm raging within him, for a blooded warrior was expected always to keep his feelings private, unlike the woman-faced white men. But worry he did. Constantly his vigilant eyes returned to the camp below, to a lone tipi which sat atop a hummock between the clan circles and the river.

Touch the Sky's tipi. From here, only its isolation from the rest marked it as different. But it *was* different. Very different, Little Horse knew. For even now, as Cheyenne mustangs rolled joyously in the new grass, the woman Touch the Sky loved with all his being was presenting him with their first child.

The timing of it could have been the work of Maiyun, the Good Supernatural. This was the time of new life springing forth throughout creation. Another hard winter was behind the tribe.

The valleys were no longer locked by ice; soon game would once again be plentiful on the hunting ranges the Cheyenne shared with their Sioux cousins. The rivers and creeks were swollen with crystal-clear snow runoff from the mountains. The new grass was green and lush, already well above the ponies' hocks. Soon the far-flung Cheyenne bands, ten in all, would unite as one for the Sun Dance.

It was a wonderful time to begin life, a time when hope filled a man's breast like rain soaking parched earth. And yet, thought Little Horse, even this time of surpassing joy was tainted by the promise of new sorrow. And it was Touch the Sky himself who said it best: For a warrior, any thing he loved was one more soft place for his enemy to hurt him.

"Still quiet," Tangle Hair remarked nervously, seeing which way his friend's eyes went.

"Quiet," Little Horse agreed. "And that stirs flies in my belly, Cheyenne. Have you noticed a thing? When the frogs and insects fall silent, trouble soon follows. Indeed, death itself is very quiet."

Little Horse had forgotten the holiness of this time and the inappropriateness of such talk right now when Honey Eater required special benevolence of the Day Maker. But as soon as the words escaped his mouth, he recollected himself. Tangle Hair only watched, approving with his silence, as Little Horse quickly scattered his best white man's tobacco to the wind.

"May the High Holy Ones forgive me," he said

contritely, facing the *Paha Sapa*, the center of the Cheyenne universe.

"We are nervous, buck," Tangle Hair assured him. "The Holy Ones know this. Just as they know you have always served Touch the Sky and his squaw honorably. I was there at Buffalo Creek when you and Touch the Sky stood back to back and defeated a score of murderous buffalo hiders.

"That limp of yours—even the old grandmothers tell the story of how you and Touch the Sky were taken prisoner and tortured on Wes Munro's keelboat. The young girls sing of it in their sewing lodge. Any moment now Touch the Sky will hold his new buck or doe. He never expected to live to see this day. If not for you, sturdy Little Horse, he would not have."

Tangle Hair was not given to speeches, but these fine words moved Little Horse.

"*Ha-ho ha-ho,*" he said in Cheyenne, thanking him. "But truly, buck, I will rest easier when he has indeed held that babe. And we both know that the end of one battle is only the beginning of the next. It matters not whether Touch the Sky has a son or a daughter, Wolf Who Hunts Smiling and the rest of his enemies do not plan to let that child live. A son, they argue, may possess his father's battle prowess, a daughter may someday foal more like him."

Little Horse spoke straight-arrow, and Tangle Hair could only agree with a glum nod. "Before he disappeared, Arrow Keeper told all of us to be patient, that we must pass through the bitter waters before we reach the sweet. For Touch the Sky,

12

all the waters seem bitter."

The two braves would be down in that camp right now, worrying with the rest of Touch the Sky's beleaguered followers, if this were not the height of horse-raiding season. The Cheyennes and their Sioux cousins had recently returned from the Bear Paw Mountains with some of the finest mustangs in recent memory. Now the Pawnees, Apaches, Crows, and other enemies too lazy to search out wild ponies would be raiding their herds. Thus the best warriors were presently riding herd guard.

"Look!" Tangle Hair said, pointing down toward the river. "They are stirring around Touch the Sky's tipi!"

"That's Sharp Nosed Woman," Little Horse said, watching Honey Eater's aunt step past the entrance flap of the lodge. "Buck, she is covered with blood! But is she smiling as all women do when a new baby arrives?"

"I cannot tell from here," Tangle Hair said, a nervous edge to his voice. "She is returning to her tipi."

"Walking slowly," Little Horse said. "Brother, I have already invited bad medicine by speaking wrong things at this time. I will not give voice to the fear in my heart right now. But I am riding down there to see which way the wind sets."

"Never mind, buck. Here comes Two Twists to tell us that very thing."

Both braves watched a young Cheyenne hurry through the clan circles toward the common corral where fully trained ponies were kept. His double braids, unusual in a tribe whose men preferred either single braids or long, loose locks, had earned him his name. Two Twists quickly cut an albino pony, a pure white with blue eyes, out from the herd and, grabbing a handful of mane, swung up onto its back.

"Here he comes," Little Horse said, "and I do not like the set of his face."

The cool apprehension in Little Horse's veins turned into cold certainty as Two Twists drew nearer, his face battle grim. The young warrior halted his pony several paces out, staring silently at his comrades.

"Well, coy one?" Little Horse demanded. "Are you a girl fresh from her sewing lodge, savoring some juicy bit of scandal? If you have hard news for us, well then, be a man."

Little Horse did not really feel the anger he feigned. Rather, the fear of bad news forced him to a deceptive blustering.

"Brothers," Two Twists said. "I have no words to say it."

At this horrible hint, all color drained from Little Horse's face. That ominous silence down below, Sharp Nosed Woman's lone journey back to her tent—did it mean the worst?

"Honey Eater?" Little Horse inquired, unable to complete the thought.

"The child?" Tangle Hair said simultaneously.

His face showing nothing, Two Twists only nodded. "Both," he said cryptically.

"Both?" It was the hardest word Little Horse ever forced out.

"Both?" Tangle Hair repeated stupidly.

Two Twists nodded again. "Both."

Before either brave could react to this, the wind made a capricious change of direction. A heart-beat later, an infant's healthy bellow split the silence below.

Two Twists laughed so hard he nearly slid from his pony.

"Both," he repeated again, "are fine, you gaping mooncalfs! Mother and *son!* It is Touch the Sky who requires calming."

Little Horse felt a great weight lifted from his chest. "Two Twists," he said angrily, "I will flay your soles for that cruel joke. But not now." A wide grin suddenly split the sturdy warrior's normally impassive face. "Hi-ya!" he shouted, raising the shrill Cheyenne war cry to the heavens. "Hii-ya!"

"Bucks," an excited Two Twists went on, "you should *see* Touch the Sky's face! You should *see* it! Do you remember his proud face when he counted first coup at the Tongue River Battle? Recall his great joy when the white children on the orphan train escaped from Sis-ki-dee and Big Tree?

"That pride, that joy, were nothing. Wait until you see him now. Now I know why we fought our way up Wendigo Mountain with him. When he arrived at this tribe seven winters ago, he wore white man's shoes and was condemned to death. *Now* his coup feathers trail the ground, and the finest woman in the Shaiyena Nation just gave him a fine son."

Little Horse and Tangle Hair savored every

word of this speech, for like Two Twists, they had been at Touch the Sky's side for many of his hardest battles.

"A son," Little Horse said wonderingly. "A fine son?"

"None finer, bucks. You heard the power of his lungs just now. He will raise a war whoop they will hear up on the Marias. But never mind my description. Touch the Sky told me to relieve both of you. He and Honey Eater insist you must both ride down now to hold the child as I have just done."

"Now?" Little Horse said.

"Buck, do I suddenly speak Navajo? *Now*. Honey Eater refuses to rest until both of you hold the baby."

This prospect struck a spark in both braves' eyes. Still, they were rugged warriors, unmarried, and this was an awkward time.

"Should we not wait until the lodgefest?" Tangle Hair wondered. The lodgefest was a public reception for the tribe's new children.

Adamantly, Two Twists shook his head. "Touch the Sky insists that you come down now. He said to me, tell them this, 'Tell them my blood flows in this child, but three other braves suffered beside me to ensure his life. Therefore, he has one mother and four fathers. And we four will hold him first.' "

Those fine words held both braves silent. Before they could speak or move, the abrupt drumbeat of unshod hooves made them glance toward the common corral. A lone brave on a pure black pony, the red streamer of the Bull Whip Soldier Society tied to its tail, raced off toward the northwest.

"Wolf Who Hunts Smiling," Little Horse said. "Where is he going in such a hurry?"

"Not toward Wendigo Mountain, at least," Tangle Hair said. "Else I would say he is going to tell his secret allies, Sis-ki-dee and Big Tree, the bad news."

"But he is riding toward the Little Bighorn," Little Horse mused. "Why? Come, Tangle Hair, for now let us go hold our honorary son. I fear we will find out, all in good time, what new treachery our wily wolf has in store."

"White Man Runs Him has finally sired his whelp," Wolf Who Hunts Smiling announced. "A son. I have long hoped for the pleasure of braining it against a tree while both parents look on. Even better than killing your enemy is the pleasure of first killing his loved ones in front of him."

Wolf Who Hunts Smiling had once been a prisoner at the Bluecoat soldiertown called Fort Laramie. His English was good enough that he only occasionally resorted to signs.

"Wolf," Hiram Steele said, "you call yourself a warrior and yet you brag about braining babies against trees?"

"If you mean to goad me, hair face, work harder at it. Even a warrior must have his pleasures, and who will stop me? You?"

"Stop you?" Steele threw back his head and roared with laughter. "*Stop* you? Listen, you slip-

17

pery red son. I'd pay gold-camp rates just to watch it happen. First his squaw and his kid, then him."

"Don't spend it till it's yours," the third man present, Captain Seth Carlson, warned both of them. "You two are damn good at *talking* Hanchon into his grave. Goddamn it, let's finally *put* him there."

The wary trio sat in a semicircle, Wolf Who Hunts Smiling keeping a wind-bent dogwood tree to his back in case this was a trap. This camp, in the high country between the Powder and the Little Bighorn, commanded an excellent view in every direction. Located a full sleep's hard ride northwest of Gray Thunder's camp, it crowned a formidable headland where, once, only ten Pawnee defenders had destroyed almost five times as many Crow Crazy Dogs. From that day on, every Plains Indian winter-count referred to the place as Massacre Bluff.

This stunning victory over fierce suicide warriors resulted from the bluff's excellent qualities as a defensive bastion. The only feasible approach was through the Valley of the Greasy Grass, where trees and other natural aids to surprise attack were lacking. The bluff itself was surrounded on all sides by long, ascending slopes of barren, wind-scoured granite. Not even a prairie dog could climb up without being seen from above.

Seth Carlson's remark did not anger either Steele or the Cheyenne. They knew he spoke from the center of his great need to kill Matthew Hanchon, known throughout the Red Nation as Touch the Sky of the Northern Cheyenne. They shared in that need, shared it so deeply it even made them hold their mutual hatred in check.

"He'll go to his grave," Steele assured both of his companions. "Seth, we took an oath on it when that aboriginal bastard trumped us in Blackford Valley. But the picture has changed a mite now. That arrogant savage has caught himself a new pup."

"So what?" Carlson said, scorn poison-tipping his words. "What, you want me to hand out cigars? That why you called me here, to tell me his squaw foaled? Hell, I already knew it from the Moccasin Telegraph. All over the upcountry there's been smoke and mirror flashes about it."

"Right there's your problem," Steele said, enjoying being in control. "You're so quick to rise up on your hind feet, you miss the main chance. Why, even the Wolf here has already figured it out. See that slyboots grinning at us? Even he knows what I got on the spit. And you, trained at West Point, can't cipher it out?"

Carlson scowled. He had unsnapped the brim of his officer's hat, and now most of his big, bluff face was shadowed by the westering sun.

"Hiram, spell it out plain. This shit gets old. How many times now have you done this? How many times have you and that gut-eating buck there grinned at me like I'm a soft-brain? How goddamn many times have you told me Hanchon's hash was cooked? And how goddamn many times has that flea-bitten blanket ass made *us* look like raggedy-assed pilgrims?"

"Now damn it, Soldier Blue," Steele said, his

tone more reasonable now, "no need to get on the peck. Simmer down and listen to me. I want you to see something, both of you."

Steele grunted as he heaved his big frame off the boulder he'd been using as a stool. His hard, flint-gray eyes lived up to his name.

"Widow Maker!" he shouted across to a group of men who were erecting a twisting network of copper tubing nearby. "C'mere!"

Even from a distance Carlson could smell the hogsheads filled with fermenting mash, a pungent smell. His face puckered as the stench filled his nostrils. "Jesus God, Hiram! That mash smells like a whorehouse at low tide."

"Hunh. That's the smell of money, Seth boy. That's why I had you hire Hardiman and his boys. That Taos Lightning you smell is going to finance Hanchon's death and bring a world of hurt to his red people."

At a high sign from Carlson, Steele abruptly fell silent, realizing he was saying too much in front of the wrong person. "No offense, Wolf," he added.

Wolf Who Hunts Smiling flashed his infamous lupine grin. "Had you offended me, you would be dead by now. But his people are not my people. As for whatever treachery you have in store for the red man—do what you will. I have banded with you to kill our enemy. Once he has been sent across, I plan to do the hurt dance on *your* people, too."

Steele, still watching the knot of men, frowned and raised his voice. "Widow Maker! I said c'mere!"

A solid man of middle height, wearing a leather weskit and the new Levi's jeans with riveted seams, peeled away from the group. He ambled over toward the trio, clearly in no hurry. As he neared, Carlson and Wolf Who Hunts Smiling saw he was a half-breed.

"Here comes the man," Steele averred, "who's going to kill Matthew Hanchon—assuming one of us doesn't have that pleasure. As for me, I'll settle for killing his woman or kid. I want to see the look in his eye when I do it."

Carlson and the furtive-looking Cheyenne with the swift-as-minnow eyes seemed unimpressed as they watched the half-breed draw nearer.

"Pee doodles," Carlson spat out. "He's not even armed."

"And if he was?" Wolf Who Hunts Smiling asked. "Why should this one succeed where legions have failed?"

"This one's different."

In a rare show of agreement, the soldier and the Cheyenne joined in contemptuous laughter.

"The Cherokee policeman named Mankiller was different, too," Wolf Who Hunts Smiling said. "His hands were so huge and powerful that, when he put the choke on his victims, they stopped both the blood and the air. Yet now he is feeding worms in the Indian Territory thanks to White Man Runs Him."

"Abbot Fontaine was different, too," Carlson said. " 'Member, Hiram? That bastard was colder than a landlord's heart, even bragged about killing his own mother. He was quick with that sawed-

21

off shotgun he wore in that sling of his. But we found him crushed to paste in Padgett's Mill—where that buck was hiding."

"This one's different," Hiram insisted again. "This time I got it all figured, right down to the 'i' dots. Face it, repeated attempts on Hanchon have all come a cropper. So this time we get at him indirectly.

"Somehow we've got to lure Hanchon out of camp for a short spell. Then—this is where you figure in, Wolf—we create a diversion at the camp itself to draw off all the security Wolf has told us about, the security around Hanchon's squaw and the brat. We grab both of them and hold them here. Hanchon will have to come to us if he wants them back."

Carlson wasn't convinced, though there was merit in this plan. "Lot of ifs," he complained. "But even *if* we can lure Hanchon out and create a diversion, even *if* we get his family up here, where's our ace in the hole? Hanchon needs killing, and bad, but how do you figure *this* hombre for the job?"

He nodded toward the half-breed. Widow Maker was still about thirty paces off, closing slowly. Nothing about the man seemed particularly intimidating; indeed, he appeared somewhat the dandy with his neat pressed cloth collar and shiny oxblood leather boots.

"To answer your question," Steele said, "there's what I can tell you and what I can show you. What I can tell you is this: Widow Maker hails from the Knife River country. He's half Hidatsa, half

French. Not only an expert tracker, but I have it straight from Big Bat Pourier himself. See, Big Bat took him back East for a spell. Taught him some interesting tricks and put him in his Wild West Show. Big Bat tells me that Widow Maker also excels in the art of silent movement and infiltration. Once we come up with the diversion, and get Hanchon out of the picture, he's going into that camp, and he's coming out with Hanchon's squaw and kid."

"That's tall, but I'll take it on faith for now," Carlson said. "What can you show us?"

Steele's weather-rawed face divided in an ear-to-ear grin. He'd been waiting for this. That was clear when he pulled three small pieces of lumber, each about the size of a slice of bread, from the saddlebags lying on the ground beside him.

"What can I show you? Those tricks Big Bat taught him." Steele raised his voice again to add, "Show 'em what you can do, Widow Maker!"

With those words Hiram pivoted hard left, hard right, then left again, tossing a board high with each pivot. Carlson and Wolf Who Hunts Smiling watched all three sail high into the air at wide intervals.

What happened next made both men stare at each other in astonishment.

Without breaking his leisurely stride, without even seeming to glance overhead, Widow Maker quickly brought his left foot up off the ground and seized something tucked into the top of the boot. Once, twice, a third time his right arm snapped out overhead, tossing the objects with incredible speed.

Three solid *thwacks*, and each of the boards was knocked hard out of its natural trajectory.

"Targets!" Steele shouted, confirming the hits with clear admiration in his tone. He ran around collecting all three boards. When he brought them back, Carlson stared at them, then looked at Wolf Who Hunts Smiling.

A narrow-bladed throwing dagger protruded through each board—precisely through the center of silver-dollar-size circles Hiram had smudged on them with charcoal.

"Not only hit the targets," Steele gloated. "Hit the goddamn bull's-eye each time!"

Widow Maker shrugged indifferently and returned to join Hardiman Burke's men. Carlson slowly shook his head. "That's not possible," he said flatly.

"Blue Blouse, I cannot hear your words because that half-breed's *aim* speaks louder," Wolf Who Hunts Smiling said. "We saw it, though I admit I can hardly credit what I beheld. A man who throws knives like this Widow Maker has surely earned his name."

"That he has," Steele boasted. "And what man has done, man will do. He can't miss within one hundred feet. You wanted to see our ace, Seth boy? Well, you just glommed him! Hanchon is smart as a steel trap, granted. But how smart can a man stay when his wife and kid are trapped between hell and high water? He'll be watching for bullets, staying out of short-gun range when we

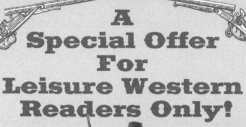

GET YOUR 4
FREE* BOOKS NOW—
A VALUE OF BETWEEN
$17 AND $20

Mail the Free* Books Certificate Today!

FREE* BOOKS
CERTIFICATE!

YES! I want to subscribe to the Leisure Western Book Club. Please send me my 4 FREE* BOOKS. Then, each month, I'll receive the four newest Leisure Western Selections to preview for 10 days. If I decide to keep them, I will pay the Special Member's Only discounted price of just $3.36 each, a total of $13.44 ($16.35 in Canada). This saves me between $3 and $6 off the bookstore price. There are no shipping, handling or other charges.* There is no minimum number of books I must buy and I may cancel the program at any time. In any case, the 4 FREE* BOOKS are mine to keep—at a value of between $17 and $20!

*In Canada, add $7.50 US shipping and handling per order for first shipment. For all subsequent shipments to Canada the cost of membership in the Book Club is $16.35 US plus $7.50 US shipping and handling per order. All payments must be made in US dollars.

Name _____

Address _____

City_____ State_____

Zip_____ Telephone_____

Signature_____

Biggest Savings Offer!

For those of you who would like to pay us in advance by check or credit card—we've got an even bigger savings in mind. Interested? Check here. ☐

If under 18, parent or guardian must sign. Terms, prices and conditions subject to change. Subscription subject to acceptance. Leisure Books reserves the right to reject any order or cancel any subscription.

Tear here and mail your FREE* book card today!

Get Four Books Totally
F R E E* –
A Value of between
$16 and $20

PLEASE RUSH
MY FOUR FREE*
BOOKS TO ME
RIGHT AWAY!

LeisureWestern Book Club
P.O. Box 6613
Edison, NJ 08818-6613

AFFIX
STAMP
HERE

lure him close to parley. He'll have to slip up.

"Granted, we got some details to work out. It's got to be done right this time, it's *got* to be! It ain't just because that savage kissed on my daughter, Seth, or that she chose a blanket ass over you. No white man will profit from this territory so long as Hanchon walks above the earth. If we expect to get rich around here, we'll have to kill that red bastard first."

Chapter 2

"Husband," Honey Eater said, "my uncle, Hat Keeper of the Sweet Medicine clan, came to see the baby. He greatly admired his lungs and said he already bellows like a little bear."

"Truly," Touch the Sky agreed. "But only look. The little one seems quiet enough *now*."

At this teasing remark Honey Eater blushed all the way to her earlobes—for as they spoke their new son was contentedly feeding at Honey Eater's breast.

Still teasing, Touch the Sky added, "At least he is not so ugly now. When first he peered forth into the world, I feared that the Day Maker gave us a Comanche monstrosity by mistake."

Before Honey Eater could protest this, the baby himself suddenly turned his mouth away from her milk-swollen nipple and loosed a bellow toward his father. The mighty roar, in the close confines of their tipi, was truly impressive. Both parents were caught by surprise and laughed.

"I regret my jest, Little Bear," Touch the Sky said hastily. "You are a handsome young buck. Your father was only disguising his great pride in you."

"Handsome?" Honey Eater held him up higher for a moment, thrusting him into the golden ray of light slanting through the smoke hole at the top. "I should say so. He could not look more like his handsome father if he were your reflection in a pool."

But something else occurred to her. "Husband? Just now you called him Little Bear. It is a simple name, but an apt one. And it was my father's infant name."

Honey Eater passed one hand in a slashing motion before her, making the cut-off sign as one did when speaking of the dead.

"Little Bear," Touch the Sky repeated. And when he said it, his son again turned his head to watch him.

Both parents laughed again, pleased at this happy discovery of a name. By custom Cheyenne males were granted two names: a birth name given by their parents and a second name earned later, conferred by the men of their clan. For several sleeps Touch the Sky and Honey Eater had discussed their child's birth name. Now he had one, one he seemed to approve of himself.

"He has a sturdy roar," Touch the Sky said. "Already his powerful little lungs show the promise of a bellowing war whoop. And already this little brave shows signs of the legendary courage of a she-grizz protecting her cubs. My wife likes the name, I like the name. So Little Bear he shall be."

Because of the dangerous situation these days in camp, Touch the Sky had ingeniously wain-scotted the tipi wall to a height of four feet with tanned buckskin. Though this blocked their firelit reflections at night and muted much of the noise from camp, it could not completely block the sound he heard now: the flat, monotonous notes of a bone flute.

He crossed to the entrance flap and threw it aside. On the far side of the huge central clearing, a knot of Bull Whip soldiers had gathered around a skinny brave with heavy-lidded eyes that made him always appear half asleep.

"Medicine Flute," Honey Eater said behind Touch the Sky, not bothering to glance outside. She laid the baby down in the soft robes and began brushing his already thick hair with the rough side of a buffalo tongue. "The coward who is trying to usurp your title as shaman and Keeper of the Arrows."

"Sweet love, you flatter that bone-blowing coward. He could not count coup on his own shadow. He is the fawning dog of Wolf Who Hunts Smiling. Every lie he tells is placed in his parfleche by our wily wolf."

The same wily wolf, Touch the Sky told himself, who raced out of camp as soon as Little Bear was of this world. Why?

As if Honey Eater were privy to his inner voice,

she now said out loud, "You know how much your enemies fear our son? They have failed often enough in their attempts to kill you. It turns their livers to milk, the thought of *two* Touch the Skys to defeat."

"Milk-livered cowards," Touch the Sky said, watching Medicine Flute, "can be the hardest enemies to defeat. Whereas a true warrior carries a gun and bow, *they* fight with lies and deceit. And truly this Medicine Flute takes to deceit like an eagle to clouds."

While still young, the intelligent and perceptive Medicine Flute had realized that visionaries were highly respected by red men, that they did not have to hunt and fight and work as other braves did. True, sometimes an angry tribe killed shamans whose medicine failed. But Medicine Flute, assisted by his master Wolf Who Hunts Smiling, always managed to take credit when medicine worked and to blame it on Touch the Sky when it didn't. By mastering simple sleight-of-hand tricks, he could keep his followers impressed between "miracles."

Such as the time when, with Wolf Who Hunts Smiling goading him on, Medicine Flute once awed the entire tribe by setting a star on fire and sending it blazing across the heavens. Or so it seemed. But in fact, Wolf Who Hunts Smiling had talked to a reservation Indian educated in a whiteskin school. This so-called miracle was really a comet, and the whiteskin shamans had predicted its passage. Nonetheless, Medicine Flute claimed credit for the spectacular celestial demonstration.

Many in the tribe were struck dumb with awe and fell upon the ground praising Medicine Flute's magic. And he challenged Touch the Sky, as the tribe's official medicine man, to best this display of power. All of this was the work of Wolf Who Hunts Smiling, all part of his ongoing efforts to wrest control of the tribe from Touch the Sky and his allies.

In the midst of this troubled rumination, Touch the Sky started when a voice suddenly spoke just outside the tipi.

"Touch the Sky. I would speak with you."

For a moment the tall warrior's dark eyes cut automatically to his Sharps percussion rifle in its buckskin sheath. But glancing outside, he spotted an old unarmed brave named Long Jaw. Curiosity replaced his wariness. True, Long Jaw was certainly not one of his supporters, for after all, both his sons were Bull Whips. But the old man walked always on the truth path and placed nothing before the good of his tribe.

"Father," Touch the Sky greeted him respectfully, "Arrow Keeper once told me you stood beside him at Wolf Creek and made the water turn red with Kiowa and Comanche blood. If you have a thing to tell me, I have ears for it. Will you come inside and share a pipe?"

It was the Cheyenne way to avoid coming at a thing too directly. Usually there must first be discussion of inconsequential matters while smoking to the four directions. But old Long Jaw shook his head.

"I have already seen your fine son," he said, "or

else I would certainly come inside to admire him again. Besides, I will be at the upcoming lodgefest with a fine gift for him. But no, young buck, for now I would speak with you out here. Alone."

Something ominous in the elder's tone made cool blood flow up the back of Touch the Sky's neck.

"As you will, father." Touch the Sky stepped outside. The warm moons had arrived, and Touch the Sky and the rest of the younger braves had laid aside their fur leggings and leather shirts in favor of clouts and elkskin moccasins. But Long Jaw was still wrapped in his winter blanket.

"Shaman," the old man began, "I will not coat my words with honey. I have heard you speak in council, and if any man insists on straight talk, that man is you. We both know that the worst trouble in the world has beset our tribe. Look, even now you are forced to glance around, watching to see who has a bead on you. Never mind guilt or blame for now. I know the stories against you. I have also seen you shed blood to save your tribe. But things are the way they are. The trouble is here, and no boil goes away until it is lanced."

Touch the Sky said nothing, only nodding. These were true words, and he waited respectfully for more.

Long Jaw made the cut-off sign as he said, "You know that I had a wife and son?"

This surprised Touch the Sky. Everyone knew the tragic story of Long Jaw's slaughtered wife and babe and how the grief-stricken brave never married again after their deaths. Everyone also knew that he never mentioned that incident to anyone. What, Touch the Sky worried, had moved him to do so now?

"I know," Touch the Sky replied. "They rode south to visit your relatives in High Forehead's camp on the Niobrara. Pawnees slew them along the way. Your grief has been terrible, a grief past all healing."

Despite his deep emotions, Long Jaw proudly held his face impassive and only nodded. "My grief, buck, and my guilt. For no one in the tribe knows this: My woman begged me to go with her. But I was keen to race my new pony against the Sioux horses, eager to win goods and respect. I stayed for the races and made my wife and babe ride south alone. I should have saved them or at least died with them. My family was slaughtered while I played games like an unblooded warrior. I drank corn beer while their blood stained the ground."

This was indeed a terrible thing, and Touch the Sky did not insult Long Jaw by trying to deny his guilt.

"We are only men," Touch the Sky said, "and men make mistakes. Our honor is not destroyed, only damaged. If all in this tribe had lived as you have, father, it would not be the hurting place it is now. But you did not come here for my praise—strong men like you do not need it. Something else sent you, old fox. Let fly the shaft and drive it straight to the grain."

Long Jaw smiled at this, nodding. His braided

hair was a dark cable shot through with streaks of silver.

"As I said, you are no man for speeches. Good. Then I will tell you why I am here. I lost my woman and child through too little love for them. Do not lose yours."

The old man's tone made the fine hairs rise on Touch the Sky's nape. "Long Jaw," he said, "I understand you. Though your words, this talk of harm to my wife and son, disturb me, I do not resent your saying them. You mean to help me. But, father, you must understand my confusion. You hardly know me. Circumstances keep our paths wide one from the other.

"Now, all of an instant, you come to speak of losing my wife and babe? I fear we still have not cracked the nut and gone to the meat. What sent you like this?"

"Not what, shaman. Who."

"Who, then?"

Long Jaw met his eyes. "Arrow Keeper."

For a moment the ground seemed unsteady under Touch the Sky's feet, as if he were standing in a canoe on a raging river. Arrow Keeper! The wily old shaman-warrior who knew that, by disappearing mysteriously, he could never be declared officially dead. Thus his name could still be spoken without fear a spirit might answer it. And truly, the brave who always said, "By indirection we shall find directions out," would indeed work through an emissary this way.

"He placed a medicine dream over my eyes," Long Jaw said. "He told me that I, of all men, must be the word-bringer when your wife and babe faced sure death."

Touch the Sky's heart turned over at these words, and the fear was on him almost to the point of panic. Only the instincts bred of the warrior kept his voice reasonably steady.

"If Arrow Keeper sent you, father, then every word he spoke to you was important. He is warning me, as he has before. What did he say to tell me?"

"Two things, Cheyenne, though I confess they seem worthless. I suspect my old brain is too frosted, and I have addled the words. He said, 'Fear the man who seems least fearsome, and make the trap come to you.' "

When Honey Eater had recovered sufficiently, the men of the Bow String Soldier Society sent the camp crier around to announce a lodgefest or public reception for Little Bear.

This ancient tradition reflected the great importance to Cheyennes of their children. Unlike white men, the Cheyennes did not have a word for "orphan." This notion was alien to them, for they believed that every adult in any camp was the parent of every child.

By custom, it should have been Touch the Sky's clan that declared the lodgefest. But the proud, aloof warrior had joined the tribe without knowing his official clan. That fact, and his constant status as a pariah, gave him an unusual position: He was in the tribe, but not truly *of* it. And Arrow Keeper had approved his decision not to join one of the soldier troops—it was his destiny to lead, not to follow.

But most of the Bow Strings, following the example of their former leader Spotted Tail, were loyal to Touch the Sky. Spotted Tail had been brutally slain for his loyalty, but the Strings' new leader, River of Winds, was a fair man who refused to persecute Touch the Sky. So the Bow Strings offered their lodge for the reception.

And as a token of their regard for this extraordinary couple, it was a ceremony that would be talked about over the firepits in the cold moons to come.

The women of Honey Eater's clan prepared Cheyenne delicacies: young puppies boiled tender and scraped of their hides; calf-brain soup with rosehips; hump steaks dripping marrow fat. The men wore their crow-feather war bonnets and brought gifts for Little Bear, whom they also lavishly praised.

Touch the Sky's three closest friends were there, beaming as if they did indeed own part share in this handsome young baby. Touch the Sky agreed it was a lodgefest to be remembered—but it was also a stark reminder that this camp was at war with itself. For more than half the Indians in Gray Thunder's camp did not stop by. Indeed, the Bull Whips and their supporters gathered in a huge circle around Wolf Who Hunts Smiling, their new leader since the death of Lone Bear, deliberately making clear their allegiance.

Chief Gray Thunder took Touch the Sky briefly aside. While the rest made merry inside the lodge, the two braves counseled alone outside.

"Touch the Sky," his chief told him, "you know that I am trapped between the sap and the bark?"

Touch the Sky nodded. Though well past his fortieth year, Gray Thunder was still a stout, vigorous warrior. However, recent events had aged him spiritually.

"As a chief, you know I am allowed even less say than a common warrior. It is my solemn duty to determine the will of the tribe, not to dictate to them."

"A duty you perform well, father."

"With Maiyun's help, buck. But although the chief in me may not take sides, the *man* believes in you. I believe old Arrow Keeper was right in his conviction that you are marked out for a great destiny."

Arrow Keeper. Hearing his name, Touch the Sky heard old Long Jaw's baffling and ominous words yet again: *Fear the man who seems least fearsome, and make the trap come to you.*

"Touch the Sky, have ears. I was baffled by the murder of our war leader. But, damning appearances aside, I cannot truly suspect you. I believe you are right. I believe Wolf Who Hunts Smiling meant to shoot you, but mistakenly killed his own cousin in that thick fog. He who may not be mentioned was shot from behind. Had you killed him, it would have been a bloody contest face to face."

These words lifted a great burden from Touch the Sky. For although Gray Thunder's influence was severely restricted, his good opinion meant much to the tall warrior. The unsolved death of

Black Elk still hung over this tribe like a trouble cloud.

And now only look: In this once peaceful camp, more weapons were carried openly. Braves were careful to always move about in groups, seldom leaving camp alone. Brother suspected brother, clan cousins no longer gossiped freely. Even the old grandmothers increased their keening wails late into the night, sensing the nearness of some great tribal catastrophe.

"Count upon it," Gray Thunder said. "Wolf Who Hunts Smiling has an overwhelming ambition burning in his young eyes. I am powerless to prevent his machinations. That wily young brave works like Maiyun in the universe, everywhere felt but nowhere seen. One can only *suspect*, one cannot pick up his treachery and examine it. But I know this. The birth of your child has put a new sheen of determination in his eyes."

Gray Thunder gripped the young brave's shoulder in a hold that was surprisingly strong. "Buck, look sharp. That wolf has trouble firmly by the tail, and sadly your new joy *must* be tempered by strong vigilance."

Widow Maker peered cautiously around the tangled deadfall, spying on the Cheyenne camp below.

His fancy boots and leather vest were nowhere in evidence now. The stone-faced half-breed wore soft fawnskin shirt and trousers, their color blending easily with the spring hues of the plains. He wore no hat, and his footgear were the savvy tracker's own invention, ugly but silent boots with soles of cork and sponge rubber.

He studied the bustling activity around the lodge below, watched the other big group on the far side of the huge camp. From up here one could truly appreciate how this was a camp divided against itself. He had watched their peace chief and that tall warrior counsel alone behind the lodge. Widow Maker had never before seen the brave named Touch the Sky, but surely this buck was he.

Widow Maker, like most men who seldom fear violent death, was generous in praising the men he killed. The more worthy one's victim, the worthier the kill. And this broad-shouldered Cheyenne below was indeed worthy. From his strong, hawk nose to the knot of burn and knife scars on his torso, this was a brave marked with menace. Widow Maker planned to only wound him with the first knife, so that he might steal his last breath from his lungs when this red giant crossed over.

It was a pleasant day, and plenty of good elk steak lay heavy in Widow Maker's belly, making him a little sleepy. Idly, secure in this thick deadfall, he watched some Cheyenne boys down by the Powder. They were ferrying firewood across the river in bull boats, small, bowl-shaped vessels of skins stretched over willow frames. Some normal life went on, even in this camp that devoured its own tail.

Widow Maker heard a pony snuffle behind him, and instantly he was nerved for action.

His own pony was tethered farther down the

back side of the ridge, this one was much closer. Resisting panic from long experience, he turned around very, very slowly. It was movement, not shape, that caught an enemy's eye.

He recognized the warrior as a Sioux instantly from his white clan feather and the clan notching. The brave had not spotted him, though he peered suspiciously into the thick tangle where Widow Maker hid. Then the half-breed saw that the brave led two ponies, his own cayuse and Widow Maker's skewbald three-year-old with her distinctive white splotches on roan.

Widow Maker regretted this. For now the Sioux would have to die. For clearly he meant to lead this pony into the Cheyenne camp.

Widow Maker was not cruel, only implacable. In a heartbeat he raised his left leg, slid two throwing knives from his boot, and leaped out into the open. His first knife deliberately punched into the brave's throat, preventing any warning shout to those below. Yet it did not instantly kill.

Widow Maker knelt and held the second knife to the dying man's heart. "Sing your death-song, warrior," he said, "that you may cross in peace after I kill you."

The Sioux understood. When the brief, minor-key chant—garbled by gushing blood and damaged vocal cords—ended, Widow Maker leaned forward and held his mouth close over the Sioux's. Then he plunged cold steel into the brave's warm and beating heart, stealing his soul as the dying man gave up the ghost.

Chapter 3

"When you approach the Sioux camp at Elbow Bend," Wolf Who Hunts Smiling explained to Hardiman Burke, "raise your right fist high in the friendship sign. Then, as you ride in, make a gift to the place. Scatter some tobacco to the wind. This will impress them and make the trading go better."

The Cheyenne brave fell silent, and Burke slewed around in his saddle to flash a disjointed smile. His teeth were crooked yellow gravestones almost hidden behind a shaggy teamster's mustache. The eyes he turned on the Indian glittered like hard chips of obsidian. He wore a floppy slouch hat, canvas trousers, and a pullover of gray homespun. A Colt Navy revolver with an engraved cylinder and a one-piece walnut grip was tied low on his right thigh.

Burke slid a bullet out of his cartridge belt and held it up. "A few a these here Kentucky pills will impress their red asses, too."

Wolf Who Hunts Smiling threw his head back and laughed with hearty derision. "Hair face, you have green on your antlers if you think you can force the Sioux under Pony Trader. His camp may be at peace with the whiteskins, but there is not a coward among them. Look over there, toward that butte."

He pointed toward a long straight column of black smoke rising from the butte.

"That is a Sioux victory signal. They are telling everyone that they just defeated the Pawnees at the Republican River. See those shorter columns on each side of the long one? Look at all of them. One for each scalp they took."

"Won't matter," Burke said, "once them red sons pull the cork on that Taos Lightning. They'll be lucky if they can find their peters, let alone their weapons."

The Cheyenne renegade and the Army deserter, unlikely allies for the time being, both sat their ponies in the Sioux country south of Gray Thunder's camp. Pony Trader's Sioux village lay a short ride to the east, closer to the Black Hills. Behind Burke, a dozen more whiteskins mounted on big Cavalry horses waited for the command to move out.

Each horse had a full gutbag of just-brewed Taos Lightning tied to the saddle horn. This was the infamous "Indian whiskey" distilled from straight alcohol boiled with gunpowder, chewing tobacco, and river water. To this already potent brew had been added strychnine, at Hiram Steele's orders. Whiskey with strychnine produced an exceptionally crazy drunk and created quicker addiction.

Steele had introduced himself to Burke as a "development agent." He told Burke he meant to acquire all the furs, ponies, and Indian trade items he could. With luck, by the time he had cleaned the local tribes out, they would have stirred up enough trouble to ensure their own destruction at the hands of the U.S. Army. The same Army from which Burke and the rest of his men had recently taken "French leave." Known as Snowbirds, they had enlisted in winter for food and warmth, then deserted with the spring melt. Hiram Steele paid cash on the barrelhead, and so long as he kept paying it, Burke held his men in check.

"Ask you something?" Burke said.

"How would I stop you?" Wolf Who Hunts Smiling demanded. "You Mah-ish-ta-shee-da never give your tongues a rest. You are like our women, always talking simply to hear your own voices."

"See, that's my very question, buck. I mean, 'pears to me you hate palefaces like horses hate bears. Yet here you are, throwin' in with the likes of Hiram Steele and Seth Carlson. That ain't quite jake, unless you got one hell of an axe to grind agin this Matt Hanchon hombre."

Burke had a thick hillman's twang, and Wolf Who Hunts Smiling missed some of what he said. But when the deserter made the vengeance sign, two fists joined in front of the face, the Cheyenne nodded.

"I will tell you how the wind sets. Do you see any coup feathers on me?"

Burke shook his head. "I don't, for a pure-dee fact. And that don't make no sense, given all I've heard about you being the Red Peril himself."

Wolf Who Hunts Smiling held silent at this. But in fact that name—the Red Peril—belonged to the Blackfoot renegade Sis-ki-dee, one of only two Indians he feared besides Touch the Sky. The third was Big Tree, the Comanche terror from Blanco Canyon. They, too, had placed old enmities aside to join this struggle against the tall shaman. However, both braves had led their men down from Wendigo Mountain during the snowmelt moons, heading back to Blanco Canyon to recruit new ponies from their magnificent herd of Spanish and Mexican stock. With luck, thought the Cheyenne, they would miss the death of White Man Runs Him. Then none but he could claim credit.

"Yes," he finally answered, "I have an axe to grind—and once honed, it will knock his skull open."

"Well, I'll take a page from your book, Wolf. No more palaver. Me 'n' my boys here are dusting our hocks toward Pony Trader's camp. And we got plans to emigrate outa there before they swaller down much o' that Old Knockumstiff."

Burke quartered his well-trained sorrel around and pumped his fist in the air twice. A cheer erupted from the men.

"Maybe we'll get some of that red cunny with

no hair around it!" somebody shouted, though Wolf Who Hunts Smiling again lost the meaning of the words.

"And the dripping disease!" somebody shouted back.

In spite of his hatred for these stinking Yellow Eyes, Wolf Who Hunts Smiling was impressed by their industry and organization. How efficiently they worked to prepare this strong water, like busy ants driven by unerring instinct. No wonder, he thought, that the red men were having such a rough time of it against this odd enemy. Few tribes were as efficient as that, nor were the red men organized to fight as one nation.

But Wolf Who Hunts Smiling planned to change all that. So far his scheme was working: First he must cooperate with Steele and Carlson to kill Touch the Sky and wrest full control of the tribe. Then, through his crucial secret alliances with Sis-ki-dee and Big Tree, he must form one giant, warring red nation camped on Wendigo Mountain. And they would hold tight to one goal, a war of total destruction against the whiteskin invaders.

He reminded himself, however, as he watched the whiteskin horses kick up dust puffs out ahead, that he must come up with a perfect lure to separate Touch the Sky from his wife and new son. And the moment he told himself this, the wily young brave instantly thought of just the lure he needed.

It was perfect. It could not fail. It was the one soft place White Man Runs Him had, besides that for Honey Eater and Little Bear. But one soft place, he reminded himself with a lupine grin, was all he required to sink his blade.

"Hi-ya!" he shouted to his uncle, the sky, raising the war cry in his excitement. "Hi-ya, hii-*ya!*"

This was too good to hold in his parfleche. Besides, it would require the blue blouse Carlson's help. That meant he must see Hiram Steele now.

Wolf Who Hunts Smiling gouged his pure black pony hard with both heels, tugging the buffalo-hair hackamore around toward the northwest and Massacre Bluff.

Soon after Sister Sun had gone to her resting place, the Sioux village under the peace chief named Pony Trader began to grow loud and unruly. At first the Sioux soldier societies, charged with the task of tribal policemen, tried to restrain the wilder braves. But as the Taos Lightning flowed ever more freely, the soldiers, too, grew crazy and wild with drink.

Pony Trader, his hatchet profile sharp in the light from the firepit, gazed into the flames with sad, fearing eyes. His wife saw this and knew real fear, for this was not a brave to be easily frightened.

Outside their tipi, another gunshot was followed by a burst of wild laughter. Unlike their Cheyenne cousins, the Sioux did not bother with entrance flaps to ensure privacy within their lodges.

"They have shot another horse," Tassel Woman reported, peering outside.

"And will shoot more," Pony Trader said bitterly.

The old brave had nearly sixty winters behind him, and had lost the use of his left arm in his final battle, the glorious victory over white militiamen at Smoky Hill. But he knew it was not just age and his infirmity that had allowed those stinking whiskey peddlers into his camp. The warriors under Young Two Moon had won a victory over the Pawnees, and they demanded strong water to celebrate.

"I will touch none of it," the old warrior said again. "But I know this devil water. The Wendigo himself could not piss a more bitter brew. Wife, hold fast to that pistol I gave you. Do not set foot from this tipi. Before this camp sees next light, we will all do the hurt dance."

As if to give credence to his words, several more gunshots erupted. A dog's sharp howl of pain was followed by another explosion of laughter.

"Now they are content to kill animals," Pony Trader said. "Soon they will kill each other."

He gathered his courage and again glanced outside into the camp clearing, lit by clan fires that sawed in the wind. Here and there, braves had already passed out, dead drunk. Desperately, their sober wives and children tried to drag them out of harm's way, for wild braves raced their ponies everywhere, heedless of whom they ran over.

Pony Trader watched a drunk brave snatch a burning log from the fire and rub it on his own head, setting his braid on fire. Another fell from his galloping pony, laughing hysterically when he realized he had broken his arm. Some of the younger women had gotten into the gutbags, too. Now couples lay in the open, making love. Pony Trader turned his head in disgust when he saw a group of adolescent boys taking turns behind a bellowing calf they had rustled earlier.

"This strong water," he said bitterly. "It turns a red man into a squaw man. Those are not warriors out there; they have turned themselves into dogs for the whites. The troop leaders gave those stinking traders a whole season's catch of fine furs. How will we obtain the powder and ball we need for the hunt? What about flour and coffee and cloth? When the short white days come, this tribe will not be ready."

Pony Trader shifted his old rifled musket in his lap so that it pointed toward the entrance. He swore that any brave trying to force his way in would be sent across the Great Divide. But his weapon held only one shot; if enough came to seize power by force, he and his woman were doomed.

Then he glimpsed something outside, and he realized they were probably doomed whether or not the young rebels came for him in the night.

Several braves of the wild Eagle's Head clan were just then riding into camp, raising a victory whoop. They leaped from their ponies and immediately began an impromptu scalp dance around the nearest fire. But that wasn't an Indian scalp that Roan Bear was waving in the firelight, Pony Trader realized with a sinking heart.

"Now we are in for the worst trouble in the

world," the old chief announced. "Death will soon come to our camp, and he will be implacable in his wrath."

The scalp Roan Bear waved was long, the color of new wheat, and obviously had been lifted from a white woman.

"If I had a half dime for every brilliant plan you've hatched," Steele said to Wolf Who Hunts Smiling, "I'd already have my fortune. You haven't come up with one yet that's worth a plugged pistoreen. What makes this one any different?"

Behind Wolf Who Hunts Smiling and Hiram Steele, Widow Maker stood before a metal mirror that he'd nailed to a tree, shaving with a straight razor. The half-breed wore cologne in his hair, and Wolf Who Hunts Smiling wrinkled his face in disgust when the breeze wafted a sniff to his nostrils. All around the camp on Massacre Bluff, Hardiman Burke's men sprawled drinking whiskey—white man's whiskey, not the Indian brew—and playing cards.

"This one is different," the Cheyenne insisted, "because it will work."

"That *would* be different, buck, for a fact. But you ain't said nothing yet."

"How can I, white eyes, when your mouth flaps constantly like a flag in the wind?"

Steele frowned, the flint-gray eyes all menace now.

"Every cock crows on its own dunghill, buck. But you ain't in your camp now, scaring women and old men. You'll watch how you talk to me."

"Then kill me, beef eater! And kill your best hope of destroying Woman Face."

Steele nodded, conceding the point. "Let's both lower our hammers. We're s'posed to be flying the same colors. Why is this new plan going to work?"

"Only think. We need to trick Touch the Sky out from camp so Widow Maker can steal his wife and babe. But only one danger would make him leave them now."

Steele grew impatient at the pause. "Well, Katy Christ! Spell it out plain."

"Is this plain enough? First Carlson must make a talking paper."

"What the hell you mean, a talking paper? A treaty?"

Wolf Who Hunts Smiling shook his head. "No. A message. Signs put on paper."

"Hell, you mean a letter."

"This. Yes."

Steele puckered his eyes in confusion. "What kind of letter?"

"One signed," Wolf Who Hunts Smiling explained, "by the white mother of Touch the Sky. It will be delivered to the youth my tribe calls Firetop."

"Corey Robinson, Hanchon's old friend from Bighorn Falls?" Steele was starting to look interested.

The Cheyenne nodded. "It will bear the woman's name. And the message will beg him to go to Woman Face, to bring him back."

"Why in the hell should he do that? What's in the message?"

"It tells him," Wolf Who Hunts Smiling replied, "that his white father is dying."

Steele immediately saw the brilliance of this.

"Wolf, you can be as sly as your name. That'll fetch him out, all right. That buck has already put his bacon in the fire twice for the Hanchons, he won't let his white pa die without him there at his side."

"No," the renegade agreed promptly, "for like all *honorable* men he never forgets a debt of the heart. And then, once he is gone, it will be a simple thing for Burke's men, with my help, to stampede our pony herd. We are in the horse-raiding season. Any stampede will appear to be a raiding party, and not one brave will remain behind in camp. It will be like picking a bird's nest off the ground for Widow Maker to slip in and take Honey Eater and her son."

Chapter 4

"Fathers and brothers!" Wolf Who Hunts Smiling called out as soon as the common pipe had made the rounds. "Have ears! It may be true that the *elders* who make up the Council of Forty have stripped me of my coup feathers. But old men have always bungled what young men have mended. It was old men who allowed these whi teskin traders to ply their filthy wares on our hunting ranges. Old men like the soft-brained Arrow Keeper, abetted by the white man's spy in our midst whom I call White Man Runs Him."

It was not Touch the Sky's way to rise to the bait that his enemies so often tossed his way. But these words sent hot blood rushing into his face. He was on his feet in a heartbeat, the veins in his temples pounding.

"Panther Clan," he said slowly and clearly, "call

51

me White Man Runs Him if it pleases you. And though you have just shown disrespect to our Headmen, I will say nothing—they are men to the last and can fight their own battles. But Arrow Keeper is not here to humiliate you into silence, as he always has done. This place hears me. Insult him one more time, pig's afterbirth, and I swear by the sun and the earth I live on that I will tear your heart out now and feed it to the camp dogs."

Wolf Who Hunts Smiling did not have a cowardly bone in his body, but at that moment, the determination in Touch the Sky's tone and manner could have moved a dead man to respect. Wolf Who Hunts Smiling's dark eyes threw off angry sparks, and the suppressed rage in him clearly sought release in a burst of murderous violence.

It was the cowardly Medicine Flute who advised him quietly, "Down off your hind legs, buck. All in good time, the worm will turn."

"The worm turns every time you roll over, Bone Blower," piped up the sharp-eared Two Twists, and the council erupted in laughter despite the danger, for they truly loved a good joke—especially one that wrapped the husk of humor around a kernel of truth.

Medicine Flute scowled, self-consciously tucking his leg-bone flute out of sight. This caused another ripple of laughter. Wolf Who Hunts Smiling had cooled off during this interruption.

"As you say," he told Touch the Sky, his mocking eyes never once running from the tall brave's. "If it hurts you so much, *sensitive* warrior, I will leave off mentioning your old favorite."

All of this was too much for Chief Gray Thunder. A good chief did not control the council, but helped make sure those who wished to speak could. Nonetheless, these two bucks had no right to lock horns and further divide his camp.

"Both of you, listen to your chief. And you also, Two Twists, for you dearly love to hurl insults. It is clear, clear as a blood spoor on snow, that Wolf Who Hunts Smiling and Touch the Sky must ultimately close for the kill. The day is coming when one will send the other under. I would give much to change this, for either of them is a brave worth ten men. But things are the way they are.

"However, so long as the ancient law-ways govern the Shaiyena people, our sacred Medicine Arrows will not be permanently stained by a murder at council. Not while I have sworn to keep the peace."

"As you say, father," Touch the Sky said, contrite now. He sat back down. "No blood will run at this council, not by my hand."

"Nor mine," Wolf Who Hunts Smiling chorused, also sitting down. This surprised Touch the Sky, but not pleasantly. The only time Wolf Who Hunts Smiling behaved so amicably was when he had treachery firmly by the tail. This was confirmed by the sly glance he shot toward his enemy.

Unbidden, Long Jaw's baffling dream message from Arrow Keeper sounded in Touch the Sky's inner ear: *Fear the man who seems least fearsome, and make the trap come to you.*

"Never mind licking old wounds," Gray Thunder continued. "We have new troubles. Serious new troubles. By now, most of us know what has passed at Pony Trader's camp. Brothers, now more than ever we must heal our tribal wounds, for we have a new enemy from without, and he means to destroy us."

This caused a respectful stillness, for it was a sobering truth. Touch the Sky once thought he would welcome anything that brought this tribe together again. But not *this*—the return of the dreaded whiskey traders.

"Pony Trader lies badly wounded as I speak," Gray Thunder went on. "Soon, we may not be able to speak his name again. The whites who attacked the camp were insane in their thirst for vengeance. Pony Trader's woman was sent under, as were a dozen more of our cousins. Twice this number were wounded. Lodges were burned to the ground, ponies throat-slashed. All this because the whiskey traders foxed their young men. The white merchants of strong water have returned, and they mean to destroy the Red Nation!"

By now Touch the Sky had learned that trouble seldom traveled alone. Was this horror at Pony Trader's camp part of the new battle that he would soon have to wage?

"River of Winds is our war leader," Gray Thunder said. "The next time this council meets, he will preside. We must take steps now to make common cause with the Sioux, the Arapaho, and our Southern Cheyenne kin. I say again, our very survival is the question now."

His pleading eyes met the gaze first of Wolf Who Hunts Smiling, then of Touch the Sky.

"The fate of the red man depends on our will to survive. Think of Uncle Pte. Does the buffalo survive by going his own way, indifferent to the welfare of the herd? True, sometimes the aggressive young bulls fight among themselves. This is natural; bulls will do what bulls have done. But seldom do they kill each other. And always, when the herd faces anger from without, the bulls close ranks to defend them. Cheyennes! If we must, let us fight among ourselves later. For now, let us make ready our battle rigs and close ranks."

Touch the Sky, with a new baby at his wife's breast, felt the weight of each word like a powerful stone when Gray Thunder concluded his speech, saying, "If we do not, bucks, our children will never know a future."

Captain Seth Carlson dipped his nib and wrote a few more lines before blotting them. When he finished with the note, he read it through to make sure he had it right this time. Satisfied, he sat back in his chair and permitted himself a tight little smile.

He had practically whooped for joy the moment he read the message that Hiram Steele had sent him by way of a runner. It was a damn good plan. Never mind that Wolf Who Hunts Smiling came up with it—a savage who couldn't even cipher or write. It was good strategy against a sentimental fool like Matthew Hanchon.

Hanchon. The very name was gall and wormwood to him. That flea-bitten, gut-eating red nigger had somehow turned Kristen Steele into an

Indian-loving ally who had turned on her own father—and even worse, had scorned Carlson's attempts at decent spooning while letting that filthy aboriginal top her.

But it didn't stop there. The arrogant savage had piled on the agony in an unrelenting campaign to thwart him. Carlson had been salting away gold hand over fist, up in the Bear Paw Mountains, until Hanchon broke up his cozy little scheme and left him with nothing but his hat in his hand. Same thing when he and Hiram had devised a brilliant scheme to seize the Powder River ranges for farmland. That series of fiascos cost the Cavalry officer a promotion and earned him a scathing conduct report for his permanent file.

Matthew Hanchon, Carlson told himself, had a bad habit of mixing where he didn't belong. And that bad habit was going to get him killed.

Three knocks sounded on the door of his company office.

"It's open."

Carlson grinned again when a spindly lad barely into his teens hesitantly entered.

"You wanted to see me, Cap'n?" Hoby Padgett said. The young civilian earned coppers and half dimes swamping out the stables and digging four-holers. And Carlson knew, from personal observation, that the kid had fallen in love with a yearling colt that was kept in the main paddock. He wanted that colt worse than sinners wanted out of hell.

"Hey there, Hoby. Yes, lad, I need a small favor. I'd like you to run a note to Corey Robinson's place. You know Corey, don't you?"

Hoby nodded. "Yessir. He's that redheaded carpenter that built the new powder magazines. He's nice. I held his tools for him, 'n' he showed me how to joint boards together."

Carlson nodded. He had counted on the fact that Corey knew the boy and trusted him.

"Yes," Carlson agreed, "he's a nice man. But I and some other friends of his are playing a little trick on him."

Hoby frowned and worked his cap around in his fingers nervously. "A trick?"

"Yes. We'd like you to pretend that this letter here did *not* come from me. We want you to pretend that it came from Sarah Hanchon."

Hoby slowly shook his head. "But that'd be a lie. My pa always says, tell the truth and shame the devil."

"Your pa is a good man, and he's right. But see, this isn't really a lie. Just a little trick."

Hoby looked as if somebody had just kicked his dog. "I don't know, Cap'n . . ."

"Of course I mean to pay you," Carlson added casually. "You do this, son, and when you come back, you can take Comet home with you tonight."

Hoby's eyes bulged like wet, white marbles. "You mean that?"

Carlson proffered his hand across the desk. "Shake on it, man to man. Will you believe me then?"

"Holy Hannah!" the boy exclaimed, grabbing Carlson's hand and pumping it up and down with brio. "You mean it, sir? He's mine? All mine?"

"All yours, boy. And I'll even throw in a Spanish bridle with silver conchos."

Hoby's final resistance to sin crumbled. He no longer cared what was in that letter or that he was telling a lie. He watched Captain Carlson slide it into an envelope and seal it.

"Remember," the officer told him, handing it across the desk. "All you know is that Sarah Hanchon asked you to deliver this. Got it?"

"Got it," Hoby said, already racing for the door.

Corey Robinson had taken the day off from carpentry to do some catch-up work around the old stump ranch he shared with his preacher father just outside Bighorn Falls. He was sitting in the slanting shade of the house, mending an old harness, when he saw Hoby Padgett riding in on his mule.

"Hoby!" he greeted the youth, grinning at the long-eared mule. "Tether that brevet horse of yours and have a glass of buttermilk."

"Can't," Hoby said tersely, not even bothering to dismount. He handed an envelope to Corey, his eyes avoiding the older youth's. "I got to get my butt back to Fort Bates and grain the horses. Mrs. Hanchon asked me to give you this."

"Sarah Hanchon? But what—Hoby! Tarnal hell, boy, where you going?"

But Hoby had already kicked the old jenny around toward Fort Bates.

"Kid must've eaten loco weed," Corey muttered, slipping open the envelope. Why in the hell would Sarah be writing to him? A bead of nervous perspiration zigzagged out of his curly red hair and across his freckled forehead. Common sense told him it wouldn't be good news.

Even so, Corey wasn't prepared for the brief but urgent message:

Corey,
John has suffered a massive stroke. Dr. Benson says it is very serious and that it is only a matter of days, at the most, before John will be taken from us. Please go to Matthew at once and tell him his father is dying. Corey, I know it's dangerous for Matthew around here. But it breaks my heart to hear John asking for him. I think he'll go to heaven with a smile on his face if he can hug his boy one last time.

Sarah Hanchon

"God-in-whirlwinds!" Corey exclaimed. John Hanchon dying! Well, he'd thickened at the waist considerable these late years. Still, Corey took him for a stout man with another twenty years in him. It was like his pa always said—the good ones die young.

"Damn," Corey said. "Damn and double damn." He'd have to go inside and dig through his poke, find that specially dyed blue feather that Chief Yellow Bear had once given him. It would assure Corey safe passage across the plains, for it declared him a true brother of the red men.

Corey debated nothing. Now it was time for action. Thank God Pa had come back from the min-

ing camp recently with a fast sabino pony some
converted sinner gave him. Corey sprinted toward
the corral, hoping he would be in time—that *Matthew* would be in time.

Chapter 5

"Why is it," Honey Eater asked her tall brave, "that you have said nothing about it?"

Touch the Sky pretended to ignore her, though in truth he never could ignore this beautiful woman he had finally married. For so long he had loved her without being able to have her. Never would he be able to take her physical nearness for granted—their lot was too uncertain, and each new day together might well be the last.

Little Bear lay on the buffalo robes between them, all his young concentration fixed on the bear-claw necklace his father dangled near his face.

"Said nothing about what, Flower Top?" Touch the Sky finally said. He called her by a teasing nickname Two Twists had recently given her, inspired by her well-known habit of braiding white columbine petals through her hair.

"About this," she said, reaching out to brush the hair away from Little Bear's right temple. Now, in the bright light beaming through the smoke hole, the mark on his scalp was clear: a mulberry-colored birthmark shaped like a flint arrowhead.

It was the mark of the warrior, the same mark buried under Touch the Sky's hairline.

Touch the Sky made such a poor show of feigning surprise that Honey Eater laughed outright.

"Husband," she said fondly, "you do many things well. But as for telling lies, you need lessons from Wolf Who Hunts Smiling and Medicine Flute."

He, too, dropped his pretense and broke into a wide grin. "Pretty, do I need to waste words on that which tells its own story? We both know what that mark means. I did not speak of it for fear of causing you more sadness."

"I was sad when I saw it," she admitted. "For perhaps the space of ten heartbeats. And then I told myself that my husband, too, bears that mark. Yes, our son has been born to a hard lot, and this mark confirms it. But this mark appeared to Arrow Keeper in an important vision. Therefore, it is an important mark, and our son will be an important man. Yes, he will suffer, as has his father. But he will be worthy of the suffering, and the suffering will be important."

"Suffer as has his father?" Touch the Sky said softly. "No Cheyenne has endured more than my wife. And I would harrow the Wendigo from breastworks if I could spare her from more suffering. I will do my best for her and my son. But Arrow Keeper was right, we can neither undo the past nor gainsay the future."

But this close moment between husband and wife was unceremoniously ruined when Little Bear loosed a roar, a mighty roar of impatience, for he wanted to touch the sharp claws his father dangled just out of reach.

Both parents winced at the force of that cry, duly impressed. Their first moments of startled confusion gave way to another shared laugh that left both of them holding their sides. Little Bear, too, caught the humor and chimed in with gleeful chortles while flailing the air with both tiny fists. This only encouraged Touch the Sky and Honey Eater to greater paroxysms of mirth.

"Brother," came the somber voice of Little Horse from just outside the tipi flap, "I would speak with you. The matter is urgent, Bear Caller, look lively."

Fear licked Touch the Sky's spine. For one thing, he and Little Horse had defied death too many times as a team. There was no mistaking that serious tone, one the fearless Little Horse seldom used, for he was one to always hold his face and tone neutral as a warrior does. Too, seldom did Little Horse use that nickname given to Touch the Sky by Pawnee enemies unless trouble was in the wind.

Honey Eater met his eyes, and she, too, knew they were in danger once again. As if some premonition warned her, she protectively scooped

Little Bear into her arms. Touch the Sky stepped outside.

"Brother," he greeted Little Horse. "Your frown tells me I need not stuff a pipe."

"Nor salute the directions, buck. You know that I have been riding herd guard?"

Touch the Sky nodded.

"I rode down to Singing Woman Creek to chase back a few ponies that wandered from the main gather. I saw a rider approaching, a paleface with a truce cloth tied to his hat. When he rode closer, I saw it was Firetop."

Cold fear slammed into Touch the Sky. Corey Robinson never risked crossing through the Crow and Ute country just to reminisce about their boyhood days in Bighorn Falls.

"I knew it was best if he did not ride into camp," Little Horse said. "Not now, when the tribe is painting for war against merchants of strong water. When he does ride in, your enemies are quick to sound their favorite theme, how you like to desert your tribe in its worst times of trouble. They are slow to remember how Firetop once helped you save this tribe from destruction."

"Memories are short when treachery is deep. He is waiting for me?"

Little Horse shook his head. "You know I have no English. But his sign talk is good. He told me you would not want him to wait. Not after you saw the message. He is hurrying back to your white mother."

"My white mother? What message?"

Now, for the first time, Touch the Sky noticed

the envelope tucked into Little Horse's parfleche. His friend, looking none too happy, handed the talking paper over. Touch the Sky tore open the envelope, unfolded the letter, and read the shaky handwriting. It had been many years since he had seen a sample of Sarah Hanchon's writing, and in his agitation it never occurred to him to doubt the letter's authenticity. Hadn't his best friend in all the white world personally delivered it?

Little Horse was genuinely pained when he saw the mask of trouble instantly cover his friend's face. "Brother, what is it?"

"A bad sadness in a world full of them," Touch the Sky replied. His troubled eyes cut toward his tipi—and his Indian family. "My white father lies dying."

Sister Sun was only a dull orange ball in the western sky when Touch the Sky finished his preparations.

He had cut his fastest pony from the herd, an ugly little paint trained as sharp as a circus mount. His legging sash was stuffed with pemmican, and he made sure his meat racks behind the tipi held enough for Honey Eater and the baby while he was gone. During these preparations, he tried to ignore all the accusing faces watching him from throughout camp.

Here it was again, said the mocking eyes of Wolf Who Hunts Smiling, Medicine Flute, and the rest of the Bull Whips. *He is riding out again without benefit of council, and at the time when this tribe needs its best warriors.*

As for Honey Eater, she had not even debated the issue. Of course he must ride to his white father's side. Every true Cheyenne believed the parent-child bond was a holy thing, like the mountains. To them, even a grizzly's claw was not so sharp as the pain of a thankless child. And truly this John Hanchon was a good man—his character, after all, had shaped Touch the Sky's.

Touch the Sky's last task was a brief but crucial meeting with the three braves he trusted most in the world: Little Horse, Tangle Hair, and Two Twists. They met in the common corral, safe from enemy ears.

"Stout bucks," he said, "you know how things are. Whether by my own fault or the plan of the Holy Ones, I am once again trapped between the sap and the bark. You three have already given much of your own time to protecting Honey Eater. And no ten braves could have kept her safer, though indeed the attempts on her life have not been lacking."

All three knew why he frowned. The memory gates had flown open and he was again seeing the brave named Skull Cracker. He had been on the verge of crushing Honey Eater's skull with a rock when she blew him across the Great Divide with a white man's hideout gun.

"Now my enemies are doubly rabid for the kill, Little Bear being the newest incentive. Bucks, you know my white parents. Would *you* ride to Bighorn Falls if John Hanchon had raised you for sixteen winters, loved you as his own blood, then called for you on his deathbed?"

"You ask this thing of us?" Little Horse chided his friend. "Maiyun forgive you for thinking it necessary. Buck, if you did *not* ride south, I would set up a grievance pole against you."

"This not-so-little horse," Two Twists chimed in, poking fun at Little Horse's stout waistline, "usually drops nothing but dung from his mouth. This time, however, he has truth by the tail. Why are you sitting here debating the various causes of the wind?"

Touch the Sky understood. His loyal band were rallying to ease his mind at this terrible decision during such a vulnerable time. Tangle Hair's words proved that Touch the Sky's sly comrades had worked this out quickly among themselves. "As for Honey Eater and Little Bear," Tangle Hair said, feigning nonchalance, "do not flatter yourself that they are safer because *you* are here, shaman. Are not Little Bear's *other* three fathers on hand? Any one of them is a match for you."

Despite the troubles he faced, Touch the Sky could not resist a grin as the spirit of these warriors infected him. They were braggarts, like most Indians, for Indians did not mind a boaster—indeed, they even admired one so long as he lived up to his brags. And no three braves matched word with deed better than this trio sworn to protect his wife and child in his absence.

Nonetheless, as he rode back to bid farewell to Honey Eater and his son, Touch the Sky suddenly whirled his little paint.

"Have ears!" he shouted.

Startled, all three comrades watched him intently.

With no trace of bravado or humor now, Touch the Sky roared from deep in his chest, "While I'm gone, protect my family!"

Little Horse thrust his lance out, streamers dancing on the wind. Tangle Hair and Two Twists crossed theirs over his. No words were needed, for the sign spoke more powerfully: We pledge it with our lives.

Before he left, Touch the Sky made Honey Eater promise she would keep her gun handy the entire time he was gone. A gift from Caleb Riley, the two-shot, over-and-under "parlour gun" could easily be tucked into her clothing. He reminded her sternly that a gun was useless unless it was available immediately when needed. Honey Eater also promised that she and Little Bear would stay with her Aunt Sharp Nosed Woman while Touch the Sky was gone.

Touch the Sky knew, as he pointed his bridle south toward the river-bend country of Wyoming, that he should feel better now. His band were the best warriors in Gray Thunder's tribe. Nor was Honey Eater a helpless female. Like many Cheyenne women, she had fought in battles so fierce that one soldier swore "the squaws are as dangerous as their savage lords." Nonetheless, the shaman sense plagued him, a vague prickling of his thoughts.

In a more serene frame of mind, Touch the Sky might have paid more attention to that shaman sense. But his worrying kept getting shunted from one track to another as he wondered, urging his pony to a gallop, if he'd be in time to see his white father once more before he crossed over.

Chapter 6

"It don' look so good," said Old Knobby, scratching at the bald hide over his pate where a Cheyenne had once started to scalp him before Knobby aired his vitals. "Young Matthew is riding into a reg'lar mare's nest. The Moccasin Telegraph has been active near here lately, smoke signals, flaming arrows, mirror flashes, the whole shivaree. There's heap big doin's up in Injun country, and it fair gives this child the fidgets."

The former mountain man fell silent when Sarah Hanchon forked a few more buckwheat cakes onto his plate. John Hanchon and Corey Robinson occupied two more sides of the deal table.

"I swear, woman," Knobby said around a mouthful of grub, "you cook almost as good as you look."

70

Normally Sarah would have responded to this in the same teasing tone Knobby used. But her pretty face was set deep in a worried frown.

She said, "The last time Matthew rode down here, his enemies almost destroyed Caleb Riley's mining camp. Could that be the plan?"

"I don't know about that," Corey said, "but I'm aching to get my hands on Hoby Padgett. He's the mother lode here, Missus Hanchon. He swore that letter came from you. Trouble is, he's hiding out at Fort Bates and I can't roust him there. If I could get that little tadpole alone, I could find out who gave him that note."

"Smart money," John Hanchon said, "is on Seth Carlson. And if that's the case, Hiram Steele might be involved. Those two're tight as ticks. If Steele is back, somebody is in for six sorts of hell."

"By God, you give us that plain with the bark still on it," Knobby agreed. "Hiram Steele is meaner'n Satan with a sunburn."

Invoking the name of Hiram Steele did nothing to improve the mood in the room. Corey scraped his chair back and rose, then crossed to the kitchen window and knuckled the waisted curtain aside. He searched for dust puffs out on the horizon.

"Anyhow," he said, "Matthew should be coming right behind me. I don't know which trail he's taking, so it's no use to try heading him off. He should be here soon."

"He's a father now," Sarah said wonderingly.

"Which makes you a grandmother," John reminded her, "so you needn't smile, old lady."

"I'm damn glad you're still walking above the ground, Mr. Hanchon. Matthew will be, too. But he sure isn't going to smile when he finds out how he was bamboozled," Corey muttered, returning to his plate.

"That's a fact," Old Knobby chimed in. The retired hostler had been cashiered from his job at the Bighorn Feed Stables for pulling the cork once too often. But his staunch loyalty to Matthew had convinced the Hanchons to take him in at their mustang spread. Now the old codger lived out his days in a line shack, mending bridles and hauling salt blocks out to the outlying herds. Occasionally he offered tips to younger wranglers on the fine points of breaking green horses to leather. Despite being long in the tooth and tied up with the rheumatics, Old Knobby still slept with his favorite gal, Patsy Plumb, his name for his old Kentucky over-and-under rifle.

"But this child'll tell you something else," Knobby added. "Whoever honeyfuggled Matthew into coming down here is gonna be doin' the hurt dance. And if anybody lays one hand on his squaw or his boy, *this* hoss don' wanna be around when Matthew goes on the warpath. It'll be ugly and bloody."

All during the night, while Uncle Moon clawed his way higher across the dark sky, Touch the Sky pushed his ugly but game little paint toward the Bighorn River.

He kept the Always Star over his left shoulder, the Dog Star straight ahead of him. But two other constant companions were exhaustion and worry. Worry about what lay ahead, worry about what lay behind. He drew some comfort from the continual reminder that none less than Little Horse, Tangle Hair, and Two Twists had pledged their lives to protect Honey Eater and Little Bear.

Nonetheless, the treachery of Wolf Who Hunts Smiling and Medicine Flute was a match for the best warriors. Nor could Touch the Sky shake this numb prickling at his nape—the shaman sense working to warn him.

This route was long familiar, and he knew where the runoff rills and water holes could be found. Thus, shortly after sunrise on the morning after he set out, Touch the Sky crested the final razorback ridge overlooking the Hanchon spread.

It lay fanned out in a fine valley lush with new bunchgrass. The log-and-stone main house, once nearly destroyed by Comanche fire arrows, sported a fine new shake roof and a new kitchenhouse connected to the living quarters by a short dogtrot. Several colts frisked in a breaking pen, where a wrangler worked them one at a time with blindfolds. A new cutting of hay was in, and tall ricks dotted the outlying pastures.

The place was clearly prospering. But what would happen now, with John Hanchon dying— or perhaps already dead?

With that last thought, the sadness was suddenly on him deep, and Touch the Sky felt the urgent need to reach the house and take his father's hand in his. The little paint, tossing her head in excitement as she whiffed the strange horses below, laid her ears back and galloped full out, unshod hooves tossing divots of soil into the air. She was not eager to approach this strange place, but her master always treated her as an equal. Thus, his will was inseparable from hers.

They must have been watching for him from the house, he realized when he saw Corey step outside and wave to him. Old Knobby followed him, and Touch the Sky felt his heart swell with love when his mother emerged, squinting into the sneeze-bright sunshine to glimpse her wild son.

But his emotions were suddenly at war with themselves when the big, hale form of John Hanchon also emerged into the yard.

The shock of it caused him to rein in. His first reaction, emotion coming before intellect, was pure joy. Not only was his father miraculously alive, but he was obviously, even from here, as fit as a rutting buck. He even had the old spring to his walk.

And then cruel logic interceded. Nobody, it assured him, recovers that fully and quickly from a massive stroke. Your mother is no calamity howler. That note said John Hanchon was on the feather-edge of death. And then, when it struck him all of a moment, the truth made Touch the Sky's blood seem to stop and flow backward in his veins.

That note was a lie. It was all a feint so his cunning enemies could get at Honey Eater and Little Bear!

*   *   *

"Brothers," Tangle Hair said, "I have not seen the camp this peaceful for many moons. Instead of milling about their lodge, hatching trouble for us, the Whips have an enemy from without. Most of them have ridden out in small groups, searching for sign of these whiskey merchants. And I am happy to report that Wolf Who Hunts Smiling rode at their head."

"Good," Two Twists said. "The Whips call themselves our policemen. Yet they have made it the goal of their troop to kill Touch the Sky. He protects the Sacred Arrows, yet they openly lust to stain those very Arrows by shedding Cheyenne blood. Now the Whips are finally living up to their duties. Perhaps this will help them remember what it means to be an honorable warrior."

Little Horse listened to all this in his customary silence. Like his two companions, he seldom let his eyes drift very far from Sharp Nosed Woman's tipi. The three braves sat filing arrow points in front of the Bow String troop lodge, which gave a good view of the entire camp. Touch the Sky had ridden south more than one full sleep ago, and now grainy darkness settled over Gray Thunder's camp. Huge clan fires had already sprung up, their flames sawing in the wind.

"Yes, it is peaceful," he said. "Ominously so."

"Just like you," Two Twists said, "to speak in riddles like a shaman. How is peace ominous, All Behind Him?"

Tangle Hair snickered when their young companion made this reference to Little Horse's increasing weight of late.

Little Horse, too, grinned, for he dearly loved a good joke and didn't mind being the cause of a laugh.

"I mean this, double braid. Medicine Flute, true to his cowardly nature, did not ride out. But he has noticed how close we are watching Honey Eater and Little Bear. Now he has sent the talk flying about camp on swift wings—talk about how three of the tribe's best warriors have held back from the warpath against their 'white masters.' And a fourth has ridden out."

Tangle Hair nodded. "I, too, have heard this. Others are saying not only that we refuse to search for the whites, but that we have left the herds vulnerable now with so many braves gone."

This last thought was sobering, for indeed they were worried about the ponies. They were extremely vulnerable right now, scattered over a wide area of graze. And this was the height of pony-raiding season. Little Horse had read smoke sign earlier. The Southern Cheyennes had lost nearly 200 fine ponies to an Apache raiding party. No ponies meant no annual buffalo hunt, and no buffalo meant no Cheyennes.

"What good to discuss it?" Little Horse said. "We know what we must do. With luck, Touch the Sky will be back soon and we can return to our duties. As for our present indolence, let the rest carp all they will. I have never hidden in my tipi when this camp was on the warpath."

"You could not hide in the council lodge, big Indian," Two Twists scoffed. "Your new pony is already swayback."

"Buck," Little Horse said while Tangle Hair chortled, "I see you have turned your tongue into a shovel."

"A shovel?" Two Twists said, frowning.

"Yes, for now you are digging your own grave with it."

Thus teasing each other, the three friends continued their vigil. Around them, despite this new threat from sellers of strong water, life went on more or less normally. Sharp Nosed Woman sat before her tipi, pounding sun-dried buffalo meat with a maul and mixing it with fat, marrow, and dried cherry paste to make pemmican for the short white days. Some elders had gathered before Medicine Flute's tipi to watch him perform sleight-of-hand tricks.

And then, as sudden as a boom-clap of thunder, disaster struck Gray Thunder's Powder River Cheyennes.

First there was a sudden volley of gunshots, so many they sounded like an ice floe breaking apart. This was followed by a noise that rolled across the tableland like gathering thunder. All three braves were still gaping when the cry went up throughout camp: "The ponies!"

A terrible grass fire could not have panicked these horse warriors more than this cry. The herd was being stolen! And now, when so many of the young braves were scouting for whiskey traders.

For the space of a few heartbeats, Little Horse thought to wonder, is this a feint? Then he recalled, Wolf Who Hunts Smiling had ridden out much earlier, as had Lone Bear and the rest of

Touch the Sky's worst enemies.

Besides, that volley had come from repeating rifles, which no one in this tribe owned. These were most likely Apaches or even Big Tree's Comanches.

"Look!" a frustrated Two Twists said, pointing. "Old women are running out to stop them. Brothers, we are in a hurting place if we lose those ponies."

There was no time for debate. Touch the Sky had not asked them to ruin the tribe by refusing to leave Honey Eater out of sight, only to keep a good watch on her. It might be possible to save the herd if they acted quickly, and then they could return to this boring sentry duty.

"Hi-ya!" Little Horse shouted, his blood up for some sharp work. "Hii-*ya!*"

Their ponies were tethered nearby, already rigged for battle. All three braves raced for their mounts even as the rolling thunder gathered force.

"Woman Face's band just rode out," Wolf Who Hunts Smiling said. "You may enter our camp easily. But work quickly, and expect Honey Eater to fight like a she-grizz. Her old aunt still has sap in her, too."

He stood with Widow Maker, hidden in thickets on the long ridge overlooking camp. Once again the stone-faced, half-breed blade expert had shed his dandy's garb for hard-to-spot fawnskin shirt and trousers.

Widow Maker flashed a tight, derisive smile.

"They call you an Indian terror? You, who warn me to beware of women?"

"And they call *you* a tracker and stalker?" the Cheyenne retorted, nodding toward Widow Maker's odd, sponge-soled boots. In fact there was no real venom in this exchange of insults, for each man was beginning to admire the other.

Wolf Who Hunts Smiling had indeed ridden out with the rest of the Bull Whips. But it was an easy matter to hide in cutbanks and coulees and quarter back around toward camp. He had led Hardiman Burke's men past the few remaining herd sentries, killing the ones they could not avoid. Now he would cover Widow Maker's crucial infiltration of camp.

"You have mocked my Indian training," Widow Maker said quietly, drawing tight the laces of one of his ludicrous but silent boots. "Do you also mock my white man's training?"

To make his meaning clear, he glanced toward the three narrow hilts protruding from his boot—precision-balanced throwing knives of casehardened steel.

A rare look of respect passed over Wolf Who Hunts Smiling's face. "No, that I do not mock. I saw your skill with my own eyes. You could knock the eye out of a hawk. Just remember, do not kill Honey Eater."

"Yet, you mean?"

The Cheyenne grinned. Truly this brevet Indian could prove useful once the Renegade Nation was established on Wendigo Mountain.

"Yet, I mean. Now go, or she will have a second child before we have stolen the first."

"If the people do not save the ponies," Sharp Nosed Woman lamented, "this season's Winter Count will record terrible sadness."

She dropped the entrance flap and turned to watch her niece feeding the baby. The sight of Little Bear's greedy cheeks forming eager bellows as they sucked life from his mother made the cranky older woman smile like a young girl.

"My own womb never bore fruit," she said. "And when I add up all the sorrows that have befallen our young, I tell myself I am glad. Suffering is the ridge a Shayiena baby lives on. But watching you two now gives the lie to those words."

"You have a baby now," Honey Eater assured her. "I am this one's mother, but this tribe is his parent. This one will grow up loving you, and you will live on in his mind. My grandchildren will know you through him and sing your name at the Spring Dance."

This was so simply spoken, the words so moving, that Sharp Nosed Woman's eyes grew bright with unshed tears.

"No man in camp speaks better than you, niece. Do not ever—"

"Do not ever," cut in a male voice behind her, speaking in the Lakota-Cheyenne mix that had become a lingua franca on the Plains, "think you are safe from the Wendigo, for here I am!"

Honey Eater felt her blood go cold. She and her aunt both whirled to confront the speaker. They had heard no one enter this small lodge. Yet there stood a grinning half-breed—with a rawhide lead line dangling from his left hand. Instinctively, Honey Eater covered her exposed breast.

"I have come," he said, obsidian eyes piercing her like a pair of bullets, "to collect my woman and child. I like that taut dug you just covered up, she-bitch! I mean to taste it, too, before I kill you and that puling whelp of yours."

All Cheyennes kept siege weapons to hand in case the camp was overrun in the night. Unleashing a banshee shriek, Sharp Nosed Woman lunged toward the Osage war club lying beside the firepit.

The intruder moved so fast he seemed a blur to Honey Eater. A few heartbeats later, she gasped in shock when her aunt collapsed, one twitching hand grasping at a knife hilt protruding from her stomach.

Honey Eater could not pull the gun from her parfleche without putting down the baby. And then—this man-monster moved with the swiftness of a snake!—all resistance was out of the question. For the intruder had leaped across the tipi and seized Little Bear from her arms. He held the point of another knife to the baby's soft belly, denting the pink flesh and making Little Bear roar with pain and rage.

"Tie this around your trim little waist," he ordered her, tossing one end of the lead line to her. "And follow me like a good mare. If you do not, I will throat-slash your colt."

81

Chapter 7

"Yes, we saved our horses," Little Horse said bitterly, his tone laced with self-contempt. "They were in no real danger, anyway. But two of our herd guards lay dead. And not one of us, those you trust most, was wise enough to understand the true reason of that feint."

"We failed you, shaman," Tangle Hair threw in. "We vowed to the directions that your woman and child would be as safe as eagles in their nest. Not once did one of us realize, until it was too late."

Touch the Sky stood stone still, stone silent just outside the entrance flap of his tipi. A crowd was still gathered around Sharp Nosed Woman's lodge, where even now the old woman fought desperately for her life. Her clan women attended to her while the singers chanted the cure songs.

"It is *never* too late," young Two Twists insisted,

desperate to rally his comrades to their usual courage and optimism. "Not until we know they are . . ."

He trailed off, realizing what he had been about to say. Sheepishly he glanced at Touch the Sky. "Not so long as we know Honey Eater and Little Bear are still alive," he corrected himself.

His comrades had never seen this baffled and defeated look on their leader before, and it unnerved them. In truth, much of Touch the Sky's apparent surrender was in fact exhaustion—he had spent only a few minutes conferring with Corey, Old Knobby, and his parents before again urging his worn pony the long distance back to camp.

True, he had advance warning of trouble. But no horror created by the white man's devil or the red man's Wendigo could match the hurt waiting for Touch the Sky when his contrite comrades explained the tragedy to him. Now, looking at his friends and realizing that they were nearly as miserable and devastated as he, his true character as a leader of men emerged.

"Bucks, have ears!"

All three started out of their torpor, alerted by something in his tone: a familiar ring of menace and danger and powerful determination.

"Never mind blame or woman-wailing grief. There is blame enough to go around. Who stupidly rode out of this camp, leaving his wife and babe to this hard fate? Not one of you, but I. I was foxed because it seemed foolish to suspect treachery. The same with you three. I, too, would have been caught up in the bloodlust for action when I heard our ponies fleeing. We are warriors, and it is our nature to bridge the gap without undue reflection, especially when attack on the herds is a real threat. All three of you have risked your lives for me. I have no interest in assigning blame, only in saving my family."

These words carried the weight of solid good sense, and struck his friends accordingly. Already the kicked-dog look had left their faces. Intently they watched and listened to their battle leader. If any man in camp could match the wily Wolf Who Hunts Smiling at speaking prowess, this tall brave was he.

"Know this," he continued. "It looks bad. So bad I cannot yet begin to seize the full meaning of it. But as Arrow Keeper always insisted, once the worst has come, all that is left is the mending.

"Consider this, brothers. Sharp Nosed Woman was cruelly left for dead. Indeed, she is so badly hurt we will get no useful information from her soon. Yet my woman and baby were obviously worth stealing. They *could* have been killed and left for me to find, but they were not. Why?"

"Ransom?" Little Horse said.

"Perhaps. But we are poor in terms of white man's barter. What we have, they get easily enough without ransoming our people."

"Perhaps they will be sold as slaves?" Two Twists said. "You know slave markets flourish down in Apacheria. The Comanches and Kiowas took our people once before and sold them to Comancheros."

"All broth and no meat, buck. That time they took two score slaves. Would *you* bother to stampede a pony herd and divert an entire tribe to steal a woman and child to sell to slavers?"

This made sense, but like a medicine dream provided no sure answers.

"What then, Bear Caller?" Tangle Hair said.

"It seems," Touch the Sky replied, "that the low-crawling Indian butcher Seth Carlson may be involved. Consider how he hates me. Often when he moves against us he is abetted by Hiram Steele. Either one of them is an dangerous as a smallpox blanket. And we already know that our Wolf Who Hunts Smiling has parleyed with them in the past. If they have made common cause against me again, how would they think?"

His comrades were silent for some time, considering this. The deep frowns that took over their faces spoke eloquently for their ability to follow their shaman's thought path.

"Leaving your family dead," Little Horse reasoned slowly, "would be a remote pleasure. They could not see your face when you found them."

"Besides," Two Twists added, "killing your family without killing you is foolish to a coldly practical man. You are the main threat. Why would they kill your family, yet leave you—a brave with coup feathers to the ground—alive to hunt them down?"

"Which means," Tangle Hair finished slowly, "they will soon send word. They took your family because there was no other way to force you into their trap."

Make the trap come to you. Recalling Arrow Keeper's cryptic words chilled Touch the Sky's skin. He nodded.

"As you say. Do you not see it, bucks, as clear as blood spoor on virgin snow? They mean to kill Honey Eater and Little Bear, all right. But their hatred for me has cankered like a festering wound. So I predict I will soon receive a message from them, luring me to their camp. For they mean to kill them in front of me—all for the momentary pleasure of watching my grief before they kill *me*."

The sheer, barbaric heinousness of such thinking struck his comrades dumb. But slowly all three nodded, seeing this thing as it was.

Touch the Sky's lips formed their grim, determined slit—the expression that always meant someone was going to die a hard death.

"No blame and no grief," he repeated. "We are the fighting Cheyenne! We four climbed Wendigo Mountain and got our Medicine Arrows back from Sis-ki-dee. They were in breastworks, while we stood with our backs to the cliffs and held for the glory of our tribe.

"We four stopped Carlson and Steele when they tried to dam our river for whiteskin farms. Two hundred white buffalo hiders with long guns could not separate us from our souls. What Cheyennes have done, Cheyennes will do!"

At this he thrust out his streamered lance. His comrades crossed their stone points over his.

"This place hears me," he said solemnly. "And so do the High Holy Ones. I will bring my family home or die with them, and there is no middle way."

To a Cheyenne who held his oath sacred, the phrase "There is no middle way" meant more than its soft sound suggested: *ha'ko u'na*. It was the familiar motto of the ancient Cheyenne Sash Warriors. In the bleak days after the People had been chased out of the homeland the whiteskins called Minnesota, they lived on the Plains with no knowledge of horses. When attacked by horse warriors, one clan of warriors stood their ground by staking their sashes into the dirt—there they stood, and there they fought and died.

"*We* will bring your family home or die with them," Little Horse corrected him, and Tangle Hair and Two Twists approved this with nods. "We failed you once, brother. We will not fail you again."

"Good," Touch the Sky said. He glanced forlornly at his empty tipi, which he had not the heart to even enter. "From this time on we do not follow the path of normal braves. Every step we take from here, we tread only the Warrior Way."

"Aw, hell, Hiram," Hardiman Burke cajoled his employer. "She ain't no virgin, she's caught her a pup. She's had a big ol' baby come out her hole, so what's a few pokes gonna hurt? Nobody misses a slice off a cut loaf."

The leering men gathered behind Hardiman laughed and whistled at this. Steele, a no-nonsense, straight-ahead type who dearly loved discipline and order, frowned. Before he spoke, he called out to a sentry at the perimeter of his high-country camp on Massacre Bluff. The sentry sat on a boulder out on the very highest point of the granite headland. He had an excellent view of the Valley of the Greasy Grass, the only direction attackers could take to reach this formidable bastion.

The sentry shook his head. "All clear!" he shouted back.

Hiram turned to face Burke. The hireling's odd, disjointed smile, and teeth the color of pond scum, made him look like what Hiram knew he was: frontier trash.

"I hired on you and your men to peddle firewater to the red Arabs and to tote barking irons. You got a brand-new batch of Indian burner ready, and a tribe of ignorant savages down near the Shoshone River. Leave half your men here on account I'm about to send a note to Hanchon. But send the rest of your men down to make medicine with those savages. Be generous. I want them red niggers to terrorize every settler in the area. Militiamen got riled down near the Rosebud and exterminated an entire village. Now white men are filing claims and proving up good homesteads."

"Now, Hiram, that's all peaches and cream for you and Seth. But me and the boys here, all we're wantin' is a quick peek at her titties."

"Yes, and after the peek, it'll be a touch. And then you'll all line up to bull her, and no work'll get done."

Hardiman grinned at this, for it was gospel truth. He glanced across the slope to the spot where Honey Eater and her baby huddled under a crude lean-to of skins and saplings. Although Hiram hardly cared for the soulless savage's dignity, he did feel sorry for her when, forced to breast-feed her child in the open, all Burke's filthy men had crowded around her gawking and heckling.

"Admit it, Hiram," Burke said in a low, wheedling voice. "You mean to top her all for your ownself. Or maybe you and Widow Maker mean to share her for your reg'lar night woman?"

This was a particularly sore point with Hiram, whose own daughter had disgraced him by desiring Hanchon, a filthy savage.

"*You* might rut on an Indian cow," he said with disgust, "but I don't have congress with animals."

Burke howled in derision at this, flecks of spittle flying through the gaps in his teeth.

"Congress? Why, what the hell kind of name is that for gettin' your best? Katy Christ, Hiram, you got a bit of the bluenose temperance biddy in you."

"Shut your damn cake-hole," Steele growled. "Just do what I told you."

The two men had not noticed when one of the men sneaked over to the lean-to and peeked inside. A sudden female shout, followed by a male howl of pain, preceded his hasty retreat.

"Hey, boys!" he screamed in triumph. "I seen her dirty loaves, and then sumbitches is big and nice! Big ol' nipples like ripe plums. And she's got her a real pretty little strawberry mark on one of her teats. I'm gonna get me some o' *that!*"

"Hell, I got to see them bodice-poppers!" another man shouted, trotting toward the lean-to.

"Emigrate, you bastard!" Steele shouted, trying to stop him. But the deserter had been imbibing good mash most of the day, and now his blood was up for the sight—and feel—of woman flesh.

Steele cursed again. He was a big man who moved quickly for his bulk as he started toward the lean-to. But he never had to finish the trip, for neither did the randy rowdy: The man was perhaps ten feet from the lean-to when something whizzed past Steele's eyes. A moment later the hireling's belt suddenly broke, his pants dropped around his ankles, and he tripped, pitching hard onto his face.

Slowly, nonchalantly, Widow Maker flicked a dust mote off one oxblood boot. Then he rose from the rock where he was perched and walked across the camp to retrieve his throwing knife.

"You got to be shittin' me," Burke muttered. "He took his pants down with a knife."

Widow Maker, who had the hearing of an elk, called over pleasantly, "I could've took off his pizzle. I see any more white dogs going after my meat, I *will* slice off his manhood."

"Your meat! You flea-bitten brevet white. Who give you clear title to that red honey?"

Widow Maker looked at Hiram. "Tell 'em . . . boss."

Hiram looked uncomfortable and didn't meet Burke's eyes. The leader of the snowbirds lost his stupid, goading expression. A deep fury made his pig eyes seem even closer together when he stared at Hiram.

"I see how the wind sets. Blade boy gets all the foofaraw, and we get the crappy end of the stick."

"Quit your damn bellyaching and do what I told you," Hiram said gruffly, turning away and crossing to his dog tent beneath a stand of wind-stunted dwarf willows. From his aparejo he removed a sheet of foolscap, a nib, and a bottle of ink.

He found a good, flat rock and squatted to compose a brief note. When he was finished he called a man over.

"Take this to the trading post at Red Shale," he told the man. "Ask for an Indian runner named Steals Ahead, a skinny Flathead who rides a mule. He's a message runner, he'll take this out to Hanchon for a couple bottles of mash."

Before he handed it over, Steele read the message one more time:

Hanchon,
It's finally come down to the nut-cutting. The terms are simple. I'm up on Massacre Bluff with your woman and kid. I don't want them, I want you. Get your red ass up here and surrender, they'll go free. If you don't, they'll die hard and the body parts will be sent to your camp.

By God, Hiram thought with a glow of satisfaction, that'll fetch him. And if it didn't, the P.S. surely would:

Best hurry, Hanchon. The white men have already discovered that little strawberry spot on your woman's tit. Won't be long, they'll know every inch of her.

Chapter 8

"Brother," Little Horse said as soon as the Flathead word-bringer had pointed his bridle back toward Red Shale, "now is the time to recall your own recent words to us. You knew a message was coming. As you predicted, it passed. Now, no matter how that talking paper turns the knife inside, is the time of the warrior."

Touch the Sky heard all of this. But for the moment, as the blood of wrath swam red before his eyes, the words were as meaningless to him as if they had been spoken in Pawnee or growled by a civet cat.

He had already crumpled the sheet of foolscap, but its brief, goading message still prodded at him. He stood with his band near the entrance of the common corral.

Tangle Hair, too, was alarmed at the murderous

rage burning in the tall shaman's eyes. It was said that the fearsome Pawnee Berserkers looked like that before they went into a killing frenzy on the battlefield—sometimes, in their blind fury, slaughtering their own comrades before their frenzy subsided.

"Shaman," he said, "tuck your rage into your parfleche and look to the main chance."

"Rage," the hotheaded Two Twists threw in, "will not get Honey Eater and Little Bear back; it will only ensure their death."

Those words struck Touch the Sky with the force of canister shot. The mad-bull glaze left his eyes as his young comrade's words replaced the Shaman's hot rage with cold fear for his family.

"Keep saying it, bucks," he told them with a nod. "I am learning. We are going to Massacre Bluff, and I swear by the Four Directions and the earth I live on, my quiver holds no rage, only fire-hardened arrows."

He gestured across the clearing. "Look. Could the story be any clearer if they drummed it?"

Wolf Who Hunts Smiling and Medicine Flute sat cross-legged before Medicine Flute's tipi, surrounded by their usual coterie of lickspittles. But now almost every Bull Whip in camp also ringed them—fully armed.

"It is clear," Little Horse agreed. "They have had a hand in the stealing of your wife and babe. And they know an entire soldier troop protects them from your—our—anger."

"Of course, everyone in camp knows by now that Honey Eater and Little Bear were taken,"

Two Twists said. "But no one should know about the talking paper but we four. Yet see! The wily wolf and the skinny bone-blower knew it was coming and prepared."

"I have ears for this." Touch the Sky's now-calm exterior was almost more frightening than his earlier agitation. "Brothers, take a little stroll with me. But keep your backs covered."

Little Horse traded desperate glances with Tangle Hair and Two Twists. He definitely did not like the look on Touch the Sky's face. But he shrugged and fell in behind his leader as the tall brave crossed camp toward their assembled enemies.

"Look here, bucks!" the voice of Wolf Who Hunts Smiling called out as they approached. "Woman Face is searching for his squaw. Look at his miserable, brooding face, where he wears his feelings for all to know. Perhaps she has run away with a mincing Ponca so she may know the thrill of being bulled by a stout Indian."

Laughter erupted at this. The Whips made a great show of flashing their rifles in warning. But Touch the Sky had stopped well back from the group. They had tried before to break him down before the tribe. Let them try now. Despite Wolf Who Hunts Smiling's words, Touch the Sky's face showed nothing besides a grim warning to the wise.

"She had a stout Indian in my cousin," Wolf Who Hunts Smiling said, making the cut-off sign. "But this one killed him, and we still have not buried his bones."

Cheyennes placed their dead on scaffolds until, after several winters, the flesh was long gone. Then the bones were gathered and buried.

"True," Touch the Sky said, "I am searching for my woman, and I mean to find her, for she cannot be replaced as can your toadies. I also mean to kill those who dug their own graves by laying a hand on her. But truly, Panther Clan, you will never have to search out *your* squaw. She sits beside you now, as always, playing love songs for you on her flute."

A few Whips found this amusing and snickered, the dolt named Swift Canoe laughing so hard he choked. But Wolf Who Hunts Smiling silenced him with a dark scowl. Before he could retort, Two Twists spoke up.

"I have always wondered a thing. When you lift each other's clout, which of you plays the bull and which the cow?"

More laughter as Wolf Who Hunts Smiling's rage deepened. But Touch the Sky was in no mood for wasting more time. As Little Horse and the rest of his admiring band had realized by now, Touch the Sky had no spirit for this clash of bulls. It was being done precisely because his enemies thought he could not. And many of them were indeed nervous and reluctant to join the laughter. Wolf Who Hunts Smiling's bold scorn was mostly smoke—he too feared this shaman-warrior, as did every sane brave west of the Great Waters.

Touch the Sky said, "Have ears, all of you. I see the grins on your cowardly faces, and I mark them well. To use your own favorite words, the worm will turn. No one is surprised that not one of the herd guards murdered during the pony raid was a Bull Whip. Your treachery is surpassed only by your cowardice in using even women and children to accomplish what your manhood cannot."

His tone and manner, the carved-stone set of his jaw, lent special force to Touch the Sky's words. Now not one of his enemies was smiling. *This* one spoke from the vital flame within, and few of them were man enough to meet his eye.

"This place hears me! It matters not if you hide in caves or breastworks—if you were involved in this coward's game, I will drive you out and gut you. Neither the power of heaven nor the power of the Wendigo will stop my wrath. The High Holy Ones may pity you, but I will not."

With this, Touch the Sky drew his obsidian knife from its beaded sheath. Before the Bull Whip sentries could lift their muzzles, Touch the Sky sank the blade into the meat of his own left thigh.

While they gaped, ribbons of his blood trailed into the dirt and gave special meaning to the words he had just spoken. As the tall brave and his band, eyes filled with contempt, turned and headed for the common corral, Medicine Flute pulled his leg-bone flute from his lips. The skinny brave looked as pale as moonstone.

"Brother," he said quietly, so only Wolf Who Hunts Smiling could hear him, "did you see his eyes? That was no woman's face. His thoughts are nothing but bloody. I fear you and Hiram Steele

97

have gone too far this time. We should bring his family back."

"Go to your sewing lodge, little sister," Wolf Who Hunts Smiling scoffed. "Too far! Buck, you are willing to fight but afraid to wound. I go for the kill and nothing less. I mean to either win the horse or lose the saddle.

"As for his bloody oath. It was a formidable show, truly. But he is like a frightened cat, puffing up and making a great show to cover his fear. Have you forgotten Widow Maker and his deadly knives? Have you forgotten what it is like up on Massacre Bluff, how not even a mouse can approach unobserved? Even Wendigo Mountain is not so impregnable. Stop your puling, squaw boy, he will not survive to carry out his oath."

"Lookit there," came a voice from just outside Honey Eater's crude lean-to. "She's givin' the little critter the dug again. Glom them 'ere catheads, boys. Goddamn, she's peart."

"Sling your hook," she heard someone else growl, followed by scuffling noises. "Let the next feller have a peek, you greedy-gutted piker."

"Christ Jesus! Boys, I ain't see woman flesh that fine since Christ was a corporal."

"You *know* them bucks're missin' her sweet red ass. I hear Injuns mate like cats. After the lead tom has mounted a queen in heat, she lets all the peeping toms have a whack, too."

"Hell, *we're* peeping toms! When we get our whack?"

Honey Eater understood none of it, and by now

she hardly cared. Her rage and shame had given way to concern for Little Bear. He was holding up admirably. But these conditions were grueling for her, so they must be deadly for such a little one.

Before, to hide herself, she had only fed him with her back to the opening of the lean-to. But that kept Little Bear cut off from badly needed fresh air. By now she knew that the one Steele called Widow Maker did not intend to let any of them touch her—right now, at least. Let them stare; she was not going to kill her son to preserve the famous Cheyenne modesty.

Little Bear was quiet now only when he could draw some milk from her. Her captors had taken care to feed her well, leaving plates of well-prepared meat and hot pan bread. At first, however, she had been unable to choke any of it down. But the need to live for her little one drove her to an appetite.

"How's 'bout some o' that gash that never heals!" one of them shouted, and whatever he said made the rest form a chorus of laughter—even the stone-faced Widow Maker cracked a slight grin, though he kept a protective eye on her.

This troubled her, this parley between Steele, the half-breed knife expert, and the filthy white who led these even filthier men now leering at her. It had not taken her long to realize Steele's identity, though she had never seen him before. Touch the Sky had already told her he was back in this territory, once again teamed up with the Bluecoat named Seth Carlson—and, most fearful of all, Wolf Who Hunts Smiling. The very Cheyenne who swore to exterminate all white men now played their dog.

Why did they keep pointing over here, she wondered. Pointing, nodding, now even laughing, especially the dirty one Steele called Burke. That sentry out on the point of the bluff kept shouting something back to them—no doubt Touch the Sky and his men were approaching. But surely they would not try to attack this imposing bastion?

Like her, poor Little Bear was cramped and cranky. He missed the tipi and his playthings, and he clearly missed his father—as did she. If only she—

Fear glazed her eyes when she saw Widow Maker crossing toward her. The gawking men outside stepped respectfully aside when he came up to the lean-to and looked down at her.

"Give me your baby," he said in Lakota.

Honey Eater shook her head and tried to crowd farther back inside the worthless shelter. He had already taken her gun, and no other weapons were at hand. Nor would she fight and risk her son.

"Give me your baby," he repeated. "I will bring him back shortly."

Honey Eater felt the hair on her nape stiffen when she looked past Widow Maker and saw Burke bent over a fire, stirring it to life. Steele held the blade of a knife down in the glowing coals. And all of a moment, she understood. She had watched Henri Lagace and his men torture Touch the Sky the same way.

"No!" she cried, shrinking back so violently that Little Bear roared out. The sound startled Widow

Maker and made him flinch.

"Give him to me, pretty. You will get him back, and you can comfort him. But if you refuse . . ."

He only needed to lift his foot a few inches off the ground to remind her of the knives tucked into the boot. He had already thrust one into poor Sharp Nosed Woman, perhaps killing her. She knew he would not hesitate to kill a baby.

Fighting back hysteria, for then she would be no use to her son, she held him up for Widow Maker. The poor child protested mightily, roaring and kicking. Carrying him carelessly under one arm, Widow Maker headed back toward his two comrades. He turned and shot her a warning glance when she started to follow.

"Maiyun, protect my baby!" she cried out. Honey Eater was in an agony of indecision; one moment she watched the proceedings, the next she was forced to look away, sobs hitching in her chest.

Widow Maker held the child so the soles of his feet were exposed. When Steele was satisfied his knife was hot enough, he raised it from the coals.

Crying out, unable to watch further, Honey Eater turned her face away and waged the fight of her young life to stay strong for her baby.

"This will be the greatest of all battles," Touch the Sky told his comrades. "You all know by now that we can trust nothing Steele tells us. In this he is like Sis-ki-dee. The trick is to expect the unexpected."

Little Horse nodded. The four of them stood

dangerously exposed near the foot of Massacre Bluff, within easy range of the sentry up on the headland. They knew Steele hoped to lure Touch the Sky up, so his men surely had orders to hold their fire for now.

"Brothers," Tangle Hair said doubtfully, "when have I ever hidden in my tipi when my tribe is on the warpath? I went up the backside of Wendigo Mountain, with the ghosts of our ancestors warning us to go down. But *how* will we rout them from that place?"

"We will not rout them," Touch the Sky answered grimly. He quoted Arrow Keeper's warning: "We will make the trap come to us."

"More shaman talk," Two Twists grumbled. It was his way to take the fight straight into his enemy's teeth.

"Yes, more shaman talk, double braid," Little Horse said sternly. "When you hear it, have ears. Are you the calf that bellows to the bull?"

Two Twists was about to retort when Tangle Hair said sharply, "Enough chatter, you two jays. Look . . . there!"

Two more figures had appeared beside the sentry, sharply outlined in the afternoon light, Hiram Steele and a man none of them recognized. Though truly, all whiteskins looked alike to most red men.

"They are looking down here," Tangle Hair said. "They mean for us to watch them."

"Steele is holding up a knife," Little Horse reported, for he had the best eyes in Gray Thunder's tribe. "Now . . ."

Little Horse suddenly trailed off. But Touch the Sky did not need his narration of events. For the tall brave recognized his son under the arm of the half-breed who had just joined the others.

All four Indians clearly understood the fierce howl of pain when Steele brought the red-hot knife to Little Bear's tender soles.

Honey Eater's screams added so much to the torturers' mirth that they did not prolong Little Bear's agony this time. Touch the Sky, on the verge of madness himself, feared she might go insane. His own face had twisted into a mask of hatred, and the muscles in his back and shoulders flexed like taut cables as he worked his hands into fists.

"Steady, brother," Little Horse said beside him. "We tread the Warrior Way now. We stay cold, we stay calm, and we stay lethal. Turn your rage into a stone and throw it away from you, or your wife and son are carrion fodder."

His strong hand gripped Touch the Sky's shoulder, gripped it hard until the tall brave nodded. Touch the Sky swallowed hard. "As you say, brother."

"Just a touch this time, Hanchon!" Steele shouted down through cupped hands, his bullhorn voice easily carrying the long distance. "Just a touch to convince you you best get your blanket ass up here quick!"

Chapter 9

For Touch the Sky, this was sheer, unspeakable torment of a kind he had never before encountered.

He had withstood torture by fire, hung from bone hooks in his chest until he passed out from the pain, been pinned to the ground by Big Tree's deadly "long arrow," its barbed shaft and tin point only a finger's width from his heart. Enemies had sicced grizzly bears and mountain lions on him, tried to kill him with grenades, had even tried to skin him alive.

But what he faced now baffled and frustrated him as nothing before had done. His innocent wife and child were suffering up there on Massacre Bluff. Yet he knew that all hope would be lost the moment he went up and surrendered as Steele demanded.

He and his comrades knew that shelter would be a high priority once the whites got tired of sporting with them and started aiming to kill. So after a brief council, they agreed that rifle pits were the wisest expedient. This would leave them close enough to monitor events, yet provide effective cover. Their ponies were left on long tethers well out of rifle range from the bluff.

Sister Sun went to her resting place and Touch the Sky spent a long night worrying.

"Brother." Little Horse's voice rallied him out of the darkness to his left. "I know you are in a hurting place. But if you can find any comfort at all, find it in this: It is quiet up there now. Little Bear's wounds are perhaps less than you might imagine them. This is grim, buck, and I am not one for sugarcoating a thing. You know that. But we have faced down the impossible before, and here I am, still alive to speak about it."

"It is quiet now," Touch the Sky agreed. "But I know these Mah-ish-ta-shee-da, Cheyenne. Right now they are filling their bellies with strong water. The noise will grow, as will their behavior that would shame an animal. They will be keen for their cowardly sport."

"Nonetheless," Tangle Hair said somewhere in the darkness to his right, "you have held back with remarkable restraint, shaman. Keep that up. They will do everything to get you up there, and once that is done, *all* is done."

"Straight arrow," Two Twists agreed. "Remember this, hard though it is to accept: They *may* kill Honey Eater and Little Bear if you don't go up.

But they will also kill them if you *do* go up. The only difference is that you will die into the hard bargain."

His comrades were right, and even Arrow Keeper's warning supported them. Still, as Uncle Moon clawed a path across the sky, it was hard to resist the temptation to be with his family.

This became even more true after the whiteskins fulfilled Touch the Sky's prediction—their drunken rowdiness increased as the whiskey flowed.

Random gunshots sounded, and the Indians knew they were not forgotten. To keep them honest, the palefaces snapped off rounds toward their position. Now and then a slug whined in, one striking so close it threw dirt in Touch the Sky's eyes.

Drunken men began to sing, bellowing lewd verses from "Loo-loo Girl." Somebody started playing polkas on a concertina. Laughter, whistles, cheers filled the night air. Touch the Sky bore all of it with the patience of a cat watching its prey. But he flinched hard when a woman's scream rent the fabric of the night.

Another scream that could only come from Honey Eater, and his muscles tensed themselves for action. But *what* action, he demanded of himself in frustrated anger.

Fortunately, Hiram Steele's bullhorn voice roared out, threatening that heads would roll if the fools didn't let him sleep. Touch the Sky calmed down somewhat as the camp up above them did likewise. Now there was no sound from

Honey Eater or Little Bear—and Touch the Sky prayed to Maiyun that silence was a good sign.

"Brother," Little Horse's voice coaxed out of the darkness. "Right now sleep is the last thing you want, but it is the first thing you need. Worry all through the night, and what good will you be for whatever trials await us?"

"Buck," Touch the Sky said, "you speak straight words. Now follow your own advice."

The rifle pits were damp and cramped and hardly invited good sleep. But Touch the Sky wrapped himself as best he could in his buffalo robe and willed himself into a fitful slumber.

His eyes blinked open just as dawn painted the eastern horizon in salmon-pink streaks.

"Little Horse, are you awake?"

His friend's head poked above the edge of his rifle pit. Tangle Hair and Two Twists, too, poked their heads out.

"Brothers," he announced, "I am going up there."

"No, you are not," Little Horse said just as firmly.

Touch the Sky shook his head. "No, you do not understand. I do not mean I am going up to fulfill Steele's demand. I will go up only partway, carrying a truce flag. I will call Steele out for a parley. I must at least try to make medicine with him."

"With Steele?" Little Horse demanded. "Have you been visiting the Peyote Soldiers?"

"This not-so-little horse is right," Two Twists said. "You would find a she-grizz with cubs more reasonable."

107

"Yes," Tangle Hair added. "And even partway up gives them a clear shot, if they mean to kill you."

"They might kill me," Touch the Sky agreed. "But if I know Steele as I think I do, his heart is set on making me suffer before I die. He has my wife and child, he will not rush things."

Little Horse stubbornly shook his head. "I do not like it. Leave it alone."

This was too much for Touch the Sky.

"Leave it alone?" he exploded. "Why not just ride back to camp and work our ponies in the corral while they torture my wife and child?"

Touch the Sky was not one for emotional outbursts. His angry words betokened well the extent of his desperation, and his comrades saw this.

"As you say," Little Horse conceded. "I still do not like it. But, brother, you will tangle your brain past all use if you do not take some action. Only remember that today is not a good day to die. We will be right behind you, covering you. Keep your eyes to all sides. Steele may wait, as you say. Or he may seize the moment he has lost so many times before."

The plucky Cheyennes waited until Sister Sun had journeyed higher in the sky. When he heard signs that the camp was awake, Touch the Sky dug the white truce flag out of his legging sash and tied it around his right arm.

He grounded his Sharps rifle, although his comrades—who stayed well behind him—carried their weapons.

"All of you listen," Touch the Sky warned them

sternly. "It is I Steele longs to make suffer. However, the rest of you are ripe for quick killing. So stay back far enough that you will have a fighting chance if they open fire. At the first sign of trouble, break for the rifle pits."

The sentry spotted them as soon as they began the long ascent up the smooth, rocky slope. Clearly they were arousing no alarm from above. Steele and the hard case with the teamster's mustache, the one who led the whiskey traders, came to the edge of the bluff to chart their progress.

"Steele!" Touch the Sky shouted when he was perhaps halfway up the slope. "I would speak with you. Come down the slope to meet me, unarmed. I will try no tricks—you have my wife and son."

"That's right, red nigger, I do!" Steele shouted back, his voice gloating. "So never mind this meet-me-halfway shit. Get your flea-bitten ass up here, and your woman and kid go free."

Touch the Sky stood his ground.

"Come on up!" Steele repeated. "Come see your woman!"

"The rest of us are seein' plenty of her, John!" Burke shouted in his hillman's twang. He used the name that whites on the frontier used in direct address to an Indian.

His comrades understood none of this. But Little Horse did not like the set of his friend's broad shoulders.

"Put it away from your mind, brother," he called out behind Touch the Sky. "I told you this was a foolish plan. Turn back now."

Touch the Sky might have done just that, but

Hiram Steele had said something briefly to Hardiman Burke. The lackey disappeared for a moment, then reappeared dragging a reluctant Honey Eater with him. She held Little Bear clutched protectively in her arms.

Her eyes met Touch the Sky's across the long distance. Even from here Touch the Sky could read the misery and fear and suffering they had exposed his wife to. And Little Bear seemed ominously still and lethargic, as if perhaps ill. The conditions up there were brutal enough for an adult; for a newborn child they spelled eventual death.

Steele divined some of these thoughts, judging from his next words.

"They're looking mighty peaked, Hanchon! I thought you were the Noble Red Man? Yet here you are, too chickenshit to save your own family. I wonder if my daughter knew what a white-livered coward you are when she was putting her ankles behind her ears for you."

"Steele! Listen to me! This thing you have in your mind about me and Kristen—it's *only* in your mind. I swear, I never touched her. You're about to kill an innocent woman and baby because of something that never happened."

"You're a bare-assed liar, Hanchon! I caught you in her goddamn bedroom down in Great Bend. And she spent the night in Blackford Valley with you and that bunch of yours."

"She had to. You told Abbot Fontaine to kill her, remember?"

By now Steele, forced to memories he never

brooked, had turned livid with rage. He said something to Burke. The next moment, Touch the Sky watched the filthy Burke tear Honey Eater's doeskin dress away to fondle her breasts. He kept his sick, disjointed smile aimed at the Cheyenne as he did.

Honey Eater knew that resistance would only jeopardize her baby. She submitted with a stoic dignity that wrenched Touch the Sky's heart—until anger at Burke burned deep within him and drove the pity out.

"Hold, shaman!" Little Horse called out behind him, seeing his comrade's muscles flex. "I swear by the four directions, I will shoot you myself if you try to go up there. I would rather wound you than let them kill you—and Honey Eater and Little Bear, too."

Little Horse's words sank in, although Touch the Sky was still poised for movement. What happened next, however, settled events for now.

Burke had dropped his mouth to taste one of Honey Eater's nipples. But Little Bear chose this moment to launch a powerful stream of vomit, catching the leering toady square in the face.

Things might have gone very badly indeed if Steele himself, as surprised as everyone else, had not suddenly guffawed.

Touch the Sky heard all three of his comrades burst into hoots.

"Brother," Two Twists shouted up, "your whelp has his father's fighting spirit, even if he still lacks his weapons!"

Steele had already pushed the enraged Burke

away so that he did not harm Honey Eater or the child. Steele, Touch the Sky knew, would not hesitate to kill them when the time came. But this was motivated by his extreme, obsessive hatred for the Cheyenne. Steele did not have the stomach for needless brutality, for he was a disciplined man.

Nonetheless, the Cheyennes were not out of danger. For Burke, frustrated in his attempt to get that goddamn kid or its mother, had turned on the Indians. He knew Steele would kill him if he plugged the tall one, so he opened up with his Colt Navy revolver against the three savages behind him.

Returning fire was out of the question, with Honey Eater and the baby standing right there. Touch the Sky did not need to shout out any orders. His battle-savvy men knew which way the wind set for now. His parley with Steele had been a waste of time, but at least Touch the Sky had verified that Honey Eater and Little Bear were unharmed . . . for now.

Burke's Colt's .36 caliber slugs chased the frustrated Cheyenne warriors back to their rifle pits.

Chapter 10

You know that I had a wife and son? said the voice of the old brave named Long Jaw.

I should have saved them or at least died with them.

I lost my woman and child through too little love for them. Do not lose yours.

I should have saved them.

Saved them!

"Brother," Little Horse's voice said firmly, "wake to the living day."

Touch the Sky started awake, the rest of a shout of protest stuck high in his throat. Little Horse looked down at him from the edge of his rifle pit. Touch the Sky sat up, his face sheepish.

"Did I wake you, buck?"

"Yes, and the birds too. Hear them?"

His friend spoke straight. Even there, on the

edge of the river tableland, thousands of birds had started their dawn chorus. Another sleep had passed. Like his comrades, Touch the Sky had grabbed fitful bouts of rest when he could. He glanced up toward the bluff as he stretched his cramped muscles. It seemed quiet enough, but he feared quiet almost as much as commotion where that bunch of animals were concerned.

"Brother," Little Horse reported, "while you slept, I saw two signal arrows sent up by our tribe. They are searching well north of here, near the Yellowstone. Have you guessed by now that we will not see them anywhere around here?"

Touch the Sky gnawed on a piece of jerked venison, eating only to keep his strength up. He nodded, again glancing up toward the headland.

"More of Wolf Who Hunts Smiling's treachery. He and the Whips will manufacture sign to keep the Bow Strings on a false trail. I truly thank Maiyun that Big Tree and Sis-ki-dee are not in this territory now, for Wolf Who Hunts Smiling would surely move in concert with them to deal our distracted tribe the death blow. At any rate, we cannot expect help from camp."

"No," Little Horse agreed. "But I have been thinking a thing."

"Well?" his friend demanded. "Are we girls in their sewing lodge, bargaining over fresh gossip? Speak it or bury it, buck."

Little Horse grinned at the rebuke, for it suggested his friend's old spirit of teasing. "Only this. Have you thought about Steele's plan? What it is based on?"

A knowing grin twitched at Touch the Sky's lips. He had been thinking about this very thing.

"I have ears, warrior. Fill them."

"His plan," Little Horse said, "is as simple as falling down. You were supposed to run up that slope in a blind fury once they pawed your woman. You have not, for your love is too strong. A lesser man would have run up in a rage when another man touched his wife, his manly pride more important than his woman's and son's lives. You put them first and held back. Now the yellow eyes have a slight trouble. For you are still alive, and they need to come down that slope eventually. Steele and his lickspittles have not considered the possibility that we may wait longer than they can."

Touch the Sky nodded eagerly. "Sweet words, buck, for your thoughts fly with mine. I have dragged you into too many battles with whiteskins. At least, however, you have studied their thinking even as you have killed them. Knowing Steele, they are well provisioned up there. But the dirty work he requires of his greedy hirelings requires much gold. He has whiskey he must peddle."

"We can interfere," Little Horse said, following this thread. "But they can retaliate by moving against Honey Eater or the little one."

"Believe me, brother, I have shed much brain sweat on that point. We must take a chance. We must strike a risky balance. We must annoy them enough to put them in a worrisome place, but not enough to panic them and cause harm to my family. Difficult as it is to believe, my shaman eye tells me Steele might help us there."

At these words Little Horse looked at his friend as if he had just flown down from the moon. "Steele help us? Did your paint kick your skull?"

Tangle Hair and Two Twists, too, were listening to all this.

"This was the shaman speaking, not Touch the Sky," Two Twists said to Little Horse.

This made Little Horse somewhat contrite, for indeed it was not the way of Touch the Sky's followers to debate things spiritual.

"For once, Double Braid," he conceded, "I will swallow the rebuke, even though it comes from a spindle-shanked colt who needs whipping. Still, this Hiram Steele, he is a man who drinks his coffee black."

"Laced with snake poison," Touch the Sky agreed. "But think a moment, stout buck. Steele is a man who is steeped in bitterness. His criminal acts have brought misery and suffering to the red man, truly. He has paid those who have killed many of us. But *he* never wields the gun, though he is not a coward. His own daughter told me that, although always a hard man, he was once fair. His wife's hard death from the yellow vomit embittered him. And once one small place went rotten, the rest became corrupt."

This was understandable and Little Horse nodded. Many Indians, too, had become bitter and hard and criminal after the death of a great love. This was a thing a warrior could understand, though it was too important to discuss openly, for words fell short of the major truths. These were felt directly, seldom spoken.

"For just a moment, the space of a heartbeat," Touch the Sky continued, "his heart softened with humor when my son puked all over his lackey. And perhaps more than humor. Maybe for a moment he remembered his own good wife, and his fine daughter Kristen when she, too, was a handful.

"Oh, I am no sentimental fool. He has the heart to order Honey Eater killed when the time comes. But a human heart, or the stub end of one, is buried deep down in him. I hope he will not have the heart to torture a woman and a small child."

"You know," Little Horse said carefully, "that sometimes the worst pain comes before a fever breaks?"

Touch the Sky understood these diplomatic words. His friend was suggesting that, even though Steele might be reluctant to inflict torture, he would certainly make life unpleasant for Honey Eater and Little Bear in some fashion. Or Touch the Sky might even be wrong, shamanic hunch to the contrary.

Touch the Sky nodded. "Nothing comes without risk. My wife knows that, and whatever happens, she will understand."

Whatever happens, Touch the Sky thought grimly, his lips pressing into a straight line. Easier words to say than to comprehend. That *whatever* included the potential death of his wife and son. If they died, he swore to live long enough to avenge their deaths. Then he, too, would join them in the Land of Ghosts. Touch the Sky would face down any terror unleashed by man or Wendigo. But the thought of life without his family made his heart hurt unbearably.

"Hardiman!" Steele shouted across the camp as he emerged from his dog tent. "What the hell you doing standing around with your thumb up your sitter? Daylight's burning! Get that latest batch of whiskey out to the aboriginals. Unless, that is, you don't give a hoot in hell about me making payroll."

"What about them red devils down below?"

Steele sneered, hunching one beefy shoulder to slip his suspenders on. "What about 'em? You think Hanchon will bust caps knowing what might happen up here? You're just reluctant to miss a chance at seeing his woman's tits. Christ, ain't you never seen a naked woman before?"

Burke shot a resentful glance toward Widow Maker. As usual, he was in clear sight of Honey Eater's little lean-to.

"Not much chance of any fun," he grumbled. "It ain't fair, you two hoggin' all the meat and the rest of us don't even get chicken-fix'n's."

"You're getting thirty a month and found," Steele shot back. "A wrangler would have to *work* for those wages. Now stow the chinwag and get humping."

"Kiss my ass, Bacon Face," Burke growled under his breath, using the men's nickname for Hiram inspired by his heavy jowls. But he spoke low enough that Steele couldn't hear him.

He barked a few commands, stirring his men to

life from their faro games and yarning sessions. They tied whiskey-filled gutbags to the saddle horns of the packhorses. Soon his little caravan of destruction was ready.

"What if them Injuns don't fade when we ride down?" demanded Fargo Danford, the "master brewer" who knew the closely guarded recipe for Taos Lightning. "Should we let daylight into 'em?"

"They'll fade," Burke said. "Don't worry."

But soon the caravan of heavily armed deserters was halfway down the slope, and the Cheyennes hadn't retreated from their rifle pits.

"Well now," Burke said, "looks like them red niggers're feeling a mite froggy. 'Pears they're ready to jump.

"Hiram!" he shouted through cupped hands back up the slope, slewing around in his saddle. "You want we should keep riding?"

Steele, who was monitoring the scene from above with a troubled frown, nodded. "Plug the others if you want, but don't shoot Hanchon!"

Burke grinned. "Fan out in a skirmish line, boys, and don't clusterfuck—hold your intervals. Face front and fire on my command."

But that command never came. An eyeblink after he quit speaking, a roaring monster opened up from below. Little Horse's revolving-barrel shotgun was loaded with four full loads of rock salt. It was normally his favorite weapon for close combat. But at this distance he knew it would not kill, just sting like terrible hornets.

Four ferocious barks, and a wall of pain swept through the surprised whiskey traders. On the heels of this, Tangle Hair's British trade rifle cracked, and Fargo Danford's packhorse buckled onto its hocks, pink foam spewing from a punctured lung.

The devastating attack amplified when Two Twists and Touch the Sky launched a flurry of flint-tipped arrows, all carefully aimed below saddle height so that several thwapped into the legs of the riders.

The arrows missed Hardiman Burke, but a few pellets of rock salt scraped a silver-dollar-size flap of skin off his right cheek, and he roared in agony. Several men cried out in pain, others in panic, and another horse began crow-hopping when an arrow pierced its rump. Almost all the gutbags of liquor had been pierced, and now whiskey spouted out in arcing streams.

"Haul ass!" Burke roared, whirling his sorrel and lunging up the slope.

Below, Touch the Sky pondered the outcome of this attack. Indeed they had done well, exactly as they had hoped: They had sent word to Steele that he and his rabble were trapped. And they had not caused a death or serious injury, knowing that white men sometimes went wild for revenge when Indians bested them in combat.

As the silence up above dragged on, Touch the Sky prayed to Maiyun that it meant good news for Honey Eater.

"We'll kill his squaw," Steele assured an incensed Burke. "All in good time. But for now, just calm down. He didn't do any serious damage."

Burke's twang, in his agitation, sounded like whining.

"What the hell you smiling about? You didn't have your ass in the grass like I done, or it wouldn't be so funny."

Hiram tried not to smirk at the crude plaster stuck over Burke's rock-salt wound. "I'm not laughing at you," he lied. "It's funny, is all, that savage thinking to put snow in our boots with that little show."

"Funny, my sweet aunt! Let's roast his squaw's feet over some coals, let him pay for his little laugh."

"Never mind that. He'll pay, all right."

Steele glanced toward Honey Eater and the baby. Then he signaled to Widow Maker. The half-breed rose indifferently and ambled over.

"Lissen up, you two," Steele told Burke and Widow Maker. "I want you to go over there and grab the baby from her. Widow Maker, you see that scrub oak over there?"

The half-breed nodded, curiosity clear in his face.

"Grab the baby around the ankles and make like you're going to brain it against the tree. Don't actually do it, just start to."

Burke scowled, liking the perverse nature of this skit but failing to understand its purpose. "What the hell for?" he demanded. "All it'll do is make the squaw scream like she's being gutted."

"Exactly." Steele flashed an ear-to-ear grin. "You have a remarkable grasp for the obvious."

Widow Maker, much brighter than the deserter,

grinned appreciatively. "Oh, she will scream. You see the love in her eyes for that whelp? If she thinks we're killing it, to somebody down below when she screams, it'll sound like she's being skinned alive."

Burke glanced at his employer with new respect. "Hiram, you do know how to hurt a man without hitting him."

"Still silent," Little Horse said. "Brother, I think your ruse may have had some effect. They must be counseling now. Perhaps they mean to bargain with us."

"My *arrows* had effect," Two Twists boasted, getting some spirit back at this apparent victory for the beleaguered Cheyennes. "They are having second thoughts about toying with the Fighting Cheyenne of the north country!"

"Did you see that Mah-ish-ta-shee-da pig scramble when I dropped his horse under him?" Tangle Hair gloated. "He did not stay for his saddle. Maybe—"

A terrible, agonized scream almost too powerful to call human suddenly split the silence surrounding Massacre Bluff. A woman's scream—a scream from so deep in the hurting place it froze all three Cheyennes like stone carvings.

Unleashing a shout that matched the scream for desperate feeling, Touch the Sky lunged out of his rifle pit and tore up the slope.

"*No!*" Little Horse yelled behind him. But when his comrade failed to halt, Little Horse did not hesitate. He scooped up a rock as big as his fist and hurled it after his friend, scoring a solid hit to the skull and dropping Touch the Sky in his tracks.

Chapter 11

"Brother," Little Horse said, no trace of apology in his tone, "I regret that lump on your skull. But I do not regret braining you with that rock. At least you are still alive, able to carry on the fight to victory. Consider the alternative had I let you charge up that bluff."

Touch the Sky nodded, albeit gingerly, the effort making him wince. "No need to consider, buck. By now I would be too dead to skin."

He glanced up toward the headland again. "Whatever happened to my wife or child, I could not have changed it nor done them any good. I swore us to the Warrior Way, Little Horse, and your timely rock has kept me there. A warrior lives to fight on until the last fight. The last fight has not come."

Sister Sun was sinking in her resting place.

Touch the Sky had recovered slowly, and for some time yet he would not walk steadily, for that rock had a good arm behind it. But he welcomed this physical pain, for somehow it helped focus the other pain that was even worse.

Somehow, too, to borrow a phrase from his paleface vocabulary, it had knocked some sense into him. For Touch the Sky suddenly realized he was taking the wrong trail here. In attacking the whiskey traders, he was applying force when he ought to be using strategy. With his family at stake, he had not been thinking clearly. But now, of all times, he must play the fox.

"Brothers," he said, still forming his plan as he spoke, "we know why our wily Wolf Who Hunts Smiling has been scarce. He must at least pretend to be hunting for these pale marauders. But have you noticed a thing? Where has the Bluecoat been, the Indian-hater named Seth Carlson?"

"At the soldiertown," Two Twists suggested. "You yourself laughed at the news from Firetop about how this Carlson was in steep trouble with his eagle chief. You said his attempts to kill you have angered his chief, for he lies and dissembles and ends up humiliating the hair-face army. Now he is confined much to the fort, and watched closely."

Touch the Sky nodded. "My thoughts fly the same way. Count upon it, however, that he plans to be here for my death. However, we cannot know what the prearranged signal is to lure him out."

"Lure him out?" Little Horse repeated. "Buck,

125

you shamans always take indirect routes. Crack the nut and expose the meat."

"Only look for it, slow wit. Is Hiram Steele the only one who can take hostages?"

His meaning dawned clear, and all three of his comrades grinned. There was no love lost between Steele and Carlson—men such as they did not care for camaraderie. But Carlson was Steele's best ally, his only link to the all-important U.S. Army. He would not treat his death lightly.

"But as you say," Tangle Hair objected, "you cannot know how Steele meant to inform him when the time has come to kill you. So how can you lure him?"

"As to that, buck, do not forget, whatever fells a tree may be called an axe. We do not know their signal, but there are other lures."

Already Touch the Sky was checking the load in his rifle and preparing to drop back and recruit his horse.

"Lure him how?" Little Horse demanded. "Time is a bird, Cheyenne, and that bird is on the wing."

Touch the Sky nodded, worry clear in his dark eyes. "The best way to lure him will be determined after I visit with Firetop. That freckled face and foolish grin of his hide a wily mind. He knows every man, woman, dog, and cat in Bighorn Falls, as well as their strengths and weaknesses. He will know the soft places where we can sink our hooks into Carlson."

"What the hell," Corey said, sealing the letter with one of the new paper wafers that were beginning to replace melted wax. "It worked with you, and you've got twice the think-piece that Carlson has. They say what goes around, comes around. Let the arrogant son of a bitch fall for the same chicanery he played on you."

The two friends sat at the crude deal table in the split-slab cabin Corey shared with his father just outside Bighorn Falls. The elder Robinson was a mine-camp preacher and seldom at home.

"You sure he's struck a spark for this woman?" Touch the Sky asked. "Carlson's not one for a soft spot."

"I'll tell you, Matthew," Corey said, slipping into old habit and using his friend's paleface name, "it ain't a *soft* spot he's got for her, if you catch my drift. This Libbie La Belle sells dances—and a few other pleasures—at the Three Sisters saloon in town. Personally, I wouldn't touch her with a ten-foot quirt. She's a soiled dove, and a blight to decent women. But I'll grant she's a fine-looking specimen of woman flesh. And I've seen Carlson look at her like a hungry dog looks at meat."

Corey pounded the wafer once with his fist to assure the seal.

"I'll ride hell-for-leather into town and roust out little Donny Hupenbecker. He always runs messages and such out to the fort, and no one will question him. For an extra two bits, he'll stay mum about who really gave him the letter. You just wait right here until it's good and dark. Then lay for Carlson along the Old Fork Road—it's the shortest way to town from the fort."

"I remember," Touch the Sky said. "I used to

drive it almost every day of my life."

Corey looked sheepish. "Yeah, o' course. Damn, buddy. That seems like a lifetime ago, don't it?"

"It was," Touch the Sky said. "A whole, white lifetime ago."

Corey was heading for the door when something else occurred to him. A sly grin split his round face and he veered toward a crude shelf in the corner made from crossed sticks.

"One last little touch," he said, pulling a bottle of violet water off the shelf and sprinkling some on the folded sheet of foolscap. He winked at Touch the Sky. "Pa converted a whore to Jesus. She give him all her fripperies and told Pa to chuck 'em. But that sly son of a gun kept the violet water to splash in his side-whiskers. Ol' Seth sniffs on this little puppy, his pecker will jump to attention."

Captain Seth Carlson held the scented letter up to his nose again, inhaling deeply as he thanked his lucky stars.

He read the brief but enticing note yet again, each word worth more than a double-eagle gold piece to this woman-starved soldier:

Captain,
A lot of men vie for my attention, but there's something special about a soldier—especially one who has that manly sneer of cold command. I must leave town tomorrow for several weeks, but I'll be alone tonight—unless you come to keep me company. The

stairs behind the saloon lead up to my door. The latch-string will be out, soldier.

L.L.B.

"Jesus Christ," Carlson muttered, pacing his narrow quarters behind the commissary stores. "Libbie La Belle!" His lust was almost overtaken by his astonishment. That beauty could have just about any man in town—and his wallet. Yet she chose him!

Why not, demanded his inner voice. *Just because that Indian-loving whore Kristen Steele chose a savage over you, you've been selling yourself short.*

Of course he would ride into town to meet her, despite the risks. He was not authorized to leave the post, and it was not without its dangers. Colonel Thompson was already on the verge of busting him down to buck private and assigning him to permanent latrine detail. But God almighty, he thought, you don't fail to pluck at a diamond for fear of a splinter. He'd bribe the gate sentries and take his chances.

Only one thought slowed him for just a moment. What if word came from Hiram? Word that Hanchon was finally feather-pinned and ready to be plucked?

But at that moment, most of Carlson's blood was not in his brain. So what, he asked himself, if Hanchon was caught? He'd be back from town soon enough, and Hiram would want to play around with Hanchon first, have some fun with that red son before he freed him from his soul.

Carlson quickly checked himself out in the little

mirror over his bunk, deciding he could skip the shave—Libbie wasn't looking for a fancy-man tonight, but a by-God animal to make her see Jesus.

He strapped on his five-shot Army Colt, gave his tunic a quick dusting, then set off for a ration of pleasure.

Touch the Sky left his pony ground-hitched a double stone's throw back from the Old Fork Road that linked Fort Bates with the growing community of Bighorn Falls. Had a series of razorback ridges not cut off the view, he might have spotted the lights from his parents' place.

But he spared them little thought right now, love them as he did. For his own red family needed him now, needed him desperately. And Touch the Sky had learned long ago one of the first lessons of his warrior training: A warrior must ignore the inner eye of memory and feeling and focus on the world around him.

Despite his contempt for Seth Carlson, he did not take the man's survival skills lightly. Carlson had arrived out here with green on his antlers, but he had learned a great deal. He was competent, if not superb, with firearms, and dangerous in a close-in fight, for he was big and strong and tenacious as a raging bull.

Touch the Sky was normally a good match for him in a fight. Indeed, he had sent Carlson sprawling in the wagon ruts of Bighorn Falls and left him bloody in a tangled deadfall. But the brave was nearing utter exhaustion now. Not only had he just covered much distance at a hard pace, but he had neither slept nor eaten well for days. On top of all that, his head was one huge, throbbing ache from the rock that hobbled his flight.

So now he relied on a trip-fall. Working quickly in the buttery moonlight, he secured a section of buffalo-hair rope to a gnarled cottonwood. Then he stretched it across the narrow road, leaving it lying on the ground and kicking dirt over it. He stretched the other end close to a second cottonwood, ready to snub it when Carlson's horse was too close to avoid it. It would take careful timing, but he should be able to send Carlson flying hard. With luck, he would be too dazed to fight before Touch the Sky got the drop on him.

He had left his Sharps in its boot, for under no circumstances did he want to shoot this Bluecoat criminal. Not just yet. He tugged his beaded sheath around into handier position to grab his knife if he needed it. Fearful of the bright moon, he grabbed a handful of dirt and spit into it, making a paste, and smeared his face to cut the light.

Then, ready once again to face an enemy, he squatted near the tree, hidden in shadows, heart thumping in his ears, waiting.

The randy Carlson did not keep him waiting long. A buckboard had rattled past, and Touch the Sky heard an obviously married couple nagging at each other. Soon after, the rapid drumbeat of pounding hooves told him a lone rider in a hurry was approaching.

He cleared his mind and focused on this critical timing. Touch the Sky peered through a cover of bushes until he spotted the big Cavalry steed galloping full out down the long slope of Bighorn Valley. Carlson, true to his mean nature, wore four-point rowels on his spurs, and had filed them even sharper. Touch the Sky winced, feeling the horse's pain as the soldier repeatedly roweled him hard, drawing threads of blood.

The Cheyenne gripped the loose end of the rope and paused on the feather edge of a breath. The big bay drew even with a line of willows near the road, and in an instant Touch the Sky wrapped the rope around the tree, lifting it above the line of the horse's fetlocks even as he snubbed it tight.

Neither Carlson nor his mount noticed the rope until it was too late. The hurling animal crashed down to one side of the trail while its rider tumbled hard down the middle of the road.

The horse whinnied piteously, too hurt to get up. But Touch the Sky was like a wolverine locked onto the kill scent. Even before Carlson came to rest, the tired but agile Cheyenne had leaped into the road and begun racing toward his quarry.

But he didn't know that the hard tumble had broken one of Carlson's latigos and the saddle had flown off. Touch the Sky's left foot hooked into the pommel as he ran, and like his enemy, he too took a tumble.

The fall wasn't hard, but it cost him the critical element of surprise. For by the time he regained his feet, a woozy Carson had struggled to his knees and unsnapped his holster.

There's nothing else for it, Touch the Sky told himself desperately. In perhaps ten more heartbeats, Carlson—a big, strong man—would be on his feet and in fighting fettle. So Touch the Sky's only choice was to race into his enemy's teeth, hoping he could not point that Colt too accurately.

Carlson still didn't know who had dry-gulched him. But he could see a figure hurtling toward him down the sloping road. The Colt bucked in his fist, bucked again, spitting red spear-tips. That's two bullets, Touch the Sky counted, even as the gun bucked again and a white-hot wire of pain creased his left cheek when the slug grazed him. A fourth slug whined past his ear loud as a bumblebee, and now he heard Carlson gasp, *"You!* You mangy red bastard, this last one's going center of mass."

Touch the Sky hadn't quite made it. He was perhaps fifteen paces away as Carlson took up the trigger slack, and the Cheyenne saw the single eye of the muzzle centered right on him. Instinctively, his hand flew to his knife and hurled it haft first in one smooth, continuous movement.

With a sound like leather bursting, the obsidian handle of the weapon chunked into Carlson's forehead only a heartbeat before he pulled the trigger, drawing his bead off. The bullet whipped past him even as Touch the Sky, unleashing a triumphant cry, smashed knees-first into Carlson with all his weight and crushed the air from his lungs.

Chapter 12

"I don't like this shit," said a worried Hiram Steele.

He turned from his scrutiny of the Cheyenne position below at the bottom of the long approach to Massacre Bluff.

"I don't like it one bit," he repeated to Hardiman Burke and Widow Maker. "Hanchon disappears yesterday before dark. This morning just before dawn, the sentry sees a lone rider leading a horse. It was too dark to see clear, but the sentry says there was a body thrown across the second horse."

"Whose body?" Burke demanded. "A dead body?"

Steele gave the man a disgusted look. "If I knew that, would I be standing here asking? Katy Christ, Hardiman, is your brain any bigger than your pee hole?"

Widow Maker grinned at this while Burke

scowled. The two men looked like total contrasts. Burke's sagging canvas trousers were almost as filthy as his drooping mustache, while Widow Maker as usual looked as if he had just stepped out of a mail-order fashion catalogue.

"Don't get so close to the edge with those," Steele told Widow Maker, for the knife expert was sharpening one of his blades on a whetstone. "Hanchon hasn't seen you wearing a short gun *or* packing a knife. Let's keep it that way. I want him worrying about everybody else but you."

"The hell?" Burke said sharply, narrowing his eyes as he peered down the slope. "What's that 'ere buck up to?"

Below, Hanchon's comrade, the sturdy Cheyenne who had given Steele almost as much trouble by now as Hanchon himself, had climbed out of his rifle pit.

"He's notching an arrow into his bow," Burke said. "Best cover down!"

"Don't bother," Widow Maker said. "It's a message arrow. He's pointing it into the sky."

Sure enough, the Cheyenne let his arrow fly in a high, short arc, expertly dropping it on top of the ridge only ten paces from Steele. The big man walked over and snatched up the flint-tipped arrow fletched with black crow feathers. A message was tied onto the shaft with rawhide.

"Hanchon must be back," he remarked to the world in general as he slid the note off the arrow. "Them other savages can't write."

The brief note puzzled him: WE BEST PARLEY. I HAVE SOMETHING YOU NEED. TAKE A LOOK.

Steele glanced back down the long, smooth granite slope, and then rage twisted his features.

"That goddamned red bastard son of a bitch!" he roared, throwing the note down.

Below, Hanchon had just risen from one of the rifle pits into plain view. And the man beside him, hands bound behind him, was Seth Carlson.

"I've got your wife and kid, Hanchon," Steele said. "So wipe that shit-eating grin off your face. You ain't got the buying power you think you have. If we opened up right now, you and your flea-bitten pards would be worm fodder."

The meeting was tense. Steele, backed by Burke and a dozen of his hardcase gunsels, had come halfway down the slope. Touch the Sky, backed by his warriors, had come halfway up.

"Go ahead," Touch the Sky invited him. "But take a close look. All three of my men have their weapons trained on *you*. One of them will score a hit before he crosses over."

Carlson, livid with rage, stood near Touch the Sky, tied to him by a lead line around his waist. A grape-colored bruise as big as a biscuit stained his forehead, the legacy of Touch the Sky's knife toss.

"All right," Steele conceded, "I'll stow the threats. But I'll tell you right now, you can forget the idea of a trade. Kill the son of a bitch for all I care, I will *not* give up your woman and kid."

"Kill *me?* Why, you yellow-bellied egg-sucker, I'll kill *you!*" Carlson roared.

The soldier lunged, but Touch the Sky jerked him back roughly.

"I knew you wouldn't trade," the tall Cheyenne said. "I'm the first one to realize this dishonorable coward is not worth my family. But you need this pond scum. It's handy to have a crooked soldier in your hip pocket when you make your living swindling Indians."

"Spare me the stump speech," Steele sneered, "and name your terms."

"My terms? They're simple. From now on out, no matter what happens up here, you agree not to mistreat my wife or son. That's all I ask. Feed them, keep these filthy white dogs away from them, and leave them alone. On the other hand, if I hear one more scream of pain from either one of them, I'm killing this son of a bitch."

"That's all you ask?" Steele demanded, surprised and suspicious.

"It's all I care about," Touch the Sky said. "And if I ask for more, you'll try a double cross."

"You callin' me a white dog, John?" Burke asked, his hand working on the walnut grip of his Colt.

"Fuck you, blanket ass!" one of the snowbirds shouted. "I seen your squaw's loaves, and I aim to top her!"

"Slap a stopper on your gobs, all of you," Steele ordered. He squinted at the Cheyenne. "You talking straight? I leave your woman and kid in peace, you won't kill Carlson?"

Touch the Sky nodded.

"Wait a minute here," Carlson sputtered. "Just a goddamn minute. You mean I got to stay down there with these stinkin' savages?"

137

"Quit whining," Steele snapped. "You're lucky I don't let them kill you."

He looked at Touch the Sky. "All right, Hanchon. I refuse to shake your filthy hand, but you got yourself a deal."

"Shake my hand?" Touch the Sky sneered. "I wouldn't piss in your ear if your brains were on fire, let alone touch your hand."

"Bastard's got a mouth on him," Hardiman Burke said. "Buck, you see this?" He slid a bullet from his cartridge belt. "This here's a Kentucky pill, and I aim to make sure you take your medicine."

"I'm cooking that red bastard's hash this time," Steele fumed as soon as his negotiating party had returned to the top of the bluff.

"Yeah, I see that," Burke said sarcastically. "He's got us wedged 'tween a rock and a hard place, and here you are struttin' like a banty rooster. I'd say you're more like a capon."

"That's why I'm the ramrod here and you're just riding the grub line," Steele boasted. "Because I'm always one step ahead of the roundup, and you're always behind the drag."

He pulled a fragment of mirror from his pocket. "You forget that Wolf Who Hunts Smiling has a man stationed north of here, watching for our signals. We catch the sun now from the back of the bluff, Hanchon will never see the flashes. The Wolf has a war party with him, bucks loyal to him. They're s'posed to be looking for us."

Burke flashed his odd, disjointed grin, baring

crooked-gravestone teeth. "Well now! And if the Wolf and his bunch was to ambush them cockchafers below from the rear, that draws them off so me and my boys could smash 'em from their front. Sort of a hammer and anvil deal."

Steele nodded. "For once your brain is riding ahead of your mouth. As for Seth, he's a big boy now. If a trained soldier can't make his break when the chance comes, to hell with him. I need him, Hanchon is right. But I don't need *any* man to live more than I need for that savage to die. Never mind the pleasure of killing his wife and kid in front of him first. We can't stay up here forever. Life is a matter of compromise. I'll trade my pleasure for the sure knowledge that Matthew Hanchon is dead."

"They surely have new treachery on the spit," Two Twists said. "But your ride to Bighorn Falls was a wise move, Bear Caller. I cannot abide the smell of this stinking Mah-ish-ta-shee-da," he added, nodding toward Carlson. "But if smelling him is the price we pay for Honey Eater's and Little Bear's safety, let him stink away."

Touch the Sky nodded. He was angry with himself for not thinking of this sooner. Nonetheless, unlike most Indians, who avoided looking into the eyes of white men for fear they might steal their souls, he had stared into Steele's. And something told him that Steele's obsession to kill him was so powerful he would sacrifice Carlson.

That something was a distinct prickling on the nape of his neck, a feeling like insects scurrying—

a warning, he had come to learn by now, from the third eye of the shaman. But frustratingly, the shaman sense was always short on specifics. One thing, however, he would not do is attack. Make the trap come to you, Arrow Keeper had warned him.

Which meant, he realized, that sooner or later the attack was coming, too.

"Hanchon!" Carlson called out. Touch the Sky had not gagged him. He preferred letting this white enemy—who relied on his mouth too much, like most whites—fail at trying to goad him. "Hanchon! They're sharing your woman up there right now. Your next pup'll have white markings."

"Do you know for a fact," Touch the Sky said, "that they're having her?"

Carlson grinned. "That I do."

Touch the Sky shrugged and quickly unsheathed his knife. "In that case, Steele broke his word. Get square with your God because I'm about to kill you."

Carlson hastily lost his grin. "Ahh, I was playing the larks with you is all. I didn't mean it."

"Tell you what, you murdering, cowardly piece of shit. You mention my woman one more time, I'm taking your tongue out of your mouth."

His three companions, of course, understood none of this. But they watched, highly amused, as Carlson's eyes widened in fear.

"Buck," Little Horse said, "what did you say to him?"

But Touch the Sky was tiring of this. He derived little satisfaction from words, for his was a warrior's legacy of deeds. Even more important, that tingle in his nape was back.

"Never mind Carlson," he said, looking uneasily toward the flat grassland beyond the Valley of the Greasy Grass. Dust puffs floated on the horizon, drawing closer. A premonitory worm of fear inched through his vitals. He glanced back up the bluff.

"Brothers," he said, "do you remember how we kept Sis-ki-dee's men pinned down on Wendigo Mountain, when they outnumbered us so vastly?"

"We made the air hum with arrows," Two Twists boasted. "We launched fifteen for every bullet they got off. We set up a wall of death, and behind it we advanced."

"We did," Touch the Sky agreed. "And what Cheyennes have done, Cheyennes will do."

"As you say, brother," Little Horse said. He, too, now glanced around uneasily. "It would seem the shaman is speaking again, and trying to warn us."

"Hanchon!" Carlson called out, having recovered his courage. "What the hell did Kristen Steele ever see in you?"

Touch the Sky shrugged. "How long is a piece of string? Never mind what she saw in me. She meant it when she said she'd rather be mounted by a Cheyenne dog than let you touch her."

"You're a bare-assed liar, Hanchon. She never said that."

In fact she hadn't, to his knowledge, but Touch the Sky only grinned, enjoying the angry blood in Carlson's eyes.

"Brother," Little Horse said suddenly, and his

tone alerted Touch the Sky. The sturdy little brave had knelt to place his fingertips on the ground. From long experience he was able to read the earth.

"A group of riders approaches rapidly. Indian riders, for their ponies are unshod."

"Riders approach from behind," Touch the Sky said. "And things have been quiet up above—as if the whites were preparing for a charge?"

His companions nodded, realizing now which way the wind set.

"Ready your rigs!" Touch the Sky commanded. "The jaws of the trap are closing. I fear that somehow they have summoned Wolf Who Hunts Smiling."

Soon enough the approaching raiders were visible, identifiable by the red streamers tied to their ponies—Bull Whips. Now, from up above, came the clear shouts and sounds of a formation preparing for the charge.

"Brothers!" Touch the Sky said. "We cannot stand and hold in a shooting battle, we are vastly outnumbered. We have only one choice. Little Horse, get in Tangle Hair's pit. Two Twists, you climb into mine. Never mind your rifles unless you run out of arrows. We each have double quivers stuffed, so it will be arrows that save us or nothing.

"The attack will come from both directions. Therefore, we will stand back to back, each supporting the other in the fight of our lives. Two of us will send a wall of arrows into Wolf Who Hunts Smiling's group, the other two into the attack force from the bluff. Never mind human targets. I, too, am loath to kill ponies, but we must aim for their mounts. If you have ever grabbed a fat handful of arrows and strung your bows rapidly, do so now. If not we are all dead, along with my wife and child!"

Chapter 13

Carlson, too, quickly realized that Steele must have ordered some kind of attack. He grinned again as he watched the Cheyennes make their combat preparations. He had seen his worst enemy in all the world glancing nervously toward those dust puffs, which by now were discernible shapes moving in fast—Indian shapes.

"Looks like your tit's in the wringer, Hanchon," he gloated. "My people lookin' to cook your hash from one direction, your people from the other. Kind of looks like you ain't welcome in neither world, don't it?"

"Tell you what, blue blouse," Touch the Sky said, climbing out of his fighting hole and slipping his hands under Carlson's armpits. "Since *your people* will be tossing lead at us, let's put you in the way of it."

144

The muscles of his chest and shoulders strained like taut cords when Touch the Sky pulled the big man out and set him on the ground out before the pits. Tied at hands and ankles, he could not rise.

"Hey!" Carlson complained. "This ain't fair! You and Steele made a deal."

"*You* talk about fair?" Touch the Sky said. "Will a skunk dream of perfumes? But never mind, I am not breaking my word. If you are killed, it will be at the hands of *your people.*"

But the time to cease talking had arrived. They could see the attackers massing above now as the first Bull Whips, rapidly approaching, opened fire. Wolf Who Hunts Smiling led the ferocious pack, his streamered lance on high.

"Ready, brothers!" Touch the Sky commanded, reaching up and behind and grasping as many arrows as he could grip in one hand. "Wait for my command. If we fire too soon, we will run out of arrows and they will overrun us from one side or both."

He faced the force on the bluff, as did Two Twists. Tangle Hair and Little Horse, braced back to back with their comrades, faced the attacking Cheyennes.

"I can see Wolf Who Hunts Smiling," Little Horse called out. "Even from here his eyes are gleaming with triumph. Clearly he believes our death is at hand."

Now the Cheyenne bullets, as the attackers drew nearer, began to find their range. Divots of soil and grass flew up all around them. A mighty roar from above signaled a coup de main, a cavalry charge in full force. And now their enemies pounded at them from both directions, across the open flat and down the hard granite slope.

"Holy shit!" Carlson screamed when the black-brimmed officer's hat was shot from his head. "Damnit, Hanchon, drag me into the pit!"

But Touch the Sky had not a split second to spare. Still, as bullets rained in on them with ever-increasing accuracy, he held his men back. Their moment of resistance would be brief indeed, and unless it was also deadly enough, it would be their last defense.

Cheyenne war cries filled the air, and the former soldiers unleashed the Cavalry kill cry. The force from Massacre Bluff was perhaps halfway down the slope; Wolf Who Hunts Smiling's group was perhaps a hundred yards out and closing rapidly.

"Now, brother?" a worried Two Twists shouted.

His mouth forming a straight and determined line, Touch the Sky shook his head. "Hold a bit longer," he commanded.

By now even Carlson was begging the Indians to fire. "Open up!" he screamed desperately when another bullet flew by so close it tugged hard on his sleeve. "What the hell you waitin' on, a chinook?"

"Now!" Touch the Sky screamed.

Fwip! Fwip! Fwip!

Fwip! Fwip! Fwip!

Deadly arrows thickened the air in both directions, so many it appeared that Comanche trick shooters must be performing their lethal art. And indeed, the Cheyennes did copy the style of their worst enemies—with a handful of arrows held close to their buffalo-sinew strings, it was a mere heartbeat's work to slip one on and deliver it without pausing to aim. Thick leather bands on their left wrists protected them from the hard slap of their bow strings.

Hardiman Burke flinched hard when, beside him, Fargo Danford threw both arms out toward heaven, an arrow skewering his neck. One horse after another went down, skidding, tumbling, throwing their riders to a hard fall and tripping more behind them. Steele, watching all of it from above, shouted obscenities as the attack lost force and began to degenerate into a rout.

Nor had the attacking Bull Whips fared much better. The advantage of the defenders' position was the attackers' lack of cover. Tangle Hair and Little Horse matched their skillful comrades, sending out a deadly hail of flint-tipped death, followed by devastating shotgun blasts. Not too many Bull Whips were hit, but almost as good, they had lost many ponies. The downed riders were forced to jump up behind their mounted brothers. Seeing the attack from Massacre Bluff fail, an angry Wolf Who Hunts Smiling ordered his men to retreat.

Quickly Touch the Sky took stock of their situation, only to marvel at their luck. Neither he nor his companions had suffered a wound.

"But, brother," Little Horse reminded him grimly as they shoved a still trembling Carlson back into his pit, "I am out of arrows, and so, I see, are the rest of us. I used all but one of my shotgun loads the last time we were attacked. One more charge like that, and we will be throwing rocks."

"God *damn* it, Steele!" Hardiman Burke fumed, dropping all pretense of respect for his employer. "Thirty a month ain't fightin' wages! A man don't mind letting daylight into the occasional smart-mouthed buck. But this here is a shootin' war! And them 'ere savages down there is the meanest damn Injuns on God's green earth or I'll eat my flap hat."

"Why, man, get a grip on yourself. Those 'soldiers' of yours didn't even try to scrap," Steele objected. "They showed the white feather the moment they encountered a little resistance. I see now why they deserted. A Sioux papoose's got a bigger set of oysters on him than that gang of yours."

Blood surged into Burke's face. "A little resistance? Are you skewed in the brainpan? Did them bad-ass renegades under the Wolf do any better? Fargo and two others was kilt, and three more got arrows in 'em. Hiram, a few of them boys need a sawbones, and bad."

Hiram didn't really dispute these points. But in his overwhelming rage at Hanchon, he was beyond reason.

"Christ almighty, Hardiman, you want me to powder their butts and tuck them in, too? I didn't hire you boys on to cool coffee and play with that squaw's tits. You knew there'd be some rough weather when I hired you."

"Rough weather?" Burke said. "It's a gully-washer straight out of hell. And besides," he added, pointing to the rock where Widow Maker sat trimming his nails with a clasp knife and watching Honey Eater's crude lean-to, "you don't pay *that* squaw-man no thirty a month and beans. How come he makes more and fights less?"

"Tell you what, hair mouth," Widow Maker called out pleasantly, not bothering to look over at them, "you apologize real sincere-like and I might not kill you."

Burke turned as pale as bleached bones, for no way in hell did he think the half-breed could have heard him across that big clearing—not with this damned wind picking up to beat jip. That flat-faced son of a bitch was spooky.

"I swallow back them words," Burke called out reluctantly. "I'm just feelin' a mite wrathy is all."

Widow Maker nodded, satisfied. He was a reasonable man. "Any man can have a foul mood," he said congenially, his tone mocking this piece of white cowardly trash.

"Damnit!" Hiram exploded. "Would you two quit measuring your dicks? If we don't pull together, we're *all* stewmeat."

Burke shook his head, not hearing whatever Steele said, for the wind had gusted to a shrieking roar just as he spoke. Impatiently, Steele grabbed Burke's arm and pulled him into the slight hollow behind the lean-to, where the wind noise was not so fierce.

"Listen, Hardiman," he said, his tone more reasonable now that he had finally realized his danger—his own hirelings might turn on him like rabid dogs. "I didn't mean to get on the peck just now. Hell, I *know* your boys need a doctor. We got to act, and damn quick, old son, or we're planted."

"Hell, I want this pukehole behind me more 'n you do. If you got a plan, trot it out."

"Oh, I've got one, right enough. It's not brilliant, but it has the virtue of being simple. I've got ink and some nibs in my saddlebags. I send a note down to Hanchon. I propose a cease-fire and an exchange of prisoners halfway up the slope. But in fact, the moment Carlson is released, every one on our side opens fire on the Indians. How's that plan pop your corn?"

"What about blade boy? Don't he earn his keep?"

"He's our ace in the hole, remember? I already played it stupid when I let Hanchon see him holding his baby. I'm the first to admit this plan could come a cropper—Hanchon likes to pile on the agony. That happens, I don't want him tipped that Widow Maker is trouble. I'm holding him back for our last play."

Burke dug at a chigger in his shaggy mustache, pondering. "Well, like you said, it's simple. Maybe too simple. Them red Arabs down there have proved they can tell 'b' from a banjo. They ain't near so stupid as I thought."

"Wild doesn't mean stupid," Steele conceded. "Hanchon is nobody's fool. And so far his clover has been mighty deep. But he *is* damn desperate, Hardiman, remember that. A desperate man thinks from his heart, not his head. Besides, what other choice does he have? What other choice do *we* have?"

Burke thought all this over, his stupid face a stolid mask as he concentrated. "No argument from me. That slick Injun has got us wedged between shit and sweat."

"There you've struck a lode. So do we give my plan a try?"

Burke finally nodded. "Let's get 'er done."

Honey Eater did not understand one word the men said. Even if she could speak English, the wind had begun howling too loud to permit eavesdroping. But she did not need language—nothing spoke treachery so loudly as their faces and huddling manner.

She carefully dropped the corner of tanned skin back into place and tried to comfort Little Bear. Nobody had fed Honey Eater recently, and her milk was thin, when any came at all. Little Bear was bravely holding up, but she could tell he was weaker. His dark eyes, usually bright with curiosity, now held a dull glaze; he had no desire to play, nor could she even coax a smile out of him.

Again she lifted the skin aside, just in time to watch both men outside glance in the direction of Touch the Sky's position, clearly laying plans.

"More trouble, little one," she said softly. "Somehow, someway, we must warn your father. May the High Holy Ones pity their red children."

Chapter 14

Seth Carlson had been humbled by his near miss during the pincers attack. He only watched, hope burning bright in his eyes, as a courier under a truce flag brought a note down to his Cheyenne enemy.

"What's it say?" he demanded the moment the tall brave finished reading it.

"Caulk up," Touch the Sky told him absently, reverting in his exhaustion to an old phrase learned from John Hanchon. But his Cheyenne comrades were asking the same thing of him in their own language.

He raised his voice to counter the howling of the wind.

"It says one of two things. Either that our enemy is desperate, and ready to strike a truce, or that he means to kill us. Steele proposes a cease-fire and an exchange of prisoners halfway up. He says our last defense has injured many men, and they need a whiteskin doctor."

Little Horse said, "Do you believe this?"

"Certainly I believe he is speaking straight-arrow about needing a doctor. Steele is too stone-hearted to care, but no doubt his lickspittles are making life hot for him. They still have dead comrades lying on that slope, reminding them of their danger."

"Hanchon!" Carlson shouted from his pit. "God-damn you, quit jabbering Cheyenne and tell me what the hell's going on."

Touch the Sky ignored him, still frowning over the note.

"Brother," Little Horse said, "this Hiram Steele would take dead flies from blind spiders. There is no honor to him. But he surely is in a hurting place by now. Do you remember down in Cherokee country, the place the whiteskins call Great Bend? Steele fought like five men. But once we had broken his fighting spirit enough, he set up a peace pole and gave in to some of our demands. Unlike the Crow Crazy Dogs, he is no suicide warrior who swears either to win or die trying. He would rather come back another day for his revenge."

This was a crucial point, and Touch the Sky gave it the long consideration it deserved. It made good sense—Little Horse had indeed described well Steele's mean, but ultimately compromising, nature. Nonetheless, it was Tangle Hair who made up Touch the Sky's mind for him.

"Buck," he said quietly, "only think. Your frail child is up there even now, perhaps shivering hard in this violent wind. Is it a trick or not? And does it matter? Do you really have a choice any longer? Trick or no trick, there comes a time for action."

Touch the Sky agreed. "Look to your weapons," he told his braves. Turning to Carlson, he switched to English. "This is your big day, beef eater. Either you're going free or I'm going to kill you."

The hair faces did not know, Honey Eater told herself, that she had seen them hatching their plan. So they had not bothered to gag her before the little "negotiating party" set off down from the bluff.

Steele headed the motley procession, Hardiman Burke a few paces behind him with the lead line tied to Honey Eater's waist. Burke's men, the healthy ones, led their horses, the seriously wounded riding. Widow Maker brought up the rear. He led several packhorses. Clearly he was being kept out of the action, but why?

Little Bear whimpered, his skin pebbled from the cold north wind. He needed a warm fire and his soft robes so that he could sleep and thus restore a healthy appetite. Honey Eater ached from her cramped position. She had crawled out of the lean-to only in the early hours before dawn, long enough to relieve herself.

She forgot her own problems, however, when she spotted Touch the Sky and his band below, leading their sullen Bluecoat prisoner. The exhaustion in their faces mirrored hers, but it also worried her. Tired men made bad decisions. She had surmised enough to guess the basic situation: The whiteskins meant to wait until the Cheyennes released their white comrade, then open fire.

Of course, Touch the Sky and his braves probably expected something along that line. But they didn't see, as she did, when the wounded men tucked lever-action repeating rifles under their coats. The Cheyennes thought they were taking another risk, but in fact they were walking into a death trap.

She slowed down too much, and Burke impatiently tugged on the line, almost making her trip. Honey Eater clutched Little Bear closer, and prayed to Maiyun that this howling, deafening wind would permit a shouted warning in time.

Honey Eater had been caught in enough battles to know the effective range of guns. Now her husband and his prisoner had entered that range, still moving slowly upward. If anything, the wind only shrieked louder. Riding a welling of panic, Honey Eater's heart surged up into her throat. He would never hear her above this racket, and after the first useless shout, Burke would silence her.

"All right, boys," Steele called out softly so his enemy couldn't hear, "get ready to bust some caps."

"Eyes front, bucks!" Touch the Sky yelled as loud as he could, barely able to make his friends hear him above the wind. "Focus hard on their eyes, for they reveal a movement even before the hands."

They were perhaps fifteen paces and closing when Touch the Sky noticed it: Honey Eater was making sign talk. Only two signs, a wavy line to indicate the snake, a straight line to indicate the arrow.

The snake: *treachery*. The arrow: *flight*. Honey Eater was telling him it was a trap, they must run.

Just on the verge of entering certain killing range, Touch the Sky whirled and ordered his companions to retreat. Even as he did, Steele realized what was happening and ordered his men to fire. Carlson leaped forward in the confusion, even as the Cheyennes scrambled for their lives.

Shooting back was out of the question with Honey Eater and Little Bear right out front. A deadly volley of fire rained down on them. Two Twists cried out and stumbled, blood oozing from a hit to the back of his thigh. But Touch the Sky grabbed one arm, Little Horse the other, and they tugged him along between them.

The Cheyennes emulated their well-trained horses and ran evasive zigzagging patterns to throw off their enemy's aim. In an unceremonious tangle of arms and legs, they tumbled into the rifle pits with slugs nipping at their heels, even as a cursing Hiram Steele ordered his men back up the bluff.

"Of course I didn't think to tie her damn hands," Steele fumed. "Did *you* want to carry that kid of hers? What the hell you bitching for, anyway? You're free, ain't you?"

Carlson scowled at this. "No thanks to you. And as a matter of fact, I'm not free. I still have to get past that red bastard Hanchon." He mimicked Steele's voice as he added, " 'This time I got it all figured out, right down to the i dots.' "

"What about you?" Steele demanded. "Letting that savage lead you out by your hard dick. Libbie La Belle, my sweet aunt, you rube."

Widow Maker, busy honing his throwing knives on a whetstone, only grinned at these two white fools. The time was approaching when their foolish, womanly quarreling wouldn't matter. He meant to kill that worthy, tall Cheyenne and steal his soul-breath as he died. And then he meant to sate his loins on his comely wife.

Carlson, still scowling, was about to hurl another insult. But abruptly the scowl disappeared, replaced by a thoughtful narrowing of his eyes.

Steele liked the look of this. "What?" he demanded.

All that wind had finally died down, but not before blowing a tumble of clouds away from the afternoon sun. Carlson glanced toward the mirror that Widow Maker had nailed to a tree, then across the plains toward Fort Bates.

"I'll tell you what," Carlson said, breaking into a grin. He crossed and slipped the mirror off its nail. "I've got mirror stations set up between here and the fort. I can get us out of here *and* cover my ass from an AWOL charge. Hanchon may be as smart as a steel trap, but I doubt like hell he knows

Morse code. This time, Hiram, his ass is nailed to the barn door."

Carlson was right, his enemy did not know Morse code. But because the Indians had their own Moccasin Telegraph, he knew all about the blue-blouse mirror stations.

"What are they saying, shaman?" Little Horse demanded, still wrapping a strip of buckskin around Two Twists's wounded thigh.

Touch the Sky shook his head. "I cannot cipher their code. But with a fort one sleep's ride from here, what would you guess?"

"He is saying he is trapped by renegades," Two Twists called out, wincing when Little Horse tied the strip tight. "He is asking for help."

"Yes, for what else could it mean? Clearly he did not bother to contact them merely to send his regards. And when more pony soldiers arrive, Steele will be free to kill Honey Eater and Little Bear."

All four braves showed the hard signs of this fight. Their faces were tired and drawn with exhaustion; huge pouches under their eyes belied their youth.

"One sleep," Little Horse said. "Or maybe even less, if hair-face soldiers are patrolling nearer. What now, Bear Caller?"

"One sleep," Touch the Sky repeated, his eyes cutting to the slope before them. "Maybe less. Unless someone were to meet the soldiers before they got here. Someone they trusted, who could then send them elsewhere. It would at least purchase a bit of time."

"It would," Little Horse agreed. "But who could do this? You speak excellent whiteskin talk, true. But you are a red man."

"I am indeed, buck." Touch the Sky's eyes focused down to one body lying off to the side of the trail, a man who had fallen during the combined attack. Like many of the deserters, he still wore his Army blouse. Indian scouts often wore partial Army uniforms—often just a blouse.

"Bucks," he told his companions, glancing up to gauge the location of Sister Sun, "after dark I am going up that slope for some new clothing. How many times has Wolf Who Hunts Smiling accused me of spying for the blue-blouses? About time I dressed for the role he loves to assign me."

Sergeant Powhatan 'Pow' Whitaker was leading a log-cutting detail near Roaring Horse Creek when one of his men spotted the mirror flashes: TRAPPED BY RENEGADES AT MASSACRE BLUFF, SEND HELP. CARLSON.

"Well, cuss my coup," he told himself when he heard the message. "So Cap'n Carlson didn't take French leave after all. Too damn bad, I was hopin' we finally got shut of that little tin god."

But duty was duty, and Whitaker took his Godsworn obligations seriously. The Army had been pretty damn good to him. Soon they would be sending him back east to Fort Defiance, where he would train on Mr. Gatling's new gun that was revolutionizing warfare. True, too much criminal trash filled the ranks. But then, men who lived in barracks weren't exactly plaster saints. This was

159

damned hard duty out here, where the "front" was all around and the rear nowhere.

He picked ten good marksmen, ordered them to crimp thirty rounds apiece for their carbines, and set out toward Massacre Bluff. They rode through the night and, just before sunup, approached the final series of ridges before reaching the Valley of the Greasy Grass.

"Rider comin' in," called out a high-private riding point. "Looks like one of our scouts. Why, he's flyin' a desperado flag!"

The soldier had used the cowboy name for the red sash tied to the rider's upper right arm. This flag alerted any soldiers to a situation of special urgency.

Whitaker halted the formation and told the men to drop their horses' bridles, for they were near a runoff rill and this would be the last water for some time. His weather-rawed face wrinkled in confusion as the lone Indian on the ugly paint rode up to them, one hand raised in the sign of peace. He wore a faded military tunic with no rank insignia, ill-fitting peg-top trousers, and a floppy-brimmed plainsman's hat.

And he was the biggest goddamn Cheyenne that Pow had ever laid eyes on. That troubled him somewhat. He didn't know all the scouts back at the fort, and hell, one Indian looked like all the others to him. But this big, strapping buck—a man would be likely to remember him.

"What is it, John?" he said suspiciously.

"Captain Carlson," the new arrival responded promptly. "Men who hold him catch him sending mirror flashes. They take him to Spotted Horse Canyon, south of this place."

"Yeah, I know where it is." Pow eyed the big Indian carefully. "How do you know all this?"

Touch the Sky asked Maiyun to help him here. He hoped the fort had not received a new commander since the time he had ridden there for help in fighting an epidemic of Mountain Fever back at camp.

"Eagle Chief Thompson send me up to Bear Paw country for heap big scout. On way back, I see riders with soldier tied up. I sneak close and see Carlson."

Pow seemed to relax somewhat upon hearing the familiar name. Why would this Indian know the Colonel if he were not a scout at the fort? But just to be safe, he said, "Tell me something, John. What color is the colonel's beard?"

"Color of water."

"The hell's that mean? Water ain't got no color."

Touch the Sky nodded. "As you say. And the colonel has no beard."

Pow was satisfied. "Form up in columns of four," he called out to his men. "We're heading south!"

Chapter 15

"That's it," Carlson said in disgust, throwing down the brass binoculars Steele had loaned him. "They've definitely turned toward Spotted Horse Canyon. We're shit out of luck."

"What is their problem?" Steele fumed. They had been watching the small squad of Cavalry for some time. At first they had formed a plumb line straight for Massacre Bluff. Then they had veered sharply. At first Steele hoped it was only a temporary detour. Clearly, however, the stupid gazaboos had messed up a signal someplace.

"This is what happens," Steele added, "when the men wearing Uncle Sam's blue haven't got the brains God gave a pissant. This man's Army is made up of the sick, lame, and lazy."

Thunder rumbled in the distance, rolling closer

162

across the Great Plains behind an ominous mass of dark storm clouds.

"No," Carlson said grimly, nodding toward the slope below them. "This is what happens when the men wearing Uncle Sam's blue have got a set of oysters on them like *that* one does."

Matthew Hanchon stood below, still wearing his scout's uniform and clearly mocking them.

"Too bad the sun isn't shining," the Cheyenne shouted up. "You could send for more soldiers. Send my wife and boy down, you all ride out of here safe and sound. Otherwise you got a nasty storm coming, and those injured men just might decide to revolt on you, Steele."

Both Steele and Carlson heard more thunder threaten. The sky to the north looked like the prelude to the Apocalypse.

"That son of a bitch knows how to stick the knife in and twist it," Steele said bitterly. "He's right. Burke is over there right now, laying plans with his men. It's come down to the nut-cutting, Seth. Only a fool keeps shoving when a thing won't move."

"You mean we just give up? Hiram, I'm AWOL right now, and I happen to be at the top of Colonel Thompson's shit list. I might end up doing bad time at Leavenworth because of this. And you're telling me it's time to fold up the tent and go home?"

Steele nodded. "More or less. We aren't going to kill him, can't you see that? Not this time. The bastard has hornswaggled us once again."

Rage compressed Carlson's big, bluff face. "All right then. We're in this together, and I don't know you for a coward, Hiram. Maybe all this scuttlebutt we hear is right. Maybe that buck's life *is* charmed."

Carlson quartered around to look at the crude lean-to. "But his wife and kid's ain't."

"No," Steele agreed. "And they're going to be our ticket down from here."

"Why just our ticket down?"

Steele cocked his head, puzzled. "Spell it out plain."

"Hiram, what's to spell? Who in the hell says we got to give them up once we get down there? We'll have weapons held right on them. He tries to move against any of us, we'll kill them right in front of him. All he can do is follow us—and if that fool wants to take his band through the gates of Fort Bates with us, let him."

Hiram considered this. "Seth, you're absolutely right. *We're* still sitting in the catbird seat, not him. I'll have Widow Maker lead the horse they ride. He'll appear unarmed. If Hanchon does make a play, he won't be looking to him, and that'll be his big mistake."

"They are coming down," Two Twists said bitterly, "and I am out of the fight. Brothers, you know they have more treachery in their parfleche."

Touch the Sky nodded, watching the little procession make its way down the steep slope. Steele had shouted down that they were sick of this siege and giving up. With that powerful storm boiling closer, and so many injured men, it was a plausible truth. But truth and Hiram Steele seldom walked the same path.

"Who is that leading the mount carrying your wife and babe?" Little Horse asked. "He appears to be unarmed. That half-breed held Little Bear while Steele burned his soles."

"Another of Steele's lickspittles," Tangle Hair suggested. "He may have a white man's hideout gun. But he looks like a stupid man, and he is dressed like those Indian squaw-men one sees east of the Great Waters. Watch the whites, especially Carlson, Steele, and the leader of the whiskey traders."

"Watch them indeed," Touch the Sky agreed. But a voice niggled at him, the voice of old Arrow Keeper. *Fear the man who seems least fearsome.*

The group reached the base of Massacre Bluff, bit rings jingling, horses snuffling. Though the half-breed was apparently unarmed, several rifles and handguns were trained on Honey Eater.

When they didn't stop, Touch the Sky shouted, "That's far enough, Steele! Let my wife and kid go."

Steele didn't even bother to look at the Cheyennes. The big man sat his saddle, hunched forward.

"Tell you what, Hanchon," he replied. "Welcome to the West, where red men eat shit and go naked."

"Steele! I said stop!"

"What the hell you gonna do, John?" Hardiman

Burke called out in his nasal twang. "You so much as spit at us, your bitch and pup are dead meat."

"I'm taking them, Hanchon!" Steele gloated. "Your squaw will be quite welcome back at Fort Bates, especially by the horny dragoons."

"And as for your kid," Carlson threw in, "I'm giving him to the Pawnee scouts. You know how *they* like a Cheyenne baby."

Evidently Little Bear did not like this prospect, for at that moment, after days of silence, he unleashed a roar to wake snakes. It sounded remarkably like the bellow of a bear cub, and all horses hate and fear bears. Touch the Sky watched the mount carrying Honey Eater and his son suddenly bolt, tearing free of the half-breed's control and crow-hopping to the side of the trail. Without hesitating a moment, Honey Eater urged the horse to a full run.

This happened in a heartbeat and left Steele's party gaping in astonishment. Hardiman Burke lifted his walnut-handled Colt, and then his face turned into a red smear when Little Horse's last shotgun load obliterated it.

Steele and Carlson knew Matthew Hanchon and his ragtag band too well to risk a fight this close. Both gave vicious spur to their mounts, leaving the rest to fend for themselves. But Touch the Sky had disciplined himself to follow Arrow Keeper's advice: He ignored everyone else and only focused on this innocuous, perfumed half-breed.

Several horses had been killed in earlier skirmishes, and the half-breed's skewbald had been loaded down with gear, including pouches of powder and shot. Touch the Sky was a little slow to notice when the half-breed began to lift his left ankle up toward his hand.

Then he spotted the three narrow hafts protruding from the half-breed's oxblood boot.

Touch the Sky had no time to precisely aim his Sharps. The half-breed's arm flashed overhead, Touch the Sky instinctively flinched, and cold steel kissed one side of his neck as the knife gouged out a gobbet of flesh and blood. Even as he fell, Touch the Sky took up his trigger slack.

The bullet flew far too wide to strike his man. But Maiyun did indeed smile on his red children this day, for just then a violent explosion literally blew the half-breed from horseback, his entrails landing all around him in a colorful spray.

"Brother!" a joyful Little Horse shouted. "You hit a shot pouch!"

White men were escaping all around them like mustangs through an open corral gate. But Touch the Sky had no desire to follow them—not when his wife and son were racing toward him even now, eager to be in his arms.

Safely back at their camp, Honey Eater brushed her son's fine but already thick black hair. "Sharp Nosed Woman will recover," she announced. "More blood on the hands of Wolf Who Hunts Smiling and his cowardly pack."

"Sharp Nosed Woman will recover," Touch the Sky repeated. "Good. But the sentries those cowardly Bull Whips killed will never bounce their children on their knees again."

"You should hear him," Honey Eater complained bitterly. "He and his Whips have gone around camp telling stories of how they defeated the whiskey traders and drove them from our ranges. That, they say, is how they lost so many ponies. Yet I watched with my own eyes while that traitor attacked you."

"Watch him long enough, pretty, and you will see him attack me again."

Touch the Sky fell silent, thinking, watching his son play contentedly on the soft robes. Little Bear had the flush of health once again. This time Touch the Sky had managed to save his family. But how long would this deadly cat-and-mouse game continue?

Idly, without realizing he was doing it, Touch the Sky brushed back his son's hair to expose the mulberry-colored arrowhead, the mark of the warrior. Honey Eater watched, not moving or saying a word.

"Twice," Touch the Sky mused, "this little fighter joined the battle. It was his angry bellow that turned the victory our way."

"Yes. He is his father's son."

Truly, thought Touch the Sky, and this troubled him. Like all parents, he wanted life to be better for his children than it had been for him. But this babe was clearly born to a hard fate. Had it been right to bring him into the world, only to fight and struggle for the simple right to stay alive?

Honey Eater knew her brave well by now. She fathomed the thoughts stirring inside him. She reached over and placed one hand against his cheek.

"Touch the Sky. Look at me."

Startled, he did so. Honey Eater seldom used his name like this directly.

"Our son was born to suffer. But Maiyun makes no mistakes. Arrow Keeper once told me that some men were sent into this world to set it right from the damage caused by others. You are one of those men, and so is your son. Never mind the justice of it. The world must have good in it, and you and my son are part of that good. And so are Little Horse, Tangle Hair, and young Two Twists."

These wise words, from this good woman, restored much peace to Touch the Sky's troubled soul.

He embraced both of them, pulling them close until their warmth was as one creature.

"Yes, my lot is a hard one," he conceded. "So it is a miracle that I have the finest woman in the Shaiyena nation to share that hard fate with me. And she has given me a son whose name will be sung until the Last Days. The fight is not over, sweet love. Our wily Wolf is rabid for power, and Sis-ki-dee and Big Tree will soon return to Wendigo Mountain. This is a tribe devouring its own tail. But I have you and my son, and thus I have all the reasons I need to fight on."

CHEYENNE

DOUBLE EDITION
JUDD COLE

One man's heroic search for a world he can call his own.

Arrow Keeper. A Cheyenne raised among pioneers, Matthew Hanchon has never known anything but distrust. The settlers brand him a savage, and when Matthew realizes that his adopted parents will suffer for his sake, he flees into the wilderness—where he'll need a warrior's courage if he hopes to survive.

And in the same volume...

Death Chant. When Matthew returns to the Cheyenne, he doesn't find the acceptance he seeks. The Cheyenne can't fully trust any who were raised in the ways of the white man. Forced to prove his loyalty, Matthew faces the greatest challenge he has ever known.

___4280-0 $4.99 US/$5.99 CAN

Dorchester Publishing Co., Inc.
P.O. Box 6640
Wayne, PA 19087-8640

Please add $1.75 for shipping and handling for the first book and $.50 for each book thereafter. NY, NYC, and PA residents, please add appropriate sales tax. No cash, stamps, or C.O.D.s. All orders shipped within 6 weeks via postal service book rate. Canadian orders require $2.00 extra postage and must be paid in U.S. dollars through a U.S. banking facility.

Name_____

Address_____

City_____State_____Zip_____

I have enclosed $_____ in payment for the checked book(s).

Payment <u>must</u> accompany all orders. ☐ Please send a free catalog.

CHEYENNE

Double Edition:
Pathfinder/ Buffalo Hiders
JUDD COLE

Pathfinder. Touch the Sky never forgot the kindness of the settlers, and tried to help them whenever possible. But an old friend's request to negotiate a treaty between the Cheyenne and gold miners brings the young brave face-to-face with a cunning warrior. If Touch the Sky can't defeat his new enemy, the territory will never again be safe for pioneers.

And in the same action-packed volume...

Buffalo Hiders. Once, mighty herds of buffalo provided the Cheyenne with food, clothing and skins for shelter. Then the white hunters appeared and the slaughter began. Still, few herds remain, and Touch the Sky swears he will protect them. But two hundred veteran mountain men and Indian killers are bent on wiping out the remaining buffalo—and anyone who stands in their way.

___4413-7 $4.99 US/$5.99 CAN

CHEYENNE

Spirit Path
Mankiller
Judd Cole

Spirit Path. The mighty Cheyenne trust their tribe's shaman to protect them against great sickness and bloody defeat. A rival accuses Touch the Sky of bad medicine, and if he can't prove the claim false, he'll come to a brutal end.

And in the same action-packed volume . . .

Mankiller. A fierce warrior, Touch the Sky can outfight, outwit, and outlast any enemy. Yet the fearsome Cherokee brave named Mankiller can snap a man's neck as easily as a reed, and he is determined to count coup on Touch the Sky.

___4445-5 $4.99 US/$5.99 CAN

Dorchester Publishing Co., Inc.
P.O. Box 6640
Wayne, PA 19087-8640

CHEYENNE

WENDIGO MOUNTAIN
DEATH CAMP
JUDD COLE

Wendigo Mountain. A Cheyenne warrior raised by white settlers, Touch the Sky is blessed with strong medicine. Yet his powers as a shaman cannot help him foretell that his tribe's sacred arrows will be stolen—or that his enemies will demand his head for their return. To save his tribe from utter destruction, the young brave will wage a battle like none he's ever fought.

And in the same action-packed volume . . .

Death Camp. Touch the Sky will gladly give his life to protect his tribe. Yet not even he can save them from an outbreak of deadly disease. Racing against time and brutal enemies, Touch the Sky has to either forsake his heritage and trust the white man's medicine—or prove his loyalty even as he watches his proud people die.

___4479-X $4.99 US/$5.99 CAN

CHEYENNE

RENEGADE NATION
ORPHAN TRAIN
JUDD COLE

Renegade Nation. Born the son of a great chief, raised by frontier settlers, Touch the Sky will never forsake his pioneer friends in their time of need. Then Touch the Sky's enemies join forces against all his people—both Indian and white. If the fearless brave's magic is not strong enough, he will be powerless to stop the annihilation of the two worlds he loves. *And in the same action-packed volume . . .*

Orphan Train. When his enemies kidnap a train full of orphans heading west, the young shaman finds himself torn between the white men and the Indians. To save the children, the mighty warrior will have to risk his life, his home, and his dreams of leading his tribe to glory.

___4511-7 $4.99 US/$5.99 CAN

WILDERNESS

WINTERKILL/
BLOOD TRUCE

David Thompson

Winterkill. The unexplored Rockies hide threats that can kill even the most experienced mountain men. But when Nathaniel King takes in a pair of strangers who have lost their way in the snow, his kindness is repaid with vile treachery. If King isn't careful, he and his young family will not live to see another spring.

And in the same action-packed volume...

Blood Truce. With only raw courage to aid them, Nate King and other pioneers brave the constant threat of Indian attack to claim the freedom they find on the frontier. But when a deadly dispute among rival tribes blows up into a bloody war, Nate has to make peace between the enemies—or he and his family will be the first to lose their scalps.

___4489-7 $4.99 US/$5.99 CAN

WILDERNESS
BLOOD FEUD

<------------------------------------->

David Thompson

The brutal wilderness of the Rocky Mountains can be deadly to those unaccustomed to its dangers. So when a clan of travelers from the hill country back East arrive at Nate King's part of the mountain, Nate is more than willing to lend a hand and show them some hospitality. He has no way of knowing that this clan is used to fighting—and killing—for what they want. And they want Nate's land for their own!

___4477-3 $3.99 US/$4.99 CAN

WILDERNESS

#25
FRONTIER MAYHEM

$\longleftrightarrow$

David Thompson

The unforgiving wilderness of the Rocky Mountains forces a boy to grow up fast, so Nate King taught his son, Zach, how to survive the constant hazards and hardships—and he taught him well. With an Indian war party on the prowl and a marauding grizzly on the loose, young Zach is about to face the test of his life, with no room for failure. But there is one danger Nate hasn't prepared Zach for—a beautiful girl with blue eyes.

___4433-1 $3.99 US/$4.99 CAN

Dorchester Publishing Co., Inc.
P.O. Box 6640
Wayne, PA 19087-8640

WILDERNESS

#24

Mountain Madness
←——————————————————→
David Thompson

When Nate King comes upon a pair of green would-be trappers from New York, he is only too glad to risk his life to save them from a Piegan war party. It is only after he takes them into his own cabin that he realizes they will repay his kindness...with betrayal. When the backshooters reveal their true colors, Nate knows he is in for a brutal battle—with the lives of his family hanging in the balance.

___4399-8 $3.99 US/$4.99 CAN

Dorchester Publishing Co., Inc.
P.O. Box 6640
Wayne, PA 19087-8640

Please add $1.75 for shipping and handling for the first book and $.50 for each book thereafter. NY, NYC, and PA residents, please add appropriate sales tax. No cash, stamps, or C.O.D.s. All orders shipped within 6 weeks via postal service book rate. Canadian orders require $2.00 extra postage and must be paid in U.S. dollars through a U.S. banking facility.

Name_____
Address_____
City_____ State_____ Zip_____
I have enclosed $_____ in payment for the checked book(s).
Payment <u>must</u> accompany all orders. ❑ Please send a free catalog.
CHECK OUT OUR WEBSITE! www.dorchesterpub.com

WILDERNESS DOUBLE EDITION
DAVID THOMPSON
MOUNTAIN DEVIL/ BLACKFOOT MASSACRE

The epic struggle for survival in America's untamed West.

Mountain Devil. In 1832, when Nate leads a hunting expedition into a valley where Indian legend says one of the fiercest creatures lives, he might become the prey of a beast that has come out of his worst nightmare.

And in the same action-packed volume...

Blackfoot Massacre. When the Reverend John Burke is trapped in perilous Blackfoot territory, Nate has to save the man—or he'll bear the brand of a coward until the day he dies.

___4327-0 $4.99 US/$5.99 CAN

Dorchester Publishing Co., Inc.
P.O. Box 6640
Wayne, PA 19087-8640

Please add $1.75 for shipping and handling for the first book and $.50 for each book thereafter. NY, NYC, and PA residents, please add appropriate sales tax. No cash, stamps, or C.O.D.s. All orders shipped within 6 weeks via postal service book rate. Canadian orders require $2.00 extra postage and must be paid in U.S. dollars through a U.S. banking facility.

Name_____
Address_____
City_____State_____Zip_____
I have enclosed $_____ in payment for the checked book(s).
Payment <u>must</u> accompany all orders. ☐ Please send a free catalog.

The epic struggle for survival in America's untamed West.

Vengeance Trail. When Nate and his mentor, Shakespeare McNair, make enemies of two Flathead Indians, their survival skills are tested as never before.
And in the same action-packed volume....
Death Hunt. Upon the birth of their first child, Nathaniel King and his wife are overjoyed. But their delight turns to terror when Nate accompanies the men of Winona's tribe on a deadly buffalo hunt. If King doesn't return, his family is sure to perish.

___4297-5 $4.99 US/$5.99 CAN

WILD BILL

DEAD MAN'S HAND

JUDD COLE

Marshal, gunfighter, stage driver, and scout, Wild Bill Hickok has a legend as big and untamed as the West itself. No man is as good with a gun as Wild Bill, and few men use one as often. From Abilene to Deadwood, his name is known by all—and feared by many. That's why he is hired by Allan Pinkerton's new detective agency to protect an eccentric inventor on a train ride through the worst badlands of the West. With hired thugs out to kill him and angry Sioux out for his scalp, Bill knows he has his work cut out for him. But even if he survives that, he has a still worse danger to face— a jealous Calamity Jane.

___4487-0 $3.99 US/$4.99 CAN